HONEYMOON INTERRUPTUS

The bottle of Brut champagne was chilling on the table. Drs. Calista and Plato Marley could hardly believe their brilliance at sneaking in this heavenly, all-free second honeymoon. "This is the life," Plato would later remember telling Cal, as they were sitting in their private Jacuzzi, up to their necks in soap bubbles, crowded together and sipping each other's champagne. Cal's face was flushed and dreamy, and Plato was more relaxed than he could ever remember.

Yet it would always seem like a dream—a bad dream—when the telephone rang and Plato reluctantly climbed out of the bath, wrapped himself in a towel, and padded across the floor to the bathroom extension. He had been thinking how decadently wonderful life could be, how *good*. But when he picked up the receiver, he heard the news that Victor Godwin had been found dead in the bright sunny courtyard just below their window—just ten minutes ago. . . .

MURDER BY PRESCRIPTION

Bill Pomidor

A Cal & Plato Marley Mystery

A SIGNET BOOK

For Alice

SIGNET
Published by the Penguin Group
Penguin Books USA Inc., 375 Hudson Street,
New York, New York 10014, U.S.A.
Penguin Books Ltd, 27 Wrights Lane, London W8 5TZ, England
Penguin Books Australia Ltd, Ringwood, Victoria, Australia
Penguin Books Canada Ltd, 10 Alcorn Avenue,
Toronto, Ontario, Canada M4V 3B2
Penguin Books (N.Z.) Ltd, 182–190 Wairau Road, Auckland 10, New Zealand

Penguin Books Ltd, Registered Offices: Harmondsworth, Middlesex, England

First published by Signet, an imprint of Dutton Signet,
a division of Penguin Books USA Inc.

First Printing, October, 1995
10 9 8 7 6 5 4 3 2 1

 REGISTERED TRADEMARK—MARCA REGISTRADA

Printed in the United States of America

PUBLISHER'S NOTE
This is a work of fiction. Names, characters, places, and incidents either are the
product of the author's imagination or are used fictitiously, and any resemblance
to actual persons, living or dead, events, or locales is entirely coincidental.

ACKNOWLEDGMENTS

Writing a novel that covers several fields of medicine—especially forensic medicine—would be difficult or impossible without some qualified assistance. My medical school and internship training featured only limited exposure to forensic pathology, so I am indebted to Kimbroe Carter, M.D., and Robert Carroll Challener, M.D., for introducing me to the world of forensic science. Dr. Carter has given me sound advice and feedback on the technical details of my plot, and Dr. Challener, deputy coroner for Cuyahoga County, provided a tour of the county morgue, along with a fascinating discussion of the intricacies of forensic science. Frank Kocab, M.D., and Mr. Dale Owens acquainted me with the autopsy suite and guided me through a typical postmortem.

Special thanks to Stuart Krichevsky, one of the most personable, supportive, and effective agents in the publishing industry, to Danielle Perez, my editor, for her perceptive comments and suggestions, and to Cathleen Jordan, editor of *Alfred Hitchcock Mystery Magazine,* for helping develop the Marley mysteries. John P. Schlemmer, M.D., and Dan Holtan, M.D., also provided invaluable guidance. So did Walter Pomidor, my father, whose support and feedback have steered my writing career. And finally, Alice K. Pomidor, M.D., M.P.H., associate director of geriatrics at MetroHealth

Medical Center in Cleveland—and my wife—has given me insights into life as a geriatrician and woman physician, and has always been there for me. This novel is dedicated to her.

CHAPTER ONE

"Think of it as a second honeymoon," Plato told his wife.

"I thought honeymoons involved *two* people." Cal frowned thoughtfully, blond eyebrows knotting together. "Or do I get to solo after the first one?"

She was perched on the pile of suitcases in the living room, a hundred pounds of dripping sarcasm with dark eyes, soft lips, and tawny blond hair that had turned Plato's heart to butter at their wedding one year ago tomorrow. Keeping a safe distance, he tried to muster his thoughts and remember how the argument had started. Something about the weight of her suitcase—why did women always have to take jokes so *seriously*?

"Yes. I mean, *no*." They were better arguers, too. Plato fumbled for words. "Come on, Cally. I thought we agreed that—"

"*You* agreed." Her eyes flashed. "I just wanted to spend our first anniversary at home—a nice romantic weekend. No patients. No autopsies. Stuff our pagers in the freezer for three days and see if they still work."

"They would. I lost mine in the snow one time, cross-country skiing. You wouldn't believe—"

"Breakfast in bed. Lunch in bed. *Dinner* in bed." She slapped one of the suitcases. Plato winced as his notebook computer toppled from the pile. "But no. You had to go lecture at the big geriatrics conference—just a couple of sessions. Like a fool, I agreed."

That wasn't the whole story. But during his first year of marriage, Plato had learned the value of silence.

"Then your best friend Miguel calls and—*bing*—suddenly it's not just a couple of sessions. We'll be spending a whole *week* at the conference—locked in some mansion, working on Miguel's textbook with a bunch of research nerds." She studied the ceiling with a martyr's pain. "No time alone. No romantic walks. No breakfast in bed."

"There's a free continental breakfast tomorrow morning," Plato volunteered.

"As if that weren't enough, you've been on call this week. Out at six in the morning, home at seven-thirty at night. And two all-nighters. I've hardly even *seen* you." She sighed heavily. "Mother warned me never to marry a doctor."

Cal didn't mention that she was a doctor herself—a forensic pathologist and deputy coroner for Cuyahoga County. She had missed more than her share of special occasions because of emergency autopsies or inquests. Plato's thirtieth birthday, for instance.

He didn't bother bringing it up, though. He always lost those kinds of arguments. Instead, he'd learned to pick his battles, fight on his own turf. And execute an orderly retreat.

"You're right," he muttered, hanging his head and sighing. "I've been thoughtless and selfish."

He shuffled across the room and slumped into the battered recliner. The cushion wheezed, and silver duct tape stuck to his elbow. The brown vinyl chair was full of holes; their Australian shepherd preferred the foam stuffing to dog food. Plato gestured at the walls of their dream house—a century-old home with a leaking roof, rotting pipes, flooded basement, and a crumbling foundation. And furniture the Salvation Army refused to haul away. Not that they could afford to replace it anyway.

"I just thought it would be nice, spending a week in

a luxury hotel for free. Working showers. Clear water you don't have to boil before drinking. A king-size bed, instead of the twins we got from Aunt Thelma. Gourmet cuisine." He brightened. "But you're right. It'll be exciting—a little like camping, since the plumber'll be ripping the pipes out this week. I can put the new sump pump in, and maybe we'll do some *wallpapering* together. I'll tell Miguel we decided—"

"I don't know, Plato." Cal shuddered visibly. "Now that we've committed ourselves, it wouldn't be right to back out. Besides, we're picking Miguel up at the airport, right?"

"Miguel can take a limo—there's service from the airport to the hotel." He felt the momentum swinging and pressed his advantage. "Hey! We could rent that machine and refinish the hardwood floors upstairs! I could start sanding them down today. Renter's Heaven is open on Saturdays—I'll call and see if they've got one—"

"Come to think of it, I *have* been looking forward to getting away. Chippewa Creek Lodge ... It does sound like a wonderful place." She swallowed hard. "Besides, it was awfully nice of Miguel to invite me in as a contributor, even though I'm not a geriatrician."

"That's true," Plato conceded reluctantly.

"It's a big opportunity for you—helping to edit a textbook. Won't hurt my résumé, either. And we've already got our outlines done; that's half the work." Cal slid down the pile of suitcases and walked across to him, heels ticking on the bare hardwood floor. She rubbed his shoulders, nuzzled his ear. A lioness making peace. "I'm sure we'll be able to find *some* time for ourselves."

"Of course we will," Plato agreed. "And it's a lot cheaper than a vacation."

"Who needs a vacation?"

Who could afford one? Buying the house had been a

mistake. The old ruin was a black hole that sucked money from their bank account and popped it into another dimension. A quarter million in student loans didn't help, either. After paying for gas and groceries, their combined salaries as junior faculty physicians left just enough for an occasional video rental, or a Boboli pizza from the Beerbelly Deli over in Northfield.

She dragged him from the chair, nestled in his arms, mumbled into his shirt. "So when're we leaving?"

The top of her head fit just under his chin, under his beard. Today, her soft hair smelled like flowers instead of formalin. "Miguel's flight comes in to Cleveland Hopkins at ten. He and Victor are meeting us at the United terminal."

"Victor?" She tilted her head back and looked up at him. "Who's Victor?"

"Victor Godwin. He directed the geriatrics fellowship at Ashbury when Miguel was training there." He slid his hands down her shoulders and rested them at the small of her back. "Victor's coming in from San Francisco; I guess he's helping out with the textbook."

"A fellowship director, huh?"

"Mmm-hmm." He brushed his lips through her soft hair and pulled her closer. Things were getting interesting. Losing an argument wasn't such a bad thing.

"Then we'd better not keep him waiting." Cal squirmed away and snatched one of her lists from atop the pile of suitcases. "Where were we? Oh, yes—did you leave a light on upstairs?"

"Yeah," he grumbled.

"Timer set on the family room lamp?"

"Yeah."

"Windows shut? Mail stopped? Got enough cash?"

"Yeah, yeah, yeah."

"Foley is at the kennel, right? Who's going to feed Dante?"

"Tommy Jorgensen."

"The paperboy? You're *kidding*." From the look on her face, Plato might as well have squashed Dante under the car. She frowned, twirled a strand of blond hair around her finger. "You know I don't trust him. I *hate* the way he skulks around our house every morning—he sneaks up the path, slinks across the porch, and slips our paper under the mat without a sound. Sinister, you know?"

"He's probably afraid of Foley." Their chair-eating dog was nearly deaf and had severe cataracts. He'd once mistaken Tommy Jorgensen for a prowler. Even with his arthritis, Foley had made a good chase of it.

"I don't know," Cal muttered reluctantly. "I've always been a great judge of character."

"Dante can fend for himself." Plato walked over to the window and glanced out at the sagging wooden porch: Project Number 396. "He left you another present this morning."

"He did?" Cal rushed over and squinted through the window. "Uh-huh. Looks like another mouse."

Plato followed his wife to the front door and watched her hurry outside to retrieve the little skeleton. She held the skull up and scrutinized it carefully, peered in the eye holes and clacked the tiny jaw open and shut. Lots of people got gifts from their cats; Cal was the only person he knew who *appreciated* them.

"Another vole—*Arvicola*—judging from the skull. Common field mouse." She tossed the skull into the bushes, kicked the other bones over the side of the porch. "Why are you staring at me like that?"

He pressed his nose against the rusty screen. "I just wish you weren't so casual about it. The poor thing's dead—why not treat it with a little respect?"

"Somehow, I think it's past caring." She wiped her small hands on her skirt and stepped to the door. "Besides, you're a geriatrician. Aren't you always telling your patients that death is a natural process?"

"Most of my patients aren't killed and munched and left on someone's front porch."

"Details." Her freckled nose wrinkled. "Can I come in?"

Plato backed away from the door and grimaced. "Go wash your hands."

"Yes, sir." She walked down the long bare hallway, her voice echoing like shouts in an empty cathedral. "How about loading the luggage?"

"I'm too hungry." Plato followed her into the kitchen and shooed the flame-colored tabby from the top of the antique refrigerator. Dante arched his back, high-stepped along the counter, and leaped onto the kitchen table. He plopped down on a stack of Medicare paperwork from Plato's office and daintily licked his paws. Plato tried to ignore him. "Any pizza left?"

"I had it for breakfast." Cal waited patiently while the tap water flowed from ruddy brown to yellow to clear. "There are some M&M's in the bread box."

"The bread box?" He opened the door and retrieved the bag.

"We can't leave them in the pantry where Dante can reach them. Remember how sick they made him last time?" She mopped her hands on a towel, then held the cat up and nuzzled his nose. He licked her forehead.

"Poor thing," Plato muttered sourly. He grabbed a mouthful of M&M's, stuffed the bag in his pocket, and headed back down the hall. "Did you get the Chevette tuned up?"

"Even better." Cal followed him back to the living room and gave a satisfied grin. "The mechanic said it'll run like new now."

"What was wrong with it?"

"I don't know." She frowned. "Something expensive, anyway. I didn't understand it all, but it sounded like normal aging. He had to replace a lot of parts."

"I see."

"Something to do with the engine."

"I see." He paused, considering. "Maybe we should get another car."

"We can't afford to now."

Plato sighed and reached into the bag for another dose of chocolate.

"Anyway, he wants to see it again in a week." She leaned over the luggage pile, grabbed her purse and the road map.

"A week? What for?" He opened a luggage carrier, piled the three suitcases on board, slung the garment bag over his shoulder, snagged the camera case with his free hand, and staggered to the door.

"Preventive maintenance," Cal replied. She held the door open for him, then pulled it shut and locked it. Following Plato down the long walk between the trees, she glanced back at the house. "Did you lock all the windows upstairs?"

Plato shrugged and grimaced at the scrunch of *Arvicola* skeletons under the luggage carrier's wheels. "What's there to steal?"

He lifted the hatch and loaded the suitcases. The back of the Chevette sagged visibly when he slammed the door again.

Cal was leaning on the fender, gazing back at the house. She took his hand and sighed. "It really is beautiful, you know. All that wonderful latticework, those half-moon windows in the little tower, the covered balcony—"

"The sway-backed roof, the peeling paint, the rotten clapboarding," Plato noted morosely. "And horrible plumbing. All rusted and clogged."

"Hardening of the arteries." She grinned. "A geriatric house."

"And a geriatric car."

She shrugged. "Well, after all, you're a geriatrician."

"And you're a forensic pathologist." He patted the car. "I think it'll be needing your services pretty soon."

"Nonsense. It runs like a top now." She swung open the driver's-side door and climbed in. "Well?"

"*You're* driving? I thought you didn't like manual transmissions." They'd only had the Chevette for a couple of months. Cal had wanted an automatic, but the old Chevette had come cheap. Now Plato understood why.

"The mechanic tightened the clutch. It's a lot easier to shift now." She revved the engine. "What are you waiting for?"

Reluctantly, Plato climbed into the passenger seat and sighed. "I'm afraid *I'll* be needing your services pretty soon."

"Very funny." She jerked the car into gear and tangoed down the drive.

Miguel was leaning on a stack of luggage just outside the terminal. Cal stalled the car at the curb and Plato hopped out. Miguel jumped up quickly, shook his friend's hand, and squeezed his shoulder. "Awfully good to see you."

He was as lean as ever, tall and wiry; the sharp angles and flat planes of his face resembled a half-finished sandstone sculpture. Dark skin and eyes, but his flawlessly styled hair had just a flicker of gray at the edges. He shot a dubious glance at the Chevette. "You've got a new car, I see."

"Well, not exactly *new*."

"Not exactly a *car,* either." Cal had stepped out and stood beside Plato. "More like a roller skate with ambition."

Miguel chuckled. "And how are you, Calista? How is married life? Is this little *picaro* treating you well?"

She tilted her head and squinted one eye at her husband. "Better than I treat him, I think."

"That's how it should be. But don't ever tell Carmen I said so."

"I won't."

Plato looked up and down the sidewalk. The loading area was empty except for a wizened old man and a plump old woman. They were deep in conversation; he was patting her hand gently. "Where's Doctor Godwin?"

Miguel gestured at the old couple. "Over there."

"He brought his wife?" Plato glanced at the roller skate, wondering how an extra passenger could possibly fit inside.

"No—his wife died years ago." Miguel smiled gently and nodded at the elderly woman. "That lady was sitting next to us on the plane—burst into tears on the runway before takeoff. I guess she's afraid of flying, never been on a plane before."

"Poor thing," Cal clucked.

"Victor talked her through it, held her hand, told her some awful jokes. She did just fine." He sighed. "It was the most amazing thing. I thought she was going to have a heart attack at first. But by the time we were ready to land, Victor had her smiling and relaxed."

Godwin finally stood and shook hands with her. Beaming, the woman folded her arms around him and squashed him to her chest. She stood a head taller than him; he looked like a child leaving for his first day of school. Gently wriggling loose, he patted her hand and straightened his tortoiseshell glasses. As he walked away, the old woman grabbed a paper bag from her purse and pressed it into his grasp.

"Terribly sorry," he said as he approached the group. "The poor woman just wouldn't let me go."

Godwin was hardly taller than Cal, and his soft voice was buried under the whine and rumble of jets and buses and cars.

"No problem at all," Cal replied quickly.

"We have plenty of time," Plato added.

"Victor Godwin, this is Plato and Cal Marley," Miguel announced formally.

"It's a pleasure to meet you, Plato. Miguel has told me so much about you." Godwin's words floated past like so much dandelion fluff. He shook Plato's hand and turned to Cal. "I'm delighted to meet you, ma'am. You're a forensic pathologist, I understand?"

She nodded.

"Fascinating field. I've read Noguchi's book, of course." He was still holding Cal's hand. His bloodshot gray eyes looked huge behind the thick glasses. They crinkled with a smile. "But I don't suppose that reflects mainstream forensic pathology."

"The reality is a bit more mundane, I'm afraid. Especially in Ohio."

"We like it that way," Plato added. "Some nights, she even makes it home in time for dinner."

"More often than *you*," Cal shot back.

Godwin chuckled and turned to the stack of luggage. "It's terribly kind of you to chauffeur us today. I do hope we haven't brought too much baggage?"

"We can just strap Plato to the roof," Miguel suggested.

But they managed to stuff most of the luggage into the hatch. Victor insisted on holding his briefcase in his lap, telling them he would have wanted to anyway, and Plato squashed a duffel bag between the two front seats.

"They're working on Route 480 again," Cal explained as they pulled away. "It'll be faster to head up into Cleveland and then catch the freeway south."

"Quite all right," Victor replied. "I would love to see Siegel Medical College—Miguel has told me so much about it."

As they headed toward the freeway, Plato glanced

into the backseat. Miguel's long legs were tucked under his chin. Godwin looked perfectly comfortable.

"This car rides remarkably well," Victor commented. He glanced over at Miguel. "You see? Diminutive size has its advantages."

Miguel moved his knee aside enough to nod.

"How was your flight?" Plato asked.

"Quite pleasant," Victor replied. "We flew in together, you know. I spent a few days with Miguel in Connecticut."

"Really?"

"Victor is a reviewer for the American Grants Monitoring Commission," Miguel explained. "He's working on a case."

Plato didn't ask for details. The AGMC oversaw most of the federal research grants. The reviewers were only called in when cheating was suspected.

"Since stepping down as fellowship director, I've had a good deal more time for my AGMC duties."

"He has to do a lot of traveling," Miguel noted.

Victor patted his protégé's knee and grinned. "It gives me the opportunity to visit my friends—all expenses paid, of course."

"I hear Carmen is quite a cook," Plato said.

"You could find out for yourself if you visited once in a while," Miguel complained.

"Good heavens!" Godwin suddenly exclaimed. "Is that *Cleveland*?"

From his tone of voice, Victor might have thought his airplane had made a wrong turn. The old geriatrician was pointing a liver-spotted hand at the side windshield where Cleveland's skyline had popped over the horizon.

"I haven't seen it in fifteen years," he continued. "Back then, the Terminal Tower was the only tall building to speak of."

"It's even changed a lot since I've been here,"

Miguel added. He and Plato had both graduated from Siegel seven years ago. Even then, Cleveland's skyline was starting to grow. Nowadays, it looked positively respectable.

"Is that new baseball field finished?" Miguel asked.

"Uh-huh," Cal replied. "More of a hitting field than Municipal was, but then their pitching is doing all right, too. First time in a decade or so the bullpen's held up past the all-star break. If they can just stay consistent through September—"

"Cal's kind of an Indians fan," Plato explained.

"I see."

While Cal detailed the history of the Tribe, Plato scrabbled in the glove box for a map.

"We'd better get off here, Cal." Plato leaned over and pointed to the 25th Street exit sign off to the right. "But don't worry about it—the next exit should be fine—"

"No problem." Cal glanced at the exit sign, studied the rearview mirror, and licked her lips. She downshifted suddenly, skated across the three lanes of heavy traffic, skittered behind a stake truck laden with riding lawnmowers and openmouthed landscapers, and sliced through a funeral procession with inches to spare. The car bumped over a last dividing curb and swerved onto the exit ramp. "That's one nice thing about this Chevette—it cuts through traffic a lot better than the bigger cars."

Plato glanced into the backseat. Miguel's eyes were bulging and his chin was down between his knees.

"Sorry, Miguel. Cal's a pretty good driver, but she gets these little fits sometimes."

"Huh." He squirmed sideways and pressed his knees against the door.

"I thought it was a fine bit of driving, myself." Godwin was still sitting primly, hands folded over his briefcase.

Cal grinned, turned the corner, and idled past MetroHealth, the near West Side, and Ohio City at a stately pace. In the backseat, Miguel had recovered enough to point out the familiar landmarks for Victor: the West Side Market, the deserted warehouses that were slowly being replaced by a thriving entertainment district, the once-combustible Cuyahoga River with its collection of rusting railroad bridges poised like steel dinosaur skeletons grazing at its banks. Down near the water in the center of the Flats, Riverside General Hospital glittered like a jewel in the morning sunlight.

Farther upriver loomed the ponderous granite towers and pillars of Siegel Medical College.

"It was built just before the Depression," Miguel told Victor. "Started by a steel baron, right, Plato?"

He nodded. "Rupert Siegel was a small fish in the high society pond over at Case Western. So he tried to build a bigger, better medical college."

They all chuckled at that. Still, the hospital served many of the city's poorer patients, and the heavily state-funded Siegel Medical College offered a shot at medical degrees for Cleveland's less affluent and well-connected youth. Like Plato Marley.

Cal caught the Innerbelt near the river, swung past the new stadium, and headed south on I-77 to the outer ring of suburbs. They exited and followed a winding country road through woods and farmland, finally arriving at the wrought-iron gate marking the entrance to Chippewa Creek Lodge.

Cal turned to Plato. "This is it?"

"I think so." The lodge had been closed for most of a decade; the new owners had just opened it this past spring. He and Cal almost had dinner there once, but an emergency autopsy had intervened. "The lady who took the reservations said we should just follow the gravel road. The lodge is about half a mile up."

She swung the car into the drive.

"I suppose that's the Chippewa Creek?" Behind them, Godwin was peering over the ridge at the black rushing water seven stories below.

"Actually, it's the Cuyahoga River," Plato replied. "Chippewa Creek joins it just south of here, I think. Down near the golf course."

"It's a beautiful view."

"Half a mile, you said?" Cal was picking up speed. Gravel pittered the floor of the car.

"Yeah. Maybe you'd better slow down, though."

"Naah." She downshifted just as they reached a turn. "This road's plenty wide enough for—*Whooooah!*"

A row of orange pylons, yellow flashers, a flare or two, all went by in a blur, crumpled under the tires as Cal pumped the brakes and spun the wheel. Slowly, sluggishly, the Chevette drifted left. Plato was treated to a close view of the Cuyahoga from directly above: nothing but empty air between his window and the scattered rocks and swirling waters below.

Cal chuckled hysterically like a mad scientist in a late-night movie, hunched over the Death Machine, twisting wheels and knobs and pulling levers.

The Chevette pivoted a half turn, wheels spinning and catching just as the rear of the car began its downward slide. A quick downshift again, the engine faltering, faltering, the sick plunk-plunk of an imminent stall, then a cough and hiccup as the tiny motor whined back to life. The clutch caught, the engine clattered, and the car finally rocked back onto solid ground.

Cal fumbled for the shifter knob and slid the car into second gear. As they crawled along the suddenly narrowed drive, Godwin's calm voice filled the silence. "Looks like part of the road slid away."

"Yes," Cal choked. "It does."

"Quite a neat bit of driving," he added.

"Thank you."

"Would anyone like a cookie?" He held up a paper

sack. "The lady on the plane gave them to me. Oatmeal, I believe."

The others shook their heads and swallowed heavily. Plato hadn't been carsick in years, but he suddenly remembered how it felt.

Just around the bend, guardrails reappeared and the road widened again. Chippewa Creek Lodge was just visible through the trees. Miguel recovered enough to speak. "Good *Lord*. Is that where we're staying?"

Plato glanced back at his friend. The deep brown color and strong lines of his face had melted away; his dark brown eyes looked like two chocolate chips in a mound of custard.

"I guess so," Plato croaked. The vision of the yawning chasm was still fresh in his mind.

Behind him, Victor Godwin might have been taking a tour through the Hollywood hills. He spoke between bites of oatmeal cookie. "Interesting. Part of it looks like a typical Victorian mansion, but the central portion—all that jagged stonework—pure Romanesque revival."

"Looks like a cross between a haunted house and a mausoleum," Miguel muttered.

"Looks like *our* house." Cal's voice quivered. Her white knuckles clutched the steering wheel at precisely ten and two o'clock. The Chevette crept across the gravel like an advancing glacier.

"I think we're staying in the haunted mansion part," Plato noted slowly. "It's called Cliff House."

"Appropriately enough," Victor observed. "And look who's out on the veranda—Eldon Gates. I see your boss decided to come after all, Miguel."

Plato squinted ahead as they entered the circle before the main entrance. A tall man in a beige suit was leaning on the curved porch railing. He pulled a cigarette from a brass case, tapped it twice on the railing, and lit it.

He looked like Sean Connery, but taller. Cal was a James Bond fanatic, Plato knew. He glanced across at his wife, but she hadn't noticed the resemblance. Cal's eyes were glazed. Her hands trembled on the steering wheel. Her pale skin was nearly translucent.

In the backseat, Miguel was frowning with exasperation. "Eldon couldn't exactly back out now, Victor. After all, he—"

"He *threatened* to, didn't he?" Godwin's voice hardened. "If Gates is hoping to convince me to drop the case—"

"Victor . . ." Miguel gave an exasperated sigh.

Godwin paused, then chuckled. "All right. Not another word—I promise. After all, this is *your* party, Miguel."

"Thanks." Miguel slumped back and closed his eyes. He opened them again, tapped Plato's shoulder and gave a ghastly grin. "By the way, happy anniversary. Tomorrow, isn't it?"

"It's been a wonderful year," Plato muttered quietly. "Hasn't it, kiddo?"

Beside him, Cal gave a brave, lopsided smile. She pulled into a parking space, slipped the keys from the ignition and fumbled them onto the floor. Her hair was damp with sweat; her freckles had vanished completely.

"I think I'm going to be sick."

CHAPTER TWO

"He's gorgeous," Cal breathed. Her brown eyes followed Eldon Gates across the parlor. "He looks just like Sean Connery."

She had finally noticed. Plato just wished Cal weren't so *enthusiastic* about it.

The sudden arrival of 300 geriatricians, fellows, residents, and medical students had taken Chippewa Creek's management by surprise. The conference rooms hadn't been ready on time, so most of the lectures were moved back an hour or so. And though the guest rooms in the main lodge were prepared, a platoon of maids and maintenance men was still scurrying around the upper floors of Cliff House. Miguel's small group—editors of the upcoming *Handbook of Practical Geriatric Medicine*—had been cooling their heels in the parlor for most of an hour.

Plato didn't blame Cal for looking. They'd finished admiring the huge octagonal parlor, curved windows on six of the walls, the grand view of the red brick courtyard surrounding the clear blue swimming pool, the Waterford chandelier, Louis XV settee, and Aubusson rug. So Cal's attention had moved on to another work of art.

Not that Plato was particularly jealous. More than once, Cal had explained that she wasn't attracted to men who looked like actors, men with suntans and powerful builds and swarthy self-confidence. No, she preferred her pale, awkward, gangly husband.

Kelvin Lorantz, another editor, was an infectious disease specialist at Riverside General. He stood beside the Steinway Grand, quietly plinking out chopsticks in the key of E flat major while sipping a dry martini and ignoring Dean Harlow Fairfax. The provost of Siegel Medical College stood beside the piano, half of his abdominal girth perched on the case, his voice rising and falling like puffs of hot wind on a dry summer day. This time it was something about the declining quality of medical school applicants. Why, back when he was in college, any one of his classmates would have killed, just *killed,* for a chance to get into medicine. These days it's business, and law, and economics. *Economics,* by God! Whatever happened to your fellow man, I ask you, whatever happened?

Judith Lorantz, a desperately boring woman, had cornered Miguel beside the fireplace. "—and big black scuff marks all across the floor in the ladies' room! Like someone had ridden their bicycle in there. *We* stay at Ritz-Carltons whenever we travel, and you can bet *their* bathrooms are clean! And their guest rooms are ready on time!"

Plato glanced at Dr. Godwin sitting quietly in a tall-backed chair in the corner of the room, feet barely touching the floor, a glass of milk perched on his knee, quietly watching the exchange between Miguel and Judith Lorantz while a half smile haunted the corners of his thin mouth.

That tall striking woman, Evelyn Something-Or-Other, had stepped outside for a while. She reappeared in the doorway and strolled over. "You're Plato Marley, aren't you?"

"Er—yes." He smiled and shook her hand, ransacking his memory for her last name.

"I read your paper in *JAGS* last month— the one on

medical education in the nursing home." A smile creased her leathery face in flashing white, like the crescent of a baseball framed in a catcher's mitt. She tilted her head and brushed her long white hair over her shoulder. "Fascinating piece."

"Thank you. That's my main interest, really. Too many doctors graduating from residency with no idea how to care for nursing home patients." God, that sounded awful—patronizing and pompous. He might have been taking lessons from Harlow Fairfax.

Cal was shooting meaningful glances at him, if only he knew what they meant. The woman seemed really familiar—Evelyn—Evelyn—Evelyn *What*? Now he was sure he'd read something of hers, something really important, just recently.

"I agree." She smiled again, accenting her high cheekbones and wide forehead. Like an American Indian. Or maybe an Eskimo, with those round, tilted eyes. As tall as Plato, and in that blue serge caftan, she looked like a priestess or something. "My own interest is in the *culture* of the nursing home."

That was it! Evelyn Baker, cultural anthropologist *cum* physician. A big name on the national scene. Her paper had been the lead article in ... what *was* it?

"I read your paper in the *New England Journal* last month," Cal finally blurted. " 'The Flux of Relationships within the American Nursing Home.' Will your section of the book deal with cultural anthropology as well?"

Baker chuckled, a deeply musical sound like a handful of marbles dropped onto a steel drum. "That, and a lot more. Nursing home architecture, social dynamics, administrative structure. And more mundane things like insurance and Medicare compensation."

"It was a fascinating piece," Plato added lamely.

Baker eyed him curiously.

"Your article," he explained. "I really enjoyed it."

James Bond sauntered over to join their little group. "Plato Marley? Eldon Gates." His grip matched Plato's and won. He was darkly handsome, despite the thinning gray hair and tall forehead with sixty years of creases. But his voice was out of character—he sounded more like a cartoon mouse than a secret agent. His blue eyes flicked across Evelyn Baker, panned slowly over Cal's blond hair and neat figure, and reluctantly fixed on Plato. "Say, I saw your name in the program—aren't you giving a lecture this morning?"

"It's been moved back—supposed to start at noon." He shrugged. "We'll see."

"Exactly." Gates's thick eyebrows lowered slightly. "I had an eleven o'clock presentation, too. First they told me it was canceled, then they said to show up at noon. I hope our editorial meetings are better organized than this."

"They should be," Baker said. "Miguel will be a fine executive editor for the book; I'm quite confident that we'll get a lot accomplished."

"As his department chair at Hartman, I couldn't agree with you more." Gates leaned forward. "Excuse me—are you a contributing editor? I didn't catch your name."

"Evelyn Baker. I'm editing the section on administrative issues: Medicare, nursing home management, and so on."

"Of course. Miguel mentioned something about that." He smiled and tilted his head. "In some ways, nonmedical issues are almost as important as medical care. I understand you're a social worker?"

"I have a Ph.D. in anthropology, if that's what you're referring to." Baker gave an icy smile. "And I have an M.D. from Harvard. Of course, some people don't know the difference."

Her voice had risen slightly, just enough to stop all conversation in the room. Kelvin Lorantz lifted his hands from the keyboard and stared, and even Harlow Fairfax paused for breath.

"My apologies—it was a silly mistake." Gates's face reddened, and he sounded almost sincere. "I read your article in the *New England Journal* last month, and I just assumed—"

"No offense taken." Baker relaxed a little. "I'm also affiliated with the university's anthropology department in Atlanta—they just merged with the social work department." She grinned. "You're not the first one to make that mistake. I've been solicited to join the National Association of Social Workers, and I've been invited to interview for a counseling position at the federal penitentiary near Atlanta."

They all laughed, and Plato breathed easier. Baker could have taken the remark personally, and Miguel couldn't afford a clash between his editors before the work even started. But she had let it slide.

He met glances with Cal, guessed what she was thinking. Gates would have never made that mistake with a man. Walking through the corridors of the hospital, Cal wore the same type of white lab coat that Plato wore, had the same "Dr. Marley" embroidered on her lapel, but she was almost always assumed to be a nurse, a social worker, a therapist, or a lab technician. Likewise, when Baker was published in the *New England Journal*—a crowning point in anyone's career—she was assumed to be anything but a physician.

Plato cast about for something to say, to break the uneasy silence. He noticed Gates was carrying a slide carousel, and felt a sudden chill. "Cal? Did you—"

"Yes, dear." She rolled her eyes. "Your slides are in the tan suitcase."

Gates smiled curiously.

Plato remembered his manners. "Doctor Gates, this is my wife. Doctor Cal Marley."

"Pleased to meet you, honey. Call me Eldon." He

shook Cal's hand and winked at Plato. "Now, that's what *I* need. Someone who can remember where my slides are!"

"Where did you say the suitcase was?" Plato asked his wife. A bellboy had disappeared with the luggage while they were signing in.

"Back at the lodge, inside a little alcove near the reception desk. Next to the ladies' room."

"Umm. Maybe I'd better be off to my lecture."

"Mind if I join you?" Gates asked. "I don't know where the conference rooms are. I feel like a rat in a maze in this place."

"Sure." Plato had flipped through one of the lodge's brochures while they were waiting, memorized the map, studied Chippewa Creek's history, counted the bricks in the hearth, and even spoken with Judith Lorantz for a minute or two.

Cal and Baker, deep in a conversation about women physicians, didn't even notice them leaving.

Cliff House was the oldest part of Chippewa Creek Lodge, Plato had learned. The gaudy Victorian mansion had been built back in the 1880s by another steel mogul from Cleveland. After he bet his fortune on the steam engine and lost, the house had been sold and converted to a hotel. The main part of the lodge was added on just before the Depression. The mansion communicated with the rest of the lodge through a long series of meandering corridors, stairways, and halls—the maze Gates had spoken of. It had its own small swimming pool and terrace; the main lodge featured a larger pool and courtyard. Despite its proximity to the main lodge and conference rooms, the mansion seemed secluded and private.

Rather than navigating the hallways, Plato decided to play it safe. He led Gates past the conservatory and library, down a short flight of stairs, and out under the porte cochière. Here, the gravel driveway swept under the ornate arched overhang and followed the edge of the cliff in a wide sweeping curve that looped to rejoin the access road. They turned left to follow the driveway back toward the lodge's main entrance.

"Quite a little woman you have there," Gates told him as they picked their way through the gravel. "Very attractive, if you don't mind my saying so. Not like that witch I had a run-in with. I'm not a chauvinist; I think women can do most men's work, almost as well as we can. With certain exceptions, eh? But women physicians are so terribly insecure. Like they've got a chip on their shoulders."

"I hadn't really noticed." Actually, it seemed just the opposite to Plato. Most of the women physicians he knew were exquisitely competent. And not ashamed of it; maybe that was what Gates meant.

"Does your wife work outside the home?" Gates was just making conversation.

"Yes," Plato replied, but he didn't elaborate. Evidently the researcher hadn't been listening during the introductions. "Are you married?"

"Never have been, never will be." He might have been a saint, or a knight, confessing his virtue and chastity. "Married to my work, like most physicians. I'm one of the few who'll admit it, though."

Plato didn't feel married to his work. He didn't even feel like he *dated* his work. At best, it was a brother-sister relationship. He felt a certain fondness for medicine, and sometimes it was a lot of fun, but it held utterly no romantic potential whatever.

Gates seemed to feel differently. After a thirty-year career, he still had that pre-lecture euphoria: the nervous chatter, tight smile, and quick breathing that would surely vanish when he started his presentation.

They mounted the smooth granite stairs beneath the arched stone entrance and stepped inside. The new owners had made the lobby into the showpiece of the lodge—from the wide mahogany stairway spiraling down from twin balconies overhead, to the carved oak woodwork and paneling of the walls and ceiling, to the wide double fireplace with gleaming antique brass trimmings, to the west-facing mullion-window, its stained glass sunburst glinting down across the slate floor. Someday, with a little work and a lot of money, maybe he and Cal would be able to remodel.

Someday, they'd pay off their student loans and buy a new car. Someday, they'd be able to afford a real vacation.

The manager, a haggard-looking fellow with blue stubbly cheeks and sad, tired eyes, stood behind the counter patiently listening to a guest's complaints about the plumbing, the linens, the size of the room, and the air-conditioning.

"I'm sorry—it's an old hotel." He shrugged mournfully. "If you'd like, I can put you down on the list for another room, should it become available."

The list was quite long.

When Plato asked about his luggage, the manager directed him to a small room almost hidden beneath the stairs. Gates twisted the knob and entered first.

"Not even locked," he grunted.

"We're probably the only people who know it's here," Plato replied. He found the tan canvas suitcase, unzipped it, and riffled through the clothes. Naturally, the slide carousel was on the bottom. He struggled to zip the suitcase back up.

"Might as well check my bag." Gates rooted through a blue Samsonite hardsider monogrammed with his initials, then snapped it shut and stood. "Everything's here."

"Good."

They headed back toward the conference rooms at the north end of the lodge. The new addition had been accompanied by a flurry of advertisement about the improved Chippewa Creek Conference Center. But few national organizations were interested in holding a conference in Cleveland at all, let alone just twenty miles south of the city. This meeting of the Society of North American Geriatricians—SNAG—was the first major conference Chippewa Creek had hosted since its reopening.

"Miguel has mentioned you several times," Gates said. "You knew each other in medical school, right?"

"We were roommates, all the way through." Plato wondered if he would have survived medical school without Miguel's help. All the time they had shared together—from the agonies of memorizing anatomy and biochemistry, to drilling each other on the nuances of pharmacology and microbiology, to the triumphs and tragedies of their clinical years. "He got me interested in geriatrics."

As a student, Miguel had grown very close to his first patient, an elderly woman with no family or friends, who showed up at the emergency room every few days with vague complaints and was released each time after a cursory examination. Miguel had taken the time to listen to her story, get to know her, gain her trust. The lump would have been obvious much earlier, but she had always refused a breast exam before. Maybe she knew.

The tumor had already spread; surgery was hopeless. She died during chemotherapy, another low blip on the survival curve for metastatic adenocarcinoma of the breast. But Miguel had written his first poem about her—based on several night-long conversations he'd had with Plato.

Gates was talking. "—awfully young to be editing a textbook, don't you think?"

"Not really." He shrugged. Miguel's achievements would never surprise Plato. His friend had always topped the class at Siegel, he'd published original research as a medical student, and he'd won the MetroCleveland Amateur Tennis title in his senior year. All while working nights as a bartender. "His research record is excellent; he's published more papers than a lot of researchers twice his age. And with his English degree, and the books of poetry he's published—he's a natural."

"Maybe," Gates conceded reluctantly.

"Anyway, he said you gave him a lot of help putting the initial proposal together," Plato added diplomatically.

"Of course. That's one of the primary roles of any department chair—mentoring the junior faculty." He frowned, and added softly, "Still, I didn't expect him to *succeed*."

Up ahead, the corridor opened into a wide modern atrium. Potted ferns hung from huge skylights in the ceiling; mirrored glass glittered in random patterns on the walls; a wire sculpture of something rusted at the center of a noisy fountain. Conference rooms A through F opened onto the atrium. Over the main entrance hung brass letters announcing that this was the "Chippewa Creek Conference Annex."

The sudden contrast with the staid dignity of the old lodge was somehow obscene—like stumbling on a McDonald's restaurant inside Windsor Castle.

"Anyway, it's a great opportunity for Miguel," Gates continued. "I just hope he comes through the grants investigation okay, or the publishers will get scared off."

"What? What are you talking about?" Miguel hadn't mentioned any pending investigation, but Victor's comments had made it sound like the old investigator was building a case against *Gates*.

"Doctor Gates! Doctor Gates!" A reception area occupied one corner of the atrium. Above, a sign read "Geriatric Sexuality Special-Interest Group." A frumpy woman with baggy jowls stood beside a potted palm and waved at them.

"If you'll excuse me—" Gates flashed a smile at Plato. "One of the graduates from our fellowship."

Plato glanced at his watch: it was almost noon. Gates darted away across the atrium, clasped the frumpy woman's hands and gave her a quick peck on the cheek. He turned and glanced at Plato from the corner of his eye.

Plato followed the signs to his room and arrived just on time, but the previous lecturer hadn't finished his presentation. He was standing at the podium near the front of the room, gesturing at the screen with a light pen, discussing another functional assessment scale. The scales were designed to measure elderly people's ability to manage in day-to-day living. A good enough concept, but functional assessment scales had multiplied like rabbits, and most of them measured the same things.

Apparently this scale was no different from the others—most of the poor fellow's audience had melted away. Besides that, he had gone overtime, worn out his welcome. Lulled by his steady baritone drone, most heads in the audience drooped forward in the classic chin-hand, elbow-knee posture for surreptitious sleep taught in medical school. Half the chairs were already vacant. The ranks of listeners were timing their withdrawal as carefully as a military retreat—slinking through the door one by one, their war-weary faces haggard with the desperation of boredom. Very soon, the speaker would glance up to find the besieged citadel abandoned.

A small crowd, Plato's future audience, was clustered just outside the door. He squeezed between them, carrying his slide carousel over his head, and glanced at the back of the room. No slide projector, yet the screen on the far wall glowed with an incredibly complex graph entitled "Correlations between Mortality, Surgical Morbidity, Quality of Life, and Self-Reported Health Status versus Nine Subcategories of the Zimmerman Scale of Functional Ability." In the dusty air, Plato traced the slide's blue beam to an audiovisual room one floor up.

He wriggled through the crowd again and stepped out into the atrium. A sign marked A-V CORRIDOR led him up a flight of stairs and down a darkened passageway spanning the backs of four conference rooms. He paused at the second booth. Zimmerman's voice rumbled through the soundproof glass to confirm his location. Down below, three attendees huddled in a tiny mass near the front. Zimmerman had them trapped; anonymous escape had become impossible.

Plato set his slides on the table beside the projector and waited. If anything, the lecturer's voice had grown louder, more insistent—almost pleading.

Watching through the glass, Plato realized that it wasn't Zimmerman's voice at all—his mouth wasn't even moving. Plato glanced down the dark corridor and saw two faces floating in the smoky glow of a distant slide projector. One of the faces belonged to a very short man with a very soft voice. His words drifted to Plato through the cottony stillness.

"I simply cannot and will not be a party to—"

The taller figure growled something.

"The report has been typed and submitted," Godwin continued calmly. "Informed consent cannot be taken lightly. You yourself—"

The growl rose to a high-pitched, whining retort.

"That is quite unreasonable and unfair, Doctor Lorantz. As matters stand, the most you will receive is a reprimand—a suspension of grant money for six months. But understand me: if you persist . . ."

Plato slid back behind the partition and tried not to listen to the rest. Poor Kelvin Lorantz—getting a grant was hard enough, but having it taken away could blackball you for life. Even getting a reprimand could make you an academic pariah. But Godwin was right—informed consent was a central issue for any research project.

A loud thump sounded down the hall, like the slamming of a door. Plato glanced out at the auditorium, then down at his watch. Twelve-fifteen. Two survivors were left in the audience, probably drawing straws to decide who would leave first.

He checked the projector. Zimmerman's carousel was on the last slide, thank goodness. A relatively simple one—"Correlations between the Zimmerman Scale of Functional Ability, the Zimmerman Mental Status Exam, and the Zimmerman Quality of Life Scale." Apparently Dr. Zimmerman was starting a franchise.

The speaker finally raised his remote and pressed the button. Blank white light flooded onto the screen, bringing the audience to life like wilted flowers meeting the morning sun. The two survivors rose to their feet and burst into grateful applause, and Plato headed downstairs to give his lecture.

CHAPTER THREE

"So how did your presentation go?" Cal asked. A picnic lunch was set up on the terrace behind Cliff House—deli meats and cheeses, fried chicken, hamburgers, and hot dogs. Plato had made a sub sandwich from everything, even the pork and beans. It had the shape and dimensions of a junior varsity football; he was wondering how to get it into his mouth.

Not that he was very hungry, really. Sitting across the table from Victor and Miguel set off flashbacks of the horrid drive and set his head spinning.

If he just squashed the sandwich flat—and stuffed a corner in—

"Mfrmbrfvphh," he finally mumbled, cheeks bulging obscenely. Maybe he *was* hungry.

"On second thought, don't answer." Cal's left upper lip wrinkled with puzzled disgust, like she'd just found something squishy under a rock and didn't really want to know what it was. "You might hurt yourself."

Miguel and Victor were watching Evelyn Baker. The older woman was already swimming, lapping the pool with the slow measured strokes of a distance expert.

"She does two miles, twice a day," Cal noted, scowling at Plato's dish: the smorgasbord sandwich, macaroni salad, potato chips, and brownie. And a pickle, Plato's concession to green vegetables. "One mile each of crawl, butterfly, breaststroke, and backstroke. She does the backstroke at night, says it helps her relax."

Plato sighed. Even *watching* her was tiring.

"I don't need that kind of relaxation," Godwin muttered with a wry smile. "Gallbladder trouble, arthritis, two mild strokes, and diabetes. If I were any more relaxed, I'd be dead."

"She's a vegetarian," Miguel mused, squinting balefully at his fried chicken. "I wonder if I could do that."

"Just to add a few months to your life?" The old geriatrician frowned at his cheeseburger and took an enormous bite. "Some things simply aren't worth it."

"Hear, hear," Plato agreed. Cal scowled again.

Godwin flipped open a bottle of Mocha-Tone and slathered it over the bare skin of his round shoulders. He gave a shy grin. "My skin's terribly sensitive lately. One of these days I'll probably just dry up and blow away."

"You've still got your feet on the ground," Miguel noted affectionately.

"One foot in the grave, perhaps." He downed the last bites of potato salad and cheeseburger. "Nothing brewing tonight, Miguel? Aside from the keynote address at seven, we have the day free?"

"Right."

"Then I may as well get some sun, perhaps even take a nap."

"The sun's bad for you, Victor," Miguel warned. "The ozone layer's all shot to hell."

"I have some ozone in a bottle here, my friend." Godwin waggled his tanning lotion at Miguel. "Mocha-Tone Number Ninety-six—like coating your skin with aluminum foil." He stood up, brown saggy belly drooping over his ancient plaid swimming trunks. "Let me know if Doctor Gates comes back—I need to discuss something with him."

Miguel sighed as the old researcher walked away.

"He's nuts about suntanning; no wonder his skin looks like boot leather. He'll get skin cancer one of these days, you watch."

"I hate to say it, but Victor is right," Plato said. "He'll probably die of something else long before skin cancer gets him."

"You'll never live to be a hundred with an attitude like that."

"Do you want to live to be a hundred?"

Miguel considered for a moment. "No."

"Plato wants to die of a massive heart attack in his sleep, on his sixty-fifth birthday," Cal said. "He's afraid of getting old. Some attitude for a geriatrician, huh?"

"Is that why he eats like he does?"

"Exactly."

They both stared at him. Plato stopped chewing, eyed the monster sandwich, and set it down. He swallowed and stroked his beard nervously. "Can't we talk about something else?"

Cal patted his hand. "Finish your sandwich, dear. We're just having a little fun at your expense."

"Glad to oblige." He picked up his sandwich again, and took a dainty bite. "You must have had a great time during your fellowship, Miguel. Victor sure is an interesting guy."

"That's one way to put it." Miguel was frowning, watching Godwin take a seat beside the pool.

"I think he's cute," Cal remarked.

"You think everyone's cute," Plato replied. He glanced at the other end of the pool. Evelyn Baker had finished her laps and was toweling herself dry. Gates was beside her, talking and smiling broadly. He nodded his head and chuckled about something, then jerked his thumb toward the woods in the distance.

Plato turned back to Miguel. "Kind of surprising, Victor being on the grants monitoring commission. I can't see him ordering physicians to give back their research money."

"Too mild-mannered, huh?"

Plato nodded.

"Too *cute*," Cal added.

"Well, all of his patients love him," Miguel replied with a grin. "But most of them have never crossed him. Back at Ashbury, he used to drive the administration crazy. I can't remember when he wasn't embroiled in some kind of dispute over funding, territory, staffing, whatever. And now that he's retired as fellowship director, he's blowing off steam with the Grants Monitoring Commission."

"Sounds like he's got his sights fixed on your boss," Plato noted.

Miguel glanced over at Gates and lowered his voice. "I think you're right. Victor just started auditing the grant records and accounts at Hartman—that's why he was in town. It wasn't just a friendly visit."

"And he found something against Doctor Gates?" Cal asked.

Miguel shrugged. "I don't know. But Eldon chairs the central research committee at Hartman, and he oversees all the accounting and administration. So naturally—"

"Hello again, folks! Enjoying yourselves?" Victor Godwin had popped up behind Miguel and Plato. He clung to their shoulders, bobbing and swaying like a channel buoy in heavy seas. Plato's sandwich suddenly tasted like tanning lotion; Victor might have taken a bath in cocoa butter. He squinted across the table at Cal and continued in a loud voice. "Have I complimented you on the appropriateness of your name? *Calista,* isn't it?"

Cal nodded, smiling politely.

"Means *beautiful,* in Italian. Or is it Greek? Well, anyway, it certainly fits." Victor's pupils looked tiny behind his Coke-bottle lenses. His face was flushed; his nose was the color of a ripe tomato. His knobby arms and legs might have been covered with radish skin. He slapped Plato's shoulder soundly. "You're a lucky fellow, Plato. *Plato!* Now there's a moniker. Course, your parents could have picked worse namesakes. I once had a patient named Fido, if you can believe it. Very proper society gentleman—Fido Percival Hector Abercrombie the Third, or some such nonsense. He said it had been in the family for generations. Imagine that! Hah!"

Actually, Plato's father had chosen his name. Funny thing, coming from a beat cop who barely made it through high school and never made it to sergeant. Plato had always been self-conscious about it.

He chuckled appreciatively.

"Are you feeling okay, Victor?" Miguel asked softly. "Maybe you should go inside, get some rest."

"I'm fine, never better, never better." His head drooped suddenly; his chin touched his chest. His voice fell. "A little tired, though . . ."

Godwin giggled softly, then tottered back to his chaise lounge. He picked up a book, set it down again, then stretched out on his back and closed his eyes. His face was drawn up in a blissful smile.

They sat in silence for a moment or two.

Finally, Cal asked, "Does Victor drink, Miguel?"

"Hardly ever. I'm worried about him." Miguel stared at Godwin's chaise and frowned. "I doubt it could be another stroke—could it, Plato?"

"Probably not." To kick off his diet, Plato left a few bites of sandwich behind. He moved on to the brownie. "Maybe he's just relaxing a little—letting his hair down, you know? Or maybe he mixed up one of his medicines."

"His skin looks terrible," Cal noted. "Like he's got sunstroke."

"No way," Plato replied. "He hasn't even been outside for an hour, and he's well-hydrated."

"Maybe you're right—maybe he's just relaxing for once." Miguel nodded to himself. "I'd better leave him alone—if I say anything, he'll just get worried. Victor tends to fixate on his health."

"Really?" Cal asked.

"Those two strokes scared him. He worries that he's not as sharp as he was. Last month he called to tell me he scored only twenty-seven out of thirty on the Kruppsberger Mental Status Scale for Professionals."

"Another scale," Plato groaned. Someday, you won't need a personality at all. You could just stamp a set of numbers on your forehead so people could decide whether you were worth talking to.

"Twenty-seven's within the normal range, anyway." Miguel shook his head and glanced at Godwin. The researcher was resting peacefully, eyes closed, still smiling happily. "Well, Victor will have to get along without me this afternoon. I've got to run to a meeting—I'm chairman of the Literature and Medicine Special-Interest Group. And then—are you two going to the governor's keynote address tonight?"

"We're taking the evening off," Cal replied. Beneath the table, she slid her bare foot along Plato's leg. "Starting our anniversary celebration a little early."

"Uhh—yeah," he agreed. "We have reservations tonight. At the Joie de Vivre downtown."

Miguel whistled. "I hope things turn out better this time. Did you ever tell Cal about the time you—"

"No," Plato growled.

"What?" Cal asked. "What?"

Miguel winked. "I'll leave the explaining to you, my friend. And happy anniversary!"

As he walked off, Cal's toe probed the top of Plato's foot, found the superficial peroneal nerve and tapped it menacingly. "What was he talking about?"

"You know, I'm not really sure—" Her toe ground into the nerve, and Plato's memory miraculously returned. It was wonderful, being married to a pathologist. "Okay, okay, I'll tell you."

The pressure and pain gradually eased, but she didn't move her foot away. "I'm waiting."

"Back in medical school, long, long before I met you, there was a girl—Cindy Brunelli, I think her name was. Not at all attractive. In fact she was so ugly that I felt sorry for her—" The toe mashed down again. "Well, she wasn't completely unattractive. She was okay-looking, if you liked that type. Couldn't hold a candle to you. We went out a couple of times, and finally I took her to the Joie de Vivre."

"Our restaurant," Cal noted. "Where you proposed to me."

"This happened years before I met you. And by the time it was all over, I wished I had taken her to Burger King."

"Go on."

"Well, I only had forty dollars with me—"

Cal smirked.

"—and she started off with some expensive wine—LaSomething Rothschild, I think it was—and then she had to have the snails, and a lobster tail along with her rack of lamb, and three appetizers, and another bottle of wine, and some kind of flaming brandy dessert—it's not funny!"

Cal bit her lip, and a spreading blush swallowed the freckles sprinkled across her nose. Tears trickled from the corners of her brown eyes, and her shoulders heaved slightly, but she wasn't laughing. "You're absolutely right. It's very sad."

"I've never seen a man or woman eat so much before or since. She was just a little slip of a thing, too—not much bigger than you. When I saw the prices, I knew I was in trouble. I called Miguel at the apart ment, begged him to scrounge up some money for me, maybe a couple of hundred dollars. He didn't have enough, so he had to call somebody else. I kept stalling the waiter, asking for more coffee, until finally Miguel showed up with practically half the senior class of Siegel Medical College, honest to God."

Cal couldn't contain it any longer. She exploded with a couple of big knee-slapping guffaws that trailed into a whistly little hoot—"Pah-*Hah*! Pah-*Hah*! Heh-Heh-Heeeeee."

"They made a big ceremony out of it," Plato complained. "Paraded up one by one, and dropped a dollar or two onto the check plate. I was never so embarrassed in my entire life."

"You poor dear." Cal wiped her eyes.

"Anyway, she finally married a plastic surgeon—he probably feeds her a lot better than I ever could."

"How much money did you have the first time you took *me* there?"

"Three hundred dollars, two Master Cards, and an American Express. And all you had was a salad."

"And I insisted on paying."

"Yes." Plato sighed dreamily. "That's when I knew I was in love."

"All this time I thought it was my fabulous figure." Cal struck a pose, ran her fingers through her butterscotch hair, and leered at him.

"We-ell. That certainly didn't hurt." Plato grinned. When they first met, he'd assumed that her perfect figure came from diet and exercise. Working out at the club, Cher-like, in a body stocking and leg warmers. Cute little bounces in an aerobics class, breaking into a pretty sweat at the weight machines.

But she never had time for aerobics, or jogging, or biking, or pretty sweats. She built her muscles at work. As deputy county coroner and a staff pathologist at

Riverside General, she did a lot of heavy lifting; she performed up to twenty autopsies a week.

Cal glanced at her watch, a cheap Timex with a cracked crystal and a second hand that always pointed down. It didn't matter; she never took any pulse rates. "We'd better start getting ready."

"What are you talking about? Our reservations are for six-thirty. It's only two o'clock."

"I know. But you haven't seen our room yet." She grinned playfully. "A king-size bed—one of those heart-shaped ones. And a Jacuzzi. I think Miguel gave us the honeymoon suite."

"Hmm." The foot brushed across the inside of his knee. "Thought we might start our celebration a little early, huh?"

"Smart boy." She stood and patted his cheek. "I married *you* for your brains."

He followed her inside, up the stairs, and down a walnut-paneled hallway. They were staying in another octagonal room, in the turret just above the parlor. The gold and green wallpaper was peeling, the carpet had a few holes, and faint water stains marked the bathroom ceiling. They had only two windows instead of six, but a wide sliding glass door with a balcony hung out over the courtyard. The sheets were clean, the bathroom had more towels than their entire house, and the water was indeed clear.

A bottle of champagne was chilling on the table, along with a cryptic prescription from Miguel's office pad:

"Brut Champagne
#: 750 cc
Sig: 120 cc every 20 min. until inebriated, repeat prn."

Cal unpacked the three bags, hung most of the clothes in the closet, tidied up, and stowed away the suitcases while Plato got more ice and watched the Indians win another game in their brand-new stadium.

"This is the life," Plato would later remember telling her, as they were sitting in their private Jacuzzi, up to their necks in soap bubbles, crowded together and sipping each other's champagne, Cal's face flushed and dreamy and more relaxed than he had ever remembered seeing her.

And it would always seem like a dream, a bad dream, how the telephone had rung and how he had reluctantly climbed out of the bath, wrapped himself in a towel, padded across the floor to the bathroom extension, thinking how decadent life could be, and how *good,* and picked up the receiver to hear the news that Victor Godwin had been found dead in the bright sunny courtyard just below their window, just ten minutes ago.

CHAPTER FOUR

The stiffening breeze was ripe with rain. A flotilla of thunderclouds had sailed across the sun. At the river's edge, poplar leaves shifted and shivered with anticipation. Already, puffs of wind tugged at tablecloths and rippled the grassy knoll between the courtyard and the clifftops. The small crowd huddled close to the body as if to ward off a sudden chill. Cal caught snatches of their conversation as she entered the courtyard with Plato.

"Pulmonary embolus, almost certainly," Eldon Gates pronounced in the slow solemn tone of a judge reading a guilty verdict. "Judging by the suddenness of it—"

"But *was* it sudden?" Kelvin Lorantz challenged. "After all, he was behaving rather oddly today."

"A subclinical myocardial infarction could do that," Dean Fairfax rumbled.

"A what?" asked Judith Lorantz.

"Subclinical, my dear. A heart attack that doesn't yield significant symptoms or signs. It may have led to atrial fibrillation, then a series of emboli to the brain causing progressive symptoms of—"

"If you ask me, all this speculation is rather morbid and pointless," Evelyn Baker scolded. "Besides, the findings point unmistakably to a single, massive stroke."

"What about his odd behavior?" Fairfax whispered.

"Excuse me." Cal shouldered her way through the

circle, knelt beside the body, and started a cursory examination. The old physician lay on the chaise as before, white hotel towel folded beneath his head, hands resting peacefully at his side. He still wore the plaid swimming trunks and the blissful, squinty grin, like the sun was shining in his face, or he was having a wonderful dream.

Cal hoped her face looked like that when she died.

"*Doctor* Marley!" Behind her, Gates was hissing at Plato. "What *is* your wife doing?"

Cal rolled the body slightly and pressed her finger against the bare skin of Godwin's back. Livor mortis was already setting in; the face, chest, and fronts of his legs were pale and gray as freshly cut granite. But the backs of his legs and trunk were stained a faint purple from the force of gravity dragging blood to the dependent areas.

"Checking whether the livor mortis is fixed," Plato replied. Cal smiled inwardly, hearing the teaching tone creep into his voice—that same kindly kindergarten lilt he used on medical students who hadn't read up on their patients. "See how the darker skin blanches when she presses on it? That helps determine the time of death."

"I'm aware of that," Gates snapped. He must have been hiking; he was wearing blue jeans, a ragged-sleeved Cornell University sweatshirt, and ankle-high mountain boots. The boots and jeans were spattered with mud, but his thinning hair was unmussed, and he smelled like a stand of aspen in springtime. "I don't see why your wife should be concerned. Is she some sort of lab technician?"

"She's a forensic pathologist and deputy county coroner," Baker interrupted. Cal looked up at her. Evelyn had traded her caftan for a madras plaid cotton suit, and her long white hair was harnessed in a stern bun. Evidently she had just returned from a lecture, or she was about to give one. The older woman's weathered cheeks dimpled slightly as she watched Gates's reaction. "I think she has a right to do whatever she believes is appropriate."

Gates stared from Cal to Baker and back again. His eyes bulged a little.

"Coroner?" he muttered softly.

Baker grinned. "That's right, *honey*."

Cal returned her attention to the body. Mild rigor mortis affecting the facial musculature. The stiffening was caused by a lack of chemical energy and began with the smaller muscles. Godwin's jaw was nearly frozen while his arms and legs still moved easily.

She ran a finger along his gleaming skin. Victor certainly liked tanning lotion; his skin was still oily and sweet-smelling. Ozone in a bottle. Like coconuts, and something sharper. No outward signs of trauma, but that didn't mean anything. A fatal blow to the abdomen, chest, or head could be almost undetectable.

Of course, it was ridiculous to think that the death of a seventy-three-year-old man under these circumstances was anything but natural.

"Who found him?" Cal murmured. They were all speaking softly, in the lowered voices people use at bedsides when the patient is asleep or dead. With Godwin, it would have been hard to tell.

"Miguel did," Baker replied.

"Apparently, he had come out to ascertain Doctor Godwin's condition," added Fairfax. "We had all gone inside when the weather changed—"

"Everyone except Godwin," Kelvin Lorantz noted.

"Where's Miguel?" Plato asked.

"Inside, trying to reach the family." Evelyn Baker gestured to the conservatory whose tall arched windows faced the courtyard. "He said Victor's brother is a doctor, too. Miguel is trying to track him down—he's practicing somewhere in Europe. Maybe someone should—"

Plato touched Cal's arm. "I'll see how he's doing."

He sounded tired. Cal glanced up at her husband. His wide mouth was drawn into a grim line. The cheery holiday spirit had drained away, leaving his broad shoulders slumped, his tall frame stooped. His deep-set eyes were almost unreadable—dark cavelike circles holding a glint of green. A pair of emeralds at the bottom of a well. But he squeezed her arm, and his heavy black beard split into a reassuring smile.

"Miguel was close to Doctor Godwin, wasn't he?" Baker noted, after Plato had walked off.

"He did his geriatrics fellowship at Ashbury in San Francisco. In Doctor Godwin's program." Jessica Novak was standing near Cal's head; her voice was almost a whisper. Cal had spoken with the geriatrics fellow earlier, while Plato was giving his lecture. Jessica was studying in Miguel's program at Hartman. He had asked Jessica to be a contributing editor—quite an honor, really. All the other editors except Cal were board-certified geriatricians with years of experience. "On rounds, Miguel was always quoting him, telling stories about him . . ."

She was tall and slender, with wide eyes, frazzled brown hair, and a thin upper lip that twitched whenever she spoke. Her voice trailed off. The group shuffled in place for several minutes and watched Cal's exam. Finally, Gates broke the awkward silence.

"We can only speculate what happened, of course. My guess is that he died from massive pulmonary embolism—a saddle embolus, most likely." He seemed to have recovered his composure. "Not that we'll ever know, since there won't be an autopsy."

Cal grabbed a stick of Big Red from her pocket and popped it in her mouth. "How long ago was he found?"

Gates picked up a bright red Land's End backpack from the ground at his feet and dragged out a massive gold pocket watch. "Must have been half an hour ago now—five o'clock, I'd say. I came back early from my hike when I saw the rain coming."

He dropped the watch back into the pack, but Cal could still hear it ticking. Like that time bomb game she played when she was a kid, except they used Mom's old brass alarm clock and whoever lost had to kiss Edith Zabrowski's nerdy little brother. Cal never lost; she always caught the clock with her finger between the clapper and the bell. Hubert Zabrowski had become a priest, Cal remembered, then wondered why she was thinking about Huey Zabrowski.

"I saw Miguel here, kneeling by the body," Gates continued. "Poor kid was about to start artificial respirations, if you can believe it. He must have been pretty shaken up; any fool could see that Godwin was long past resuscitating. Even in the heat, his skin was cold as a slab of marble."

"It's a terrible thing—terrible. I don't see how anyone can bear to—I mean, to touch a dead body—" Judith Lorantz hugged herself and shivered. Her lips pressed to a thin white line and her jaw muscles worked. But curiosity flickered in her pale blue eyes. "How long ago do you think he died?"

"Around a couple of hours," Cal replied. Not long after they went inside. It had happened awfully quickly. A fat raindrop splashed Victor's half-closed eye; Cal almost expected him to blink.

Kelvin Lorantz spoke up. He patted his wife's shoulder and rolled an olive around the bottom of his glass. "I called for an ambulance when I heard what had happened, but Doctor Gates told me to cancel it."

"It's just as well," Cal said. "The morgue likes to send their own equipment."

She looked up at Plato, who had returned in time to

hear her last comment. He slumped further and stared up at the lowering sky.

"Then you *are* doing an autopsy?" Lorantz frowned.

Gates looked astonished. "The idea that his death could be anything but—but—"

"At his age? Preposterous!" Harlow Fairfax pronounced. The dean mopped his wide forehead with a handkerchief. "Simply preposterous. And disrespectful. *Del mortuis nil nisim bonus.*"

Cal grimaced. Fairfax's Latin was terrible, and the saying wasn't even appropriate. "In the first place, *I* won't be doing anything—I'm not on call tonight."

Plato's eyebrows lifted slightly.

"In the second place, I agree. Doctor Godwin almost certainly died from natural causes."

"Then why—"

"Regardless of his age, his death was sudden, unexplained, and unexpected. Most of the coroner's cases in Cuyahoga County are just like this—maybe a heart attack, maybe a stroke, maybe something else. If we stopped doing autopsies on everyone over age sixty-five, I'll bet a lot more elderly people would start dying suddenly and unexpectedly." She stood and glared at the group. "I'm only explaining all this because I'm tired of physicians making lame rulings on cause and manner of death and preventing autopsies when they don't know the first thing about how some of their patients died."

Plato coughed, and Cal stopped speaking. Kelvin Lorantz was studying his feet. Harlow Fairfax's mouth hung open, huge rubbery lips slack with astonishment. The dean supposedly distrusted women physicians; Cal's tirade had probably strengthened his prejudice. Gates had overcome his shock at finding she wasn't just an adoring housewife. He was smiling slightly, eyes twinkling at her, arms crossed, shoulder muscles bulging. Amused, faintly respectful—and patronizing. Like those old Virginia Slims commercials: *"You've come a long way, baby."*

"Excuse us." Two uniformed paramedics from Petrelli's Ambulance Service and Funeral Home had rolled a gurney to the edge of the crowd. Behind them stood a white-coated pathology technician from the county morgue.

Cal looked at Plato. "How did they—?"

"I rang them up before we came outside," he replied. Apparently, he knew her better than she realized.

The scattered raindrops had coalesced to a drizzle, and thunder grumbled faintly. The spectators moved aside for the gurney, then drifted off toward the back porch. Miguel appeared just as Victor was being loaded onto the cart. Evelyn Baker lagged behind, flashing worried glances at Miguel.

Cal turned to Marcus, the pathology technician who helped with most of her autopsies. He was tall, with gray hair and beard, very distinguished-looking. Like many of the assistants—or *dieners,* as they were generally known—Marcus had started at a desk job in the department, with little or no medical knowledge at all. An interest in the pathologist's work and prospect of higher pay had drawn him to part-time work in the lab downstairs. After fifteen years of it, he was as deft with a scalpel as many of the deputy coroners. Newcomers to the department often assumed he was Cal's boss. He was good enough that she didn't really mind.

"How are things over at the lab?" she asked.

Marcus shook his head. Two weeks ago, a small fire had broken out in the basement of the Cuyahoga County Morgue. There wasn't much damage, but the fire inspector had ordered a massive overhaul of the sprinkler and alarm systems. The ceilings throughout the entire basement—including the two main autopsy suites, holding area, and freezer—had been torn apart. The cooling and ventilation units weren't working properly. Even if you *could* perform an autopsy there, you wouldn't want to. At least, not for another week or so.

"Jim Cartwright's got three posts stacked up—he's working on them over at University. Doesn't want to go home until he's done."

"Poor Eeyore," Cal sympathized. Jim Cartwright was another deputy coroner, one with a perpetual black cloud hovering over his head. His outlook was as gloomy as Milne's donkey, and with good reason. Whenever he was on call, Cleveland's homicide rate skyrocketed. Most of the other deputy coroners kept pretty regular hours, postponing autopsies until the following day if necessary. For Eeyore, though, procrastination would be pointless. Cartwright assumed tomorrow's caseload would be even worse, and he was usually right.

"How about taking him over to Riverside?" she asked.

Marcus shrugged. "No problem. You going to do the post?"

"I don't know." Cal glanced over at her husband. Plato was talking with Miguel. "Probably. I don't think we'll be doing much celebrating tonight."

"Celebrating what?" Marcus draped a sheet over the body and cinched the straps tight.

"Oh, nothing, really."

Marcus shrugged. "You want the full prep?" Hands in his pockets, he watched the paramedics wheel the cart across the courtyard and onto the sidewalk running between the house and the jagged cliffs.

Cal considered. "Yeah. Draw a blood sample and run a tox screen as soon as you get back. Have them phone the results to me as soon as they're ready."

"Sure, Doctor Marley." Marcus turned to follow the gurney.

Cal glanced over at Evelyn Baker. The older physician was biting her lip, shaking her head sadly. Their eyes met.

"Such a shame," Baker said.

Cal nodded slowly, watched Baker drift away to join the others on the porch, then walked over to her husband's side.

"I finally got hold of his brother's home telephone number, but he's out on a house call," Miguel was saying. "He's somewhere in England, if you can believe it—has an office near Liverpool. I'll try again later."

"And he doesn't have any other relatives?" Plato asked. No wonder Godwin had been so close to Miguel.

"None—just the brother."

"Was he married?"

"Widowed. No kids. Spent all his holidays with us—he got to be pretty fond of Roberto and Maria." He took a deep breath, opened his eyes wide, and stared up at the sky. "Damn. I've got to call Carmen— she'd want to know.'"

"Good idea," Plato agreed.

After Miguel left, Cal slid her arm through Plato's. "Maybe you should stay here with him. He still seems pretty upset."

"He's not in a really talkative mood." He looked down at Cal, considering. "Miguel gets like that. I think he wants to be alone. And besides—"

"It's okay, Plato." She took his hand. "There's no reason we can't move our dinner back a day or two."

Plato sighed again. No reason except for the dozen long-stemmed Madame del Bard roses, boxed and tied with a red velvet bow, waiting at the restaurant to be sent out with the wine. Just like when they got engaged—same florist, same restaurant. That was almost two years ago, back when he didn't have enough money for a ring—*the* ring, that was burning a hole in his pocket now.

But Plato had seen her like this before. Her eyes shone bright as mint-proof pennies, and she leaned forward on the balls of her feet, like a runner at the blocks. And she chewed gum. "Why don't we just head over to the lab?"

Cal acted surprised. "What for?"

"I heard you talking to Marcus."

"Yeah." She shrugged. "Jim Cartwright's on call again—he's got a lot of cases stacked up."

"Poor guy. Then again, I don't remember Eeyore ever coming back from vacation to help *you* out."

Cal scuffed her feet and stared at the sidewalk. "You're right. I was just getting carried away. A couple of things seemed a little strange, that's all. I'll call Eeyore and—"

"Forget it." Long ago, Plato had learned that Cal was almost impossible to live with once she got her teeth into a case. Every death, from acute glomerulonephritis to malignant hyperthermia to ligature strangulation, was a mystery—one that only Cal could solve. Her mother had been an investigative reporter for the Chicago *Tribune*; the drive was probably genetic. "Let's just go to the lab."

"You don't mind—really?" Cal's eyes lit up. "It won't take long, I promise."

"No." Plato would have to make a few phone calls of his own. "No, I don't mind."

Cal's tenacity had been one of the few snags in their marriage. Barely a month after their wedding, she had failed to come home from work. Plato had planned to surprise her with a romantic evening—dinner at the Top of the Town, a couple of hours with the Cleveland Orchestra at Severance Hall, a suite reserved at the Ritz-Carlton. After a long search, he'd finally found her at the county morgue, just about the time *The Moldau* was probably winding down.

He canceled the room reservations and watched her

complete the autopsy, then drove her home in glum silence. She explained it all to him then, told him the
story of her mother's supposed suicide. The mystery
no one had ever solved, or even taken much of an interest in. Sometimes, looking back, Cal was certain it
was a cover-up. Other times, she was just as sure
someone had simply dropped the ball, bungled the investigation and wouldn't bother to admit it.

So now, when Cal lost her perspective on a case,
went tearing after a mystery that wasn't there, Plato
just smiled and nodded, tried to understand.

He was smiling and nodding now, trying to understand. "Come on—I'll drive you over to Riverside."

Cal sighed. "You think it's all right, leaving Miguel
alone?"

"He likes to chew on things for a day or two." Plato
was remembering Miguel's first patient, the old woman
with breast cancer. "He saves it up, then talks it all
out—for five or six hours. He's in the chewing stage
now."

The spectators were still clustered on the back
porch, so they followed the sidewalk around the mansion. At the front of Cliff House, Godwin's body was
being loaded into the ambulance beneath the shelter of
the porte cochière. Marcus slammed the door and the
ambulance headed off with no sirens or flashers.

They mounted the steps and stood inside the door.
Cal looked up at him. "Why don't I call the restaurant
while you tell Miguel where we're going?"

"Fine," he replied, then shuddered. "But this time,
I'm driving."

CHAPTER FIVE

"So what is it?" Plato asked as they hurried across the main lobby of Cleveland Riverside General. The storm rumbled like a freight train on the huge skylight overhead. "What's the story with Godwin?"

"Story?" Cal shouted above the din. "What do you mean?"

The main lobby was emptier than Plato had ever seen it. During the day, it looked like the trading floor at the New York Stock Exchange. Harried clerks cowered behind tiny windows labeled LABORATORY, X-RAY, and SPECIAL PROCEDURES. Patients were herded like milling cows or airline passengers through a velvet-roped maze. A dozen televisions carrying different channels would blast from every corner of the wide, oak-paneled room. Above it all, a mechanical voice whispered a constant mantra through the public address system: "The orange floor stripes lead to Outpatient Surgery. The yellow floor stripes lead to Radiology and Special Procedures. The green floor stripes—"

But now, Saturday evening, the offices were all closed. Visiting hours were almost over. The admitting windows were blinded, the televisions were still, and even the public address system was stifled by the force of the pounding rain. A single old man lounged in an arm chair, eyes closed, mouth open, head lolling on his shoulder at an impossible angle.

"The autopsy—you said you suspected something, remember?" A drip splashed onto Plato's forehead; he mopped it away with his sleeve. Yellow buckets were scattered around the lobby like mushrooms, and were every bit as effective at catching water. "And I heard you asking Marcus to run a tox screen."

Plato's ears rang in the sudden silence of the elevator. They were the only passengers on the long ride to the subbasement.

"I wouldn't exactly say I *suspect* anything," Cal explained. She was leaning against the steel handrail, watching the indicator flick slowly from L to B. "Tox screens are cheap and pretty routine. But some things just didn't seem to fit."

"Like what?" The doors squealed open at the basement, one floor before their stop. A tall man in a clown suit and enormous orange shoes stood there, wrestling with a flock of Mylar balloons.

"Which way to the orthopedic floor?" he asked. His mouth was painted in a wide smile, and his eyes were outlined with red diamonds. A tiny black top hat nested in a fringe of orange hair. A brass horn dangled from the belt of his plaid pants.

Plato shook his head. "We're going down. Wait till this car comes back, then go up one floor—to the lobby. Follow the blue lines and take that elevator to six."

The clown nodded and gave a grateful honk as the elevator door closed.

After years of practically living in hospitals as interns, residents, and fellows, he and Cal had grown accustomed to the surreal atmosphere of hospitals at night.

Cal was silent while they entered the subbasement and navigated the maze of concrete corridors, footsteps echoing hollowly down long-forgotten passages and empty classrooms. She retrieved her keys, opened the double doors marked AUTHORIZED PERSONNEL ONLY, and flicked on the lights.

Plato blinked in the sudden brightness and glanced around the room. With its yellow tile walls and green linoleum floor, it might have been one of the operating rooms. But the autopsy suite lacked the usual tubes and masks and compressors for anesthesia. There were no crash carts or autoclaves or fiberoptics or lasers. And no racks of sutures and staples and bandages for closing the incisions again.

It wasn't even very neat. Specimen containers were scattered across the countertops like jars of ingredients collected by some mad chef. A set of knives was drying in a rack beside the sink; one still had flecks of blood on the handle. And papers covered every remaining inch of usable space—death certificates and lab results and consent forms, sprinkled like windblown autumn leaves across shelves, refrigerators, equipment carts, even one of the autopsy tables.

Although Riverside General didn't house the county morgue, autopsies still were frequently performed here. Even when patients died in the hospital, physicians often requested postmortems to learn precisely what had happened. And because Riverside was a teaching hospital, doctors-in-training often attended and learned from the autopsies as well. Postmortems allowed the young physicians a look inside the machine, which was wondrous even in its failure.

As part-time faculty in the hospital's pathology residency, Cal helped train the residents in anatomic and forensic pathology. She spent most of her time at Riverside in this room, performing autopsies with assistance from the residents. She called the dissecting suite her second office. Plato called it her second home.

The table was occupied by a white-sheeted lump. Cal grabbed a white coverall and flipped one to Plato. They both donned masks and gloves, and she slipped

into her bloodstained Keds high-tops; the paper shoe
covers never worked perfectly.

Plato stood across from her at the L-shaped table.
Godwin's body looked pitifully small on the gleaming
metal surface. Dozens of perforations punctured the
shelf holding the body, allowing fluid to drip onto the
polished aluminum below. The far end of the table held
two deep sinks with adjustable drain levels and constantly running water. At a right angle to the sinks was
another table, where the organs were examined in de-
tail after they were removed from the body. The sloping aluminum planes beneath both tables converged at
center drains leading to an outlet in the floor.

Cal lifted the sheet from Victor's head. The scalp
had been folded forward and down over his face, and
the cranial vault—the top of his head—was removed.
"I didn't want to talk about it at the hotel, or even in
the elevator. But didn't you notice something strange
about him? The things he said at lunch this afternoon,
the way he looked?"

"He looked like a cherry tomato," Plato replied.
"With red pipe cleaners for arms. Victor *said* he was
sensitive to the sun, Cally."

Her forehead wrinkled and an invisible frown
formed behind the blue paper mask. "But what about
the way he was acting? Some of the things he said—
they were totally inappropriate. That business about
my name. It was almost like he was coming on to me.
And I'd hardly expected him to poke fun at you like
that."

Plato shrugged. "He wasn't poking fun at me—he
just wanted to tell a funny story. Just a goofy old guy
having a good time."

Cal shuffled to the other wing of the L, where
Marcus had laid out the contents of the thoracic cavity:
heart, lungs, windpipe, all connected at the mediasti-
num. Their weights, along with those of the brain, kid-

neys, adrenals, and liver, were already entered on the chalkboard. A notebook hung from a hook on the wall; Cal walked over and studied it closely. "Good—the pathology resident was here. He didn't find anything unusual on external exam or during the prep, but that doesn't surprise me. . . . Marcus sent for the tox screen at six-thirty; we should be getting the results soon."

"Why are you interested in the tox screen?"

Cal drifted back to the body. "Victor was acting pretty unrestrained, didn't you think? Frontal disinhibition—happens with alcohol, cocaine, narcotics."

Plato snorted. "Is that what this is all about?" He chuckled and shook his head. "You've got to admit, psychiatry isn't exactly your field. Most of your patients are too far gone even for psychoanalysis. If he had frontal disinhibition, which I doubt, it could have been caused by a series of small strokes. Microinfarct dementia. The control areas of his brain were probably just—"

"Then how do you explain his pupils?"

"Pupils?" He glanced down at the body. "I can't even *see* his pupils—you've got his scalp folded down over his face."

"This afternoon, idiot. Didn't you notice how tiny his pupils were?" Cal freed the brain from the cranial vault and gingerly placed it on a plastic board. She plucked a long gleaming blade from the rack beside the sink. It passed through the brain with virtually no pressure. Thin, even slices curled into a neat pile. Plato remembered his father carving the Thanksgiving turkey with equal precision and grace.

"His eyes," Plato mused. He glanced over at the countertop, where Godwin's belongings were heaped in a pile. Swimsuit, towel, shoes . . . "His *glasses*. That's why his pupils were so tiny—didn't you see how thick his glasses were? Like a pair of telescope lenses."

"Exactly," Cal agreed. "So his eyes looked huge. But his pupils still looked tiny—have you ever seen a heroin addict?"

"Stop it, kiddo. Your imagination's getting—"

They both jumped when the telephone rang. Cal flipped her gloves into an orange hazardous waste bag and grabbed the receiver. "Pathology. Uh-huh. Yeah. Go ahead and run that, too. How long do you think it'll take? Okay, I'll send someone over now."

She hung up and turned to Plato. "How'd you like to run a little errand for me?"

"Pizza? Great idea, but let's leave the anchovies off this time. You want to try Player's again?"

"How can you think about food at a time like this?" She donned a new pair of gloves.

"Why not?" He glanced at his watch. "It's almost seven-thirty. Besides, you pathologists are always talking about food. Look at your terminology—chicken fat emboli, caseous necrosis, currant jelly clots . . . marmalade mucosa."

"There's no such thing as marmalade mucosa. You're making that up." Her forehead wrinkled again. "But you know, I had one case a couple of years back—some kind of bizarre stomach infection. Syphilis, I think. Sort of like cherry marmalade, but a lot more—"

"I get the picture." Plato grimaced. His wife had an unsettling talent for description.

"Then forget the pizza and run over to chemistry for me, okay? They're just getting the results in." She poked his belly with her index finger. "You shouldn't need to eat until tomorrow—that sandwich you ate this afternoon had enough cholesterol to choke a horse."

"Horses don't eat cholesterol. They're vegetarians."

"Exactly. That's why they run so fast." She patted his rear. "Git."

"Nei-ei-eigh." He kicked off his gown and trotted to the door.

Cal called after him. "Don't go all the way back to the elevators; there's a stairwell just down the hall. Two rights and a left. It'll take you straight up to the chemistry lab."

Half an hour later, Plato finally reached his destination. Two rights and a left had taken him down a short hallway that ended in a broom closet. He couldn't find the autopsy suite again, or the elevators, or a single familiar landmark. Riverside General's subbasement was a catacombs—dank, tortuous, and poorly lit, the foundation of decades of poorly planned additions, renovations, and modernizations. After twenty minutes of walking, the only individuals he had met were three dead cockroaches and a Happy Tooth beanbag chair. And cigarette butts everywhere; the hospital's no-smoking policy was being strictly implemented. One cavernous room held hundreds of boxes of hospital equipment—syringes, IV tubing, bedpans, sterile gowns—all submerged beneath a thick patina of dust. Back in the '70s, Plato remembered, a medical shipment from Chicago had gone missing. The thieves were never caught; now he knew why.

Water pipes, electrical lines, and asbestos-covered steam fittings twisted and turned overhead in a crazy weave. Walking to the pathology lab, he'd often imagined one of the steam lines blowing open, roasting him lobsterlike with live steam. In these deserted hallways, no one would hear his screams.

The pipes overhead were dramatically smaller than they were near the autopsy suite. He tried using pipe gauge to measure his progress, and gradually worked his way back. He finally found the elevators and arrived at the chemistry lab—weary, bedraggled, but triumphant.

"What took you so long?" the lab secretary asked.

She was sitting behind the desk, feet propped on the computer keyboard, watching *Jeopardy!* on the waiting area TV, and eating pizza.

"I got a flat tire. Are all the tests in?" The delicate scent of herb chicken, roasted garlic, and pesto sauce wafted past his nose from the half-open box atop the counter. He glanced at the lid: *Player's Pizza and Pasta.*

"Yeah." Reluctantly, she lifted her feet from the keyboard, pedaled her chair across the linoleum, and grabbed a sheaf of lab results. She grunted, leaned forward, and slid the printouts across the counter. "Here."

"Thanks." Plato smiled then glanced at the pizza. "What kind is it?"

"Pollo Pesto." She grabbed another slice and took a bite.

"Never tried it," he lied hopefully.

"It's pretty good." She nabbed the box, rolled back to a refrigerator marked BLOOD/URINALYSIS SPECIMENS ONLY! and placed it inside. "Guess I'll save this for lunch tomorrow. Doc says I've got to lose weight, exercise more."

"Tough break. I'll bet this job keeps you running."

"You ain't kidding."

He stopped by his office in the Professional Center across the street, then headed back to the autopsy suite. When he reached the morgue again, Cal was cradling a familiar-looking package. It was the biggest box the florist had, but the buds were so huge that they were packed in four staggered rows—the stems stuck out through a hole in one end. A fat velvet ribbon was drawn up in an enormous red bow.

"Oh, Plato—they're *beautiful!*"

"You haven't even opened the box," he observed wryly.

"I wanted to wait till you got here." Cal slipped the ribbon off, dropped it in a specimen bag, and placed it in her purse. Slowly, she lifted the lid. The red roses, big and round as tangerines, were just starting to open. "I think I'm going to cry."

"Me, too. I didn't think Georges would send them over from the restaurant. He hemmed and hawed, said he'd have to send a waiter over. I never really expected him to—"

She pulled his head down, planted a long lingering kiss on his lips, then turned away quickly. "I've got to find something to put these in."

She bustled around the room, found a clean knife, whacked the ends off the roses, and grabbed a tall plastic container from a shelf. She peered at the date, dumped the contents into the orange hazardous waste bag, and filled it with water.

"What was in there?" he asked.

"It's not important. Besides, the formalin will probably preserve the flowers."

"You're so romantic."

"What did the lab results show?"

"I didn't look at them. Let's see—" He glanced down at the forms. "Tox screen: negative, negative, negative, negative, *positive*. Positive?"

"For what?"

"Opiates." He scowled at her, but couldn't find even the faintest flicker of a gloating smile.

"That's what the lab tech told me, but she hadn't finished the test. I had her run blood levels, but since we haven't identified the substance, they may not be very accurate."

"Pretty low—take a look at this." He flipped to another sheet and showed her the blood level. "Certainly not high enough to have killed him."

She frowned at the papers and shook her head. "It doesn't make any sense. I was *sure* he had—"

"I think you're getting a little carried away." He patted her shoulder. A familiar adage popped into his head—the one he used on his medical students: *When you hear hoofbeats, don't look for zebras.* Cal didn't look for zebras—she looked for unicorns. "It's awfully hard to murder somebody with a narcotic. You'd need a huge dose orally; you'd have trouble sneaking that much codeine down someone's throat. And intravenously, well . . . Any needle marks?"

"No." She folded her arms. "I wasn't thinking about murder. I was worried about suicide—that's why I wanted to take the case. It may need some delicate handling."

"You shouldn't have worried. Victor probably took a pain pill today. That would explain why he was acting goofy—you know how potent narcotics can be in older people."

"Maybe."

"He could have died from any number of things—a stroke, a heart attack, pulmonary embolus, who knows?"

"I know it wasn't any of those things," she replied, donning a fresh pair of gloves and grabbing a white plastic container from a shelf beneath the table. She doffed the lid with a flourish. Godwin's thinly sliced brain was arrayed in a tasteful arc around the brainstem. "I've done several sections and traced the arterial tree thoroughly. There's no sign of a new stroke."

Plato pointed at a purplish blob poking out from the Circle of Willis, the arterial roundabout at the base of the brain. "What's that? Looks like a clot."

She snagged it between her fingers. The blob pulled loose easily, slid out and onto the table. "Currant jelly clot—you were just talking about them, weren't you? Anyway, it's postmortem; it formed after death."

"Yum."

"I haven't found any sign of a heart attack either," Cal continued, burping the container before snapping the lid down.

She sorted through a pile of organs, found the heart and gestured at the vessels clinging like vines on a tree trunk. The finely sectioned coronary arteries resembled minced green onions. She gestured at their gleaming whitish interiors. "He was in remarkable health— virtually no sign of thickening or blockage."

Cal pointed a probe at the large arterial trunk leading from the heart to the lungs. The huge artery had been neatly slit lengthwise; its interior was a clean pinkish-white. "No clotting or blockage—no pulmonary embolus."

She held up a wax-bottomed dissecting tray. A pair of kidney halves had been neatly sectioned and pinned. Near the glistening round surfaces, they were pink and healthy. But closer to the cup-shaped collecting system, scattered areas of purplish discoloration had appeared.

"Acute tubular necrosis. From what I can see, his blood pressure just bottomed out. End of story."

Plato crossed his arms. "So you don't know what killed him."

"Not yet, anyway." She replaced the heart and lungs and closed the splayed chest cavity, then cradled a length of intestine and "played the violin," dragging her glittering fifteen-inch surgical steel blade back and forth across one surface, freeing it from the sail of omentum and arteries and veins flapping from its base. Finally, she slit the tube lengthwise and collected a specimen in a glass vial. "I wanted to get some samples from the gastrointestinal tract. This should show whether he took the drug orally. We'll send samples of the blood and fluids over to the county lab, and try to identify the drug with the mass spec."

Cal had shown him the mass spectrophotometer once. The device identified drugs and toxins by matching their light reflection patterns with a huge electronic library of known patterns. A certain substance might produce a large spike at one wavelength, and two smaller spikes at two other wavelengths. The mass spec, combined with a computer, could identify the substance as codeine, or morphine, or arsenic, or whatever, all in a matter of minutes. Conventional chemical-based techniques could take days or weeks, or might never identify the substance at all.

After she finished, Plato helped her slide the body onto a gurney and roll it into the huge refrigerator. She tossed her gown and gloves into the trash and washed her hands. Reluctantly, she plodded to the battered oak desk, dragged a blank form from the drawer, and rolled it into the antique Underwood typewriter. With one finger, she started filling the spaces. "Let's see—*External Description* . . ."

Plink . . . Ploink-Ploink . . . Plonk!

The cafeteria was closed by now, Plato reflected; only the vending machines were working. Stale crusty sandwiches with rank cheese and wilted lettuce. Microwave hamburgers and pizza that melted to mushy blobs and then hardened like clay sculptures. Coffee that tasted like the rusty brown water back home, only warmer.

While Cal typed, he delved into the bag he'd gotten from his office. Emergency supplies—animal crackers and a can of chocolate cake frosting. He perched a ruler above the frosting can and balanced a mama kangaroo on its end. "And now, performing a layout double somersault with one and a half twists—Wheeee!"

Cal watched the performance critically. "She overrotated. Five-point-five, at best."

Plato fingered the ruler. "Too much spring in the board."

"Where'd you get those?"

He popped the diver into his mouth. "Office."

"Well, don't eat too many. I still want to go out—somewhere." She plodded through the rest of her report, then drew out a fresh sheet of paper and rolled it into the typewriter. " '*O-p-i-n-i-o-n*. Manner of death remains uncertain. The subject died of unknown cause or causes between 2:00 P.M. and 3:30 P.M. Saturday, August—' "

"That's a pretty wide time span—it covers most of the time he was out there."

Cal sighed. "Rigor mortis was just beginning—that usually starts around two hours after death. Livor mortis was just beginning, too. So he probably died shortly after we saw him—most likely around two-thirty."

"Then why not say so?" He slid an elephant down the ruler and into the frosting, then scooped it up.

"This isn't a movie. Establishing a time of death is notoriously unreliable. Everyone's body chemistry and metabolism are different." She eyed the cookie longingly, then pursed her lips. "Other things like air temperature and illness of the victim can louse up your estimate, too."

"Huh." He peered at a cookie, then held it up for Cal to see. It looked like a snake with mumps. "What do you think this is? A cobra?"

She took it from him, held it up to the light and studied it from several angles. "A giraffe. The neck and head broke off; the body's probably still in the box."

Plato scrounged in the box and pulled it out. "*Voilà!* An excellent reconstruction of the victim. I guess that's why you're a forensic pathologist."

"I guess so. Anyway, Victor shows no sign of infection—that's the only other cause of death I haven't considered." She paced across the floor and leaned against the teaching mannequin propped in the corner. His rubber liver and spleen lay beside him on the counter, and most of the skin and muscle of his face was peeled back. His bulging eyeballs looked shocked or dismayed, perhaps at his misplaced organs.

"If it weren't for the opiate, I might have written it off. Sometimes we just can't find a solid cause of death. But with the narcotic, and the kidney findings, and the absence of other disease, I just don't know. Maybe some kind of toxin, or poison, or—"

"Maybe he just choked on an animal cracker. These things can be pretty lethal if you don't get just the right amount of frosting." Plato sandwiched a generous dollop of chocolate between two antelopes. "You'd better wrap it up—it's almost midnight."

"I know." She stood behind him and ran her fingers through his hair. Her voice was husky. "True gentlemen *share,* you know."

"There's enough saturated fat here to choke a horse."

She snorted in his ear. "Nei-ei-eigh."

"Open wide." He dropped the antelope sandwich onto her tongue.

A glint of ecstasy brightened her face. "Mmm."

He retrieved the flowers and made a centerpiece for the desk. "Who needs duck Sauternes, anyways?"

"Can you make me another—just like that one?"

"I'll try. The cooking—eet ees a fine art, *n'est-ce pas?*"

CHAPTER SIX

"I can't believe you're still hungry," Plato muttered. He and Cal were bumping through the Flats downtown, looking for a restaurant. They hadn't left the hospital until almost midnight. Even in the downpour, the narrow streets by the Cuyahoga were still choked with people. Finding a parking space on a Saturday night, even for the little Chevette, would be next to impossible. "You ate half of that box of animal crackers."

"A *quarter* of the box," Cal protested. She leaned across the gearshift, tucked her shoulder under his arm, and rested her head on his chest. "Mostly crumbs. Besides, I get hungry when I work."

"I know. What's wrong with room service?"

"They don't have room service at Cliff House—not after midnight, at least. I checked." She was staring out the window; the lights near the Powerhouse blinked pale red in her eyes. "Hey, what about that place you took me to on our first date—remember? After that Arnold Scharzenegger movie. It was really late and you took me to this place way up the river, near the mills. What was the name? Roasted Goose? Basted Otter?"

"The Rusted Penguin." Plato was hoping she had forgotten.

"Yeah, that's it. Didn't you used to go there during medical school?"

"Sometimes. After final exams."

"They served drinks in those penguin-shaped glasses, and they had a band and a dance floor—"

"Three greasy teenagers and a plywood four-by-eight," Plato grumbled. It was like going back to your old grade school and seeing how short the desks were, how tiny the rooms were, how human the teachers were. As a medical student, he had seen the Rusted Penguin as a place with character, style, a gritty sort of ambiance. He and Miguel adopted the bar and spent every Friday night there with the ritualistic urgency of lemmings. But years later, when he brought Cal there, he saw it through her eyes and knew he'd made a mistake. Everything was so drab, so dull. So ordinary.

"At least the bartender was nice," Cal was saying.

"He felt sorry for us."

"The food was good, too. Hottest wings I've ever had. And half-pound burgers, all slathered in grilled onions and that melty cheddar cheese sauce—"

Plato's stomach grumbled indignantly. He looked at Cal with surprise. "You really want to go?"

"I'm *hungry*."

He turned left onto 25th Street and headed south, then cut back toward the Cuyahoga and the steel mills. "You know, everyone's talking about this new place up on Murray Hill—real nice appetizers, a great wine list. They've even got a jazz band some nights."

Eyes closed, she was still murmuring. "Hot buttery mushrooms. Greasy french fries. Big fat dill pickles. Beer."

The rain had stopped by the time they reached the bar. Plato found a parking space and crossed the gleaming street with Cal. The air had that sharp tang of burning coal and hot slag. The sky flashed blue and red from bonfires dancing on the smokestacks of the nearby mills.

Iron bars covered the windows of the restaurant, and a sliding steel cage was pulled back just outside the door. Overhead hung an enormous steel penguin, salvaged or stolen from the old Euclid Beach amusement park. A single tube of orange neon circled the icon, fizzing on and off and turning the brown rust a bloody red.

They glanced back at their car once, then stepped inside.

It was the kind of bar where everyone knows everyone else, where everyone stops talking when you walk in. White faces, black faces, most pretty old, even a woman or two, all staring that same millworker's stare like you were a big fat shiny ball bearing with a chip or a bubble or a crack. Pine walls stained dark with grease and cigarette smoke. Black-and-white pictures on the paneling—faded photos of the old mills back in the glory days, photos of union bosses tossing back a couple of beers with the commoners, photos of Euclid Beach. And the faces beneath, eyes staring, frozen just like the pictures, rusted in place like a lot of this part of Cleveland since the mills started closing.

Until Ray, fat old Ray, jolly as a fairy godmother, clucked over to them and slid his good arm around Plato's shoulder. "Plato! Doctor Marley, now, right? Come in, come in, it's been such a long time. Too long."

"We dropped by once last year, but you weren't on duty."

"Duty? Pah!" Ray pulled them back toward the bar and found a couple of empty stools. He rested his elbow on the fake wood surface and swatted the air with the stump of his left arm. For Ray's generation of millworkers, missing parts were almost as common as nearsightedness and didn't attract any stares. Usually it was just the tip of a finger or part of a hand, but Ray was injured by hot metal.

Plato glanced around the bar. "Where's the band?"

"You're kidding me, right?" Ray grunted. "Listened

to my wife and hired a manager for a while. Genius boy, screwed everything up. Said we needed entertainment, hired this bunch of hoodlum teenagers, scared all my paying customers away. Then he wants to change the menu—alfalfa sprouts and all that. Lasted two weeks before I kicked him out on his ass—beg pardon, ma'am."

"No problem. I've heard lots worse." Cal looked a question at Plato.

"Oh—Ray, this is my wife, Cal Marley."

They shook hands. Ray leaned forward, suddenly serious. "Say, I know you guys are here to meet Miguel, but—"

"What do you mean?" Plato stood to get a view of the booths in the back. "Is he here?"

"Shhh." The owner hunched down and lowered his voice. "Yeah, he's back there. I thought you were meeting him, but never mind that. He's awful gloomy—I guess a good friend of his died today."

"We know. Cal just finished his autopsy."

Ray glanced at her appraisingly. "So you're a doctor, too, huh?"

"Yes."

"Good for you. Maybe you'll keep this kid in line." He squinted sidelong at Plato. "Anyways, Miguel's pretty down, been drinking a lot of beer. Even more than he did after that whatchacallit National Board exam."

Plato whistled. "That's a lot."

Ray stood and gestured toward the booths. "I'm glad you two showed up. I worried about him getting home okay and all. Pleasure meeting you, ma'am."

Ray hadn't changed the floor plan much. Plato led Cal to a table in the back, the one with a tiny framed Polaroid of Ray's boat, the *Spirit,* a smart little ketch berthed down by the Ninth Street docks. Miguel was hunched over a bottle of Killian Red, twisting his glass back and forth, back and forth, glaring at the puddle it left behind.

"Still drinking that stuff? I keep telling you it's not even Irish—it's made in the States." Plato sat down beside him and Cal slid into the seat across the table.

Miguel looked up, bleary-eyed but not surprised. "Ray send for you?"

"Nope. We just finished up at the lab, thought we'd have a little supper."

"You didn't go to Gates's little party, then?"

"What party?" Plato frowned at his friend.

"That's right—you left before he told us. Eldon had planned to throw a little party in his room after the governor's address." He shook his head. "He invited all the editors, acted like nothing happened. They all did."

"Miguel—"

"I couldn't take it, so I left. All those people talking and laughing and having a great time." Miguel's head dropped; he muttered into his beer. "Probably the happiest day of his life."

Plato wasn't sure he had heard him right. "What do you mean? Happiest day of whose life?"

"Gates's. Remember? Victor had just started an investigation at Hartman." He lowered his voice. "I think he was on to something."

"Easy, now." Plato patted his friend's arm. "This is *Eldon Gates* you're talking about. The premier researcher. The guy you said you'd always dreamed of working for."

"That was two years ago." Miguel scowled. "I've learned a lot since then. Gates just—"

"What'll it be, folks?" Ray propped his arm against the table—a lump of pig iron tightly wrapped in tattooed skin. The curvy female on his bicep had grown stretched and blowzy; the name "Rose" was swollen like the print on a rubber balloon.

"A Penguin Burger for me, please. With everything." Cal licked her lips. "And a big mug of Iron City."

"A lady after my own heart." Ray rested his pad on the table and jotted their orders down. As he wrote, Rose swung her hips to the beat of Creedence Clearwater Revival's *Bad Moon Rising* thumping through the ceiling speakers:

> Looks like we're in for nasty weather.
> One eye is taken for an eye . . .

After Ray turned and waddled through the swing doors beside them, Cal touched Miguel's hand. "I finished the autopsy, you know."

He looked up from his beer, suddenly alert. "How'd it go?"

"I don't know." She shrugged. "He seemed pretty healthy, really. No sign of a new stroke or heart attack, no clots in the pulmonary arteries, nothing that could explain a sudden death."

"What about the way he was acting?" His voice was suddenly clearer; he gave almost no sign that he'd been drinking. Except his eyes were a little unfocused, and he had a flicker of an accent now, like a falling star glimpsed from the corner of the eye.

Cal looked at Plato, who shook his head slightly. "Nothing obvious, but we wouldn't really expect to see anything. If it was Alzheimer's or something like that, the changes were too subtle to see on gross exam. And strokes can be too small to see with the naked eye, unless there are enough of them."

"So you don't have a cause of death?"

"It's not uncommon, especially in older people." She stared at her hands. "Sometimes even the best autopsy by the greatest pathologist isn't conclusive. You know the death wasn't caused by certain things, but you don't know what it *was* caused by."

"No sign of foul play?"

Plato frowned. "Come on, Miguel—"

Their beers arrived just then, snowy cold, in huge frosted penguin mugs. Cal took a long drag, wiped the foam from her lips, and sighed. "What do you mean— foul play?"

"I was wondering if you found anything unusual, anything at all." He sounded almost hopeful.

"Why?"

"Oh, nothing." He shrugged and stared down at his beer again. "Just a little coincidence, maybe."

Plato studied his friend's face. Back in medical school, every death had struck Miguel as a personal failure. He probably felt the same way about Victor, though Plato couldn't imagine why.

With Miguel's attitude toward death, God only knew how he survived in geriatrics.

"What kind of coincidence?" Cal asked.

"Victor telephoned me late one night to tell me about it, a couple of months ago. First time it happened, I think it was a phone call. Not a death threat or anything, but this guy sounded really creepy—knew some things about Victor. Really shook him up." He looked at Plato. "You ever had a crank phone call?"

"Yeah."

"Then you know what I mean. That's all I figured it was. I told Victor maybe he should report it to the police, but I knew he wouldn't. Not about a little thing like that. It happened again, two more times. He called me each time—I didn't know what to think. To tell you the truth, I wondered if it went along with the memory problems he'd been having."

He shook his head and poured some more beer from the fresh bottle Ray had brought. "Then he got a letter—just last week. He read it to me over the phone;

it sounded totally cracked. Threatening, talking about retribution and swords and flames or something. I made him promise to send it on to the police, but I don't think he did. You know how he is—how he *was*."

The food arrived, Cal's rare half-pound burger, mushrooms and onions and cheddar slathered in a great messy heap on top, a pile of greasy french fries, Plato's bacon burger crowned by a thick slab of raw onion, Miguel's ham and corned beef sandwich glued to the plate with stringy Swiss cheese.

"Maybe I *am* hungry," he sighed, slicing the sandwich from its tethers. "Anyway, Cal—I thought you said the autopsy didn't turn up anything."

She swallowed noisily, had another pull of beer. "Do you know which medications Victor was taking?"

"Motrin and DiaBeta. He kept them on the counter in our bathroom when he was in town."

"Nothing else? No back problems, no recent falls or injuries, no chronic pain?"

"Nothing he mentioned, anyway." Miguel frowned. "Why?"

"Our drug screen was positive for opiates. We didn't want to tell you about it at first—"

Plato interrupted. "Cal was wondering if he might have committed suicide."

"*Victor?*" He tossed his head back and laughed for the first time that evening. "Never in a million years."

"Are you sure?" Cal asked. "Sometimes people—"

"Yeah, he was a little worried about his memory. And he'd been talking about death a lot lately. But he's not the type—not at all." He chuckled softly. "Victor used to joke about going into a nursing home, how he'd give some geriatrician a huge pain in the butt before he died. I think he was looking forward to it. His brother sounds just the same way."

"You talked to Victor's brother?" Plato asked.

"Yeah. I finally reached Martin around seven; it was

midnight in England. He'd just gotten back from a late
house call." Miguel stared at the patterns in the
stamped metal ceiling. "If I didn't know better, I'd
have thought it was Victor talking. Anyway, Martin's
tied up—can't fly in for a few days. He wanted me to
take care of the arrangements. And he wanted you to
call him with the autopsy results."

Cal nodded. "No problem."

He started on the other half of his sandwich. "Oh.
By the way, dinner's on me. I'm executor of Victor's
estate."

Plato raised his eyebrows.

"That's not all," he continued. His voice was oddly
flat. "Martin told me the details of the will. He said
Victor changed it last year, so half would go to his
brother and half to me. Even worked out a trust fund
for Roberto and Maria."

"That's really great." Plato smiled and patted
Miguel's arm. "I didn't know him very long, but he
seemed like quite a guy."

Cal nodded. "He must have felt very close to you, to
your family."

"Yeah. I never knew how close, I guess . . . I never
said—" He swallowed hard and stared at the table.
"Martin told me how much it was—not that I asked.
Victor was saving pretty hard for his retirement, and
bachelor physicians can put away quite a bit of money.
Even after taxes and everything, it should run well into
seven figures."

Plato whistled. "You must have done great in the
fellowship. When I graduated, they gave me a Cross
pen and pencil set."

"*Plato!*" Cal scolded.

"He's right," Miguel agreed, setting his sandwich
down and waving his hands in the air. "That's just
what I keep asking myself. What did I do to deserve
this? Sure, Victor was like part of the family, but . . ."

"But what?" Plato challenged. "You said it yourself—he was part of the family. He didn't have any family of his own, except for his brother. And real friends are pretty hard to find in medical research. Especially for someone who investigates grants fraud and ethics violations."

Miguel shrugged, then turned his gaze to the other photograph hanging over the table—a color shot of three steelworkers posing in front of a red-hot blast furnace, lines of sweat cutting through the dirt and grime on their faces, grinning with the cocky confidence of guaranteed employment and a powerful union.

Plato reached up to straighten the picture. "It sounds like you feel guilty."

Miguel shrugged.

"Well, ask yourself this—would you feel the same way if his estate was only worth a few thousand dollars?"

"That's different," he protested. "That's—"

"The principle is exactly the same. The decimal place is just moved over a little bit." Plato transferred a few of Miguel's potato chips to his own plate. "Inheriting money doesn't make you responsible for Victor's death. You should feel honored."

"I do." He swallowed again, met Plato's gaze.

"Well. Now that we've got that settled . . ." Plato grinned and signaled for Ray. "One last round of beers and then my friend here would like the check."

"You're a heck of a guy, Plato." Miguel stole some chips back and smiled slowly. "How'd I ever survive medical school with a roommate like you?"

"You're tougher than you think."

"I must be."

When the bill came, Plato passed it over. "Thanks for dinner."

"No problem." Miguel laid some cash on the plate.

"Maybe you folks could give me a ride back to the lodge—save me the taxi fare."

Plato pulled the keys from his pocket. "Your chariot awaits."

"Uh-uh." Cal snatched the keys from his hand. "You've had three beers, and I haven't even finished my first. We've had enough driving adventures for one day." She dropped the keys in her purse and grinned at Miguel. "A millionaire rates a sober chauffeur."

Plato drifted off to sleep on the way back to the hotel and woke just as Cal was piloting the car past the narrowed part of the cliff. Miguel was sprawled across the backseat, body twisted in an impossible position. Cal parked the car and they dragged him through the double doors, up the winding staircase flanking the main hall, and down a twisting corridor to his room. Plato had to fish the key from his friend's pocket before they could open his door, urge him inside, and tuck him into bed.

"Finally," Plato sighed, once they closed the door to their own room. "The kids are asleep, the dog's been walked, the garbage is out, and we've got a little time to ourselves. Who's taking the two o'clock feeding?"

Cal consulted her watch. "It's past two o'clock already."

"Technically speaking," he said, pulling her close, "this is now our first anniversary."

"*Technically,* huh?"

"Yeah." His hand slid down the small of her back. She gave a little quiver of response and tilted her face up. He brushed his lips across hers. "Want to get a little . . . technical?"

"Hmm. Seeing that you're so well-equipped . . ." Cal hovered a minute, then slipped eel-like from his grip. She tripped across the room, turned the lights down, and flicked a switch beside the fireplace. The ceramic logs roared to life. "How about getting ready while I set up some atmosphere?"

Brushing his teeth, he caught serial glimpses of her fiddling with the radio, combing her hair, slipping into the satin and lace teddy she'd worn only once since last Valentine's Day. She was all the atmosphere he needed—high slim waist, dancer's legs, generous curves and sleek softnesses all hidden and hinting under a shifting satiny landscape.

She was already in bed by the time he finished. He fiddled with the fireplace knob and just stood there a minute, listening to the hiss of the gas jets, the whisper of rain pattering against the sliding glass door, the soft melody playing on the radio—an old Nat Cole tune, something about lingering sunsets and lonely seas. And he heard Cal's rhythmic, throaty hum; she really had a beautiful voice.

Except that her timing was all wrong, and she kept humming the same line over and over again. Even after the song ended and an ad came on.

He crept over to the bed. She wasn't humming at all. Her mouth was open, her lips gently pursed, soft snores rustling away like dry leaves skittering down an empty street.

"Cally? Kiddo?" He slid between the sheets and gently rocked her shoulder. "Honey?"

Her eyes fluttered open and she smiled sweetly. "Liver contusion transected aorta uterus spleen."

"Oh."

"Pheochromocytoma," she pronounced finally, as though that explained everything.

"I see."

She nodded firmly, then rolled over and spooned herself against him. The dry leaves started skittering again. Cal reached back, instinctively tucked his arm around her middle, and sighed.

She'd wake up soon enough, with a little persuasion.

He snuggled up against her back, tugged her close, slid his hands beneath the satin, and nuzzled her neck. He breathed into her hair, kissed her ear. He closed his eyes, and promptly fell asleep.

CHAPTER SEVEN

Somewhere in the darkness, a telephone was ringing. Plato reached for the nightstand, for the switch on the bedside light, before realizing he wasn't at home. He cranked his eyelids open and peered around the dimly lit hotel room. The phone jangled again—somewhere to his right. He crawled across the vast plain of the king-size bed, slumped over Cal's unconscious form, and fumbled for the receiver.

"Hullo?"

"Plato?" It was Dan Homewood—his partner in the geriatrics fellowship at Riverside General. Dan was on call this weekend; Plato had been a free man since signing out to him on Friday. "Sorry—were you sleeping?"

"Nuh-uh," he croaked, glancing over at the clock. Its cheerful blue letters sang the obscenity of the hour. "I always get up this early on weekends. Makes going back on Monday so much easier."

"Good." Dan's sense of humor was a mystery to Plato. "Hey, I ran into that Gates guy at the keynote address last night. He's one of the people working on that book with you, right?"

"Yeah." Plato fell back onto the bed and rubbed his eyes. Cal snuffled over to him, pillowed her head on his shoulder and softly snored. She was wrapped up like a linen croissant; only some hair, the top of her forehead, and her left ear were visible. Unlike most people, Cal tossed and turned in just one direction while she slept.

"Gates is lecturing at Riverside General this morning—to the Internal Medicine Department," Dan explained. Regardless of the time of day or night, or whether he'd been awake for thirty-six hours straight, he always sounded cheerful, vigorous, alert. It was nauseating. "He's discussing memory problems and dementia—wants to cover the typical workup. He plans to demonstrate the mental status exam, of course, but he needs a good case . . ."

"Yeah." Plato was shivering; it was a chilly August night—morning—whatever. Cal must have turned the fireplace off last night, before she stole all the covers.

"Anyway, this Gates guy said the internal medicine folks don't have any good case studies in-house, asked me if we had any dementia cases. So I remembered your patient—Marietta Clemens."

Plato wondered where all this was leading. He buried his feet under the croissant. "That's fine, Dan. She'll probably be glad to help. Just explain it to her, get her permission, and stay there while he—"

"That's just it," he interrupted. "I'm giving a lecture up at the conference this morning. I knew you wouldn't want to leave Marietta alone with a roomful of strangers. Since you're off this weekend, I thought you might have a little extra time on your hands to run over there, stay with her during the exam."

"Thanks for thinking of me."

"No trouble at all. By the way—we've only got two other patients in-house. Seems like an awful waste for *both* of us to go in today."

Among doctors, call schedules were as sacred and inviolate as the Hippocratic Oath or the latest Medicare reimbursement schedules. Since their third partner had left to take a cushy nursing home directorship in Florida, Plato and Dan had been on call every other week.

Last week's call had been particularly grueling, as Cal had reminded him yesterday. Dan had no right to ask him to go in for Sunday rounds. But Homewood could make even the most outrageous request sound perfectly reasonable—he'd be a department chairman someday.

Wistfully, Plato glanced down at his wife. A ruffle of black lace peeked out from beneath the bundle of bedding. He thought of waking her with kisses, unraveling the blankets like a Christmas present. But thoughts of Mrs. Clemens kept intruding, like they would if he stayed. He sighed, loud enough for Dan to hear. "You know, today's our anniversary. Our first."

"Is it?" Homewood sounded genuinely pleased. "That's great! Hey, tell Cal I said congratulations, okay?"

"Sure."

"Listen, I've got to run. I still have to shower and shave and put my slides together. Thanks a lot—I owe you one."

"You sure do," Plato began, but Homewood hung up quickly, before he had a chance to change his mind.

Two hours later, the first rays of morning sunlight were squeezing through the heavy dark glass of Mrs. Clemens's window. Plato had showered, dressed, left a note for Cal, who still hadn't stirred, taken a taxi to the hospital, visited the other two patients, and explained the upcoming procedure to Marietta. She agreed readily enough, but she was more interested in other things.

"But why *can't* I walk?" she asked again, for the third time. Two years ago, she was one of the first patients in Plato's geriatrics practice—a sweet old woman with silver hair, dimpled elbows, and confused eyes. She'd put on some lipstick for this morning's event, a little unevenly. Bright red polish coated her long fingernails. Her tiny feet were swaddled in a pair of cheap green foam hospital slippers with little smiley faces pressed into the upper surfaces. She picked at the flimsy coverlet and frowned. "I so love to walk in the evenings. Look out the window—there's a path in the backyard that goes out through the woods—"

"It's morning, Marietta. Sunday morning." Plato had told her this once already. He spoke slowly and distinctly and patiently. "You're in the hospital. You broke your hip a while back, and the doctors had to fix it. They put in a new hip, but it's still healing. See your cast?"

Her lacy yellow nightgown and pink terrycloth robe were pulled back around her left hip; the pins and soft cast looked like a piece of abstract sculpture. She stared as though the surgeons had attached an elephant's leg to her body. Astonished comprehension dawned slowly; she crossed her arms and frowned. "Why didn't anyone *tell* me?"

"Doctor Marley?" Eldon Gates stood just inside the heavy steel door. Behind him, a herd of long-coated residents and short-coated medical students were milling in the hallway. "Mind if I come in?"

"Certainly. We're all ready for you."

Gates strode briskly into the room and shook the patient's hand. A score of residents and students crowded in behind him, clustering around the bed and out the doorway. The trainees were noisier than usual today. They had spent the last twenty-four hours on call duty in the hospital, and they would leave as soon as they finished rounds and signed out their patients to the next group. But tomorrow was Monday, another full workday. Plato could almost feel their restlessness.

"I'm Doctor Gates." The guest lecturer wasn't restless at all. He might have been planning on spending the whole day with Mrs. Clemens. His speech, his manner, his very clothes oozed professionalism and competence. His voice held concern, sympathy, and warmth. His face was open and honest, eyes gentle and caring. The gray silk jacket flowed from his shoul-

ders like a waterfall. He wore a vest despite the season;
the heavy gold chain of his pocket watch was clipped
to one of the buttons. "Thanks for agreeing to help us
this morning. As Doctor Marley explained, I'm going
to give you a little quiz to test your memory. Do you
have any questions?"

She glanced anxiously at Plato. "Can Doctor Marley
stay here? He might be able to answer some of your
questions if I can't."

"I'm staying right here," Plato said, giving her hand
a squeeze. With Marietta's arthritis, it felt like a bag of
marbles. "And don't worry about the questions. There
aren't any right or wrong answers—just do the best
you can."

"First off, can you tell me your full name?" Gates
snapped his fingers at the chief resident. She sighed
and passed him a pad and pencil.

"Marietta Clemens," the patient replied. She spoke
quickly, and her hands twitched in her lap like they always did when she was nervous. "My mother picked
that name—it's a city in Ohio, you know—down on
the river. That's where my mother was from."

"How interesting." He smiled, nodded his head. "It's
a very pretty name."

"Thank you."

Gates gestured around the room with his pencil. "Do
you know where we are right now?"

"Doctor Marley *says* I'm in the hospital." She looked
around the room and gave a little gasp, patting her chest.
"My, my. Does that mean all of you are doctors?"

Near the front of the crowd, a pair of medical students chuckled; they looked like a couple of nervous
teenagers at a prom. Gates's glare cut their laughter
short. He turned back to his patient. "Most of them are.
Some haven't graduated yet."

"That's okay, I don't mind." She smiled and
straightened the lapel of her fluffy pink robe.

"Can you tell me what day it is today?"

"Hmm." She glanced over at the bedside table. A vase of yellow roses and a telephone rested on a stack of newspapers. On top was the brightly colored comic section. "Let me think—Sunday? Is it Sunday?"

"Aren't you sure?"

Her hands had stopped twitching. She shook her head and smiled shyly. "The days all seem the same around here—it's hard to tell one from the next."

"I know just what you mean," he sympathized. "Do you know what month we're in?"

"Of course I do . . ." Marietta Clemens stared up at the ceiling, eyes clear blue and cloudless as a sunny winter's day. She looked out the window. Across the street, a stand of tall maples waved in a sea of dappled green. "Summertime—summertime. July? August?"

"That's right—August." Gates scribbled a note on his pad. "How about the year? Can you tell me what year it is?"

"Oh . . . I don't know if that's really *important*." She grinned sheepishly. "Once you get to be my age, the years just don't seem to matter much."

"If you don't mind my asking, how old are you?"

"You should never ask a lady her age—don't you know that?" She giggled, turned to Plato and squeezed his arm. "I always tell Doctor Marley that I stopped counting after twenty-nine—don't I still look twenty-nine?"

Gates smiled patiently. "You certainly do. Can you tell me your birthdate?"

"Oh, sure—July 8th, 1927." She rattled off the date without a hint of hesitation.

He turned to his audience, pointed a long finger at one of the medical students who had snickered earlier. "You. Why did Mrs. Clemens remember her birthday so easily?"

The student's face reddened. Tall and gangly, he

towered over most of the room's other occupants. Every limb, even his neck, was long and thin like stretched Play-Doh. He stared down at the floor, fiddled with the cheap stethoscope in the pocket of his short white coat. "Uh. Umm. I guess—I guess because, like—because it's so *important* to her. You know—she *uses* it a lot; it's just something you have to know. And because she's known it a long time. I guess."

"I won't dignify that answer with a comment. Other than to ask, rhetorically, how you ever gained entrance into medical school." He turned to the rest of the crowd. "Anyone else care to try?"

In the silence, Plato could hear Gates's pocket watch ticking. All eyes had suddenly flicked away, like a school of tropical fish under a searchlight. They thoughtfully studied the floor, the window, the ceiling. The restlessness, the holiday atmosphere, had suddenly dissipated. Now every student and resident seemed content to spend the day with Mrs. Clemens, too, as long as they could avoid meeting Gates's gaze.

Except for the chief resident; she was watching the medical student, whose eyes were glazed and unfocused, like a prizefighter ready to topple. Plato had worked with the chief resident several times before. The plump red-haired physician was tough and competent, and tended to get overinvolved with her patients. She squared her shoulders and broke the silence. "Mark was partially right; Mrs. Clemens *has* known her birthdate for a long time. That's important because dementia affects short-term memory first. Longer-term memories—like birthdates, childhood events, important relationships—are preserved until the dementia is relatively advanced."

"Hmmph." Gates scowled and gave a grudging nod. "That's correct, though I might have *phrased* it a little differently."

A nurse threaded her way through the crowd and appeared at the foot of Mrs. Clemens's bed. She looked over at Plato. "Excuse me—Doctor Marley? The pharmacy was late sending up the new tube of nitroglycerin paste. Mrs. Clemens was supposed to get it two hours ago. Do you mind if I interrupt?"

"Not at all," Plato replied. "Go right ahead."

Gates flipped open his pocket watch and frowned. He turned to his audience and discussed the patient's condition while the nurse took Mrs. Clemens's arm and timed her pulse.

"I guess I'm not doing very well," the old woman whispered to him.

Plato smiled gently and patted her shoulder. Beneath the hospital gown, it seemed as thin and fragile as the backbone of a kite. "Don't worry about it. There aren't really any right or wrong answers—you just do the best you can."

"I know. But I'd do a whole lot better if I could use my notes."

Mrs. Clemens was a compulsive note-taker. Plato had visited her house once, back before she moved to the nursing home. Yellow Post-It notes were everywhere—stuck to the cupboards, the refrigerator, the walls, tables, television, even the bathroom mirror. She went through about a dozen pads per week. And every night, before she went to bed, Mrs. Clemens wrote a letter to herself. She would read it the following morning to learn what day it was, what she planned to do, who was coming to visit and when, what she needed to tell her son when he called. She was awfully intelligent; she'd survived remarkably well with remarkably little memory.

"What's *that*?" Mrs. Clemens was asking him. The nurse had opened a tube of medicine, applied an inch-long ribbon to the skin of her belly, and covered it with a clear bandage.

"Your nitroglycerin, remember? So your heart

doesn't have to work as hard," Plato explained. "You got headaches from the pills, so we're giving you paste instead. It's absorbed more slowly through the skin."

She frowned. "I *still* get headaches."

"Not as bad, though. Right?"

"I guess not."

Gates waited until the nurse had left, then resumed his questioning. "Mrs. Clemens, I'm going to ask you to remember three things for me—three objects. I want you to concentrate hard and put them away in your memory. Later, when we're almost through, I'll ask you to tell me what they are. Okay?"

"Okay."

"The three things I'd like you to remember are apple, tree, and ball." He smiled genially. "Can you say that for me? Apple, tree, ball."

"Apple, tree, ball."

"Good!" The swaying inflections in Gates's voice brought back memories of Plato's first grade teacher. "Now, what were those again?"

"Apple, tree . . ." She put a finger to her lips and tilted her head. "Oh, and ball. Apple, tree, ball."

"Good. Now tell me—are you better at adding or subtracting?"

"Hah!" She chuckled. "Neither. Tom—my husband, rest in peace—always used to balance the checkbook. Now that he's gone, I let my children take care of the money. I just sign the checks."

He shrugged. "Would you rather do some spelling?"

"Oh, sure." Mrs. Clemens nodded happily. "I do the crossword all the time."

"Then would you mind spelling 'world' for me?"

"W-O-R-L-D." She was sure of herself.

"Excellent." Gates nodded and made another note on his pad. "Now, can you spell it backward?"

"Am I allowed to write it down? No? Let's see. D-L-O . . . R-W?"

Plato had tested her with the same questionnaire many times over the past couple of years; she scored a little lower with each assessment. She probably didn't have classic Alzheimer's disease; her memory problems more likely stemmed from a number of tiny strokes—multiinfarct dementia. And yet she had periods of startling lucidity, moments when she remembered names, places, events with remarkable clarity, episodes that led her family to believe she was actually improving. But they never lasted long.

Gates was wrapping up his questions. He tore a sheet from his notepad and placed the paper and a pen on her table. "Mrs. Clemens? Would you mind writing a sentence for me?"

"Yes?" She lifted the pen and waited expectantly.

"Just make up a sentence—anything you'd like."

"Oh. Okay." She closed her eyes and took a deep breath, the way she always did when her patience was running thin. She studied the pad and scribbled in a tiny ragged hand, speaking as she wrote. " 'I—don't—want—to—be—here.' "

This time, the audience laughed again, and even Gates cracked a smile. "Okay, Mrs. Clemens—we're almost done."

He held her note up to view, then passed it around. "Micrographia—small, nearly illegible handwriting. Quite common with dementia and a few other neurologic diseases."

He turned back to Mrs. Clemens. "Do you remember a while ago, how I asked you to remember three things?"

"You did?"

"Yes—before we did our spelling exercise, I asked you to remember three objects. Is that familiar to you at all?"

"Hmm." Her fuzzy white eyebrows knotted. "Let's see . . . 'world'? Did you say *three* things?"

"Yes."

"How do you like that?" She shrugged. "My memory's not what it used to be. Getting old, I guess. But I always say, I stopped counting birthdays after twenty-nine. Don't I still look twenty-nine? Hah!"

Later, after Gates had thanked her and the crowd of medical students and residents had filtered from the room, she opened her purse and sifted through a sheaf of notes. "Hmm. Says here Tom's birthday is tomorrow. I've got to go out and pick up some flowers for the grave. Can you drive me to the florist, Doctor Marley?"

"You're in the hospital, Marietta. Remember?"

"Oh. That's right." She pursed her lips. "But then who's going to take the flowers out to Tom's grave? He'll think I've forgotten him."

A tear spiraled down the wrinkles and crevices of her weathered cheek. Plato sat on a corner of the bed and patted her hand. "Maybe your son could—"

"Oh, I'm a silly old fool!" She had turned the note over and glanced at the back. "Says here Dorothy called last night—that's my daughter. She ordered a wreath and she's taking it out tomorrow."

"That's nice."

"The good Lord only knows where I'd be without these little notes of mine—they're lifesavers." She frowned at Plato. "I don't understand why I couldn't use them before, when that doctor was questioning me."

Plato smiled, then patted her hand again. "Don't worry about it. There aren't any right or wrong answers—you just do the best you can."

Marietta rolled her eyes and sighed. "You *said* that already."

CHAPTER EIGHT

"What's for lunch?" Plato asked as he entered the suite. The bathroom door was open, and the bedroom was clouded with great gouts of steam. Cal stood in front of the bureau, drying her hair with a heavy white hotel towel. "I'm famished. I haven't eaten anything since last night."

"Me neither." She wrapped herself in the towel, peered in the mirror and frowned. "Speaking of digestion, I got a call from the lab this morning. The ileum was negative for narcotics."

"Ileum?" he asked blankly.

She tossed her head back and fluffed her fingers through her hair. "Victor's ileum, remember? Those intestinal samples I took turned up negative. If the test had shown something, we might have gotten some idea about when he took it."

"Too bad." He dropped his coat on the bed and loosened his tie. "Hey, maybe they'll have some more of those hamburgers, like yesterday. Or pizza—I could go for one right now. Sausage, anchovies, pepperoni, green onions. Remember that place in Chicago?"

"You have *such* refined tastes." She yanked open a bureau drawer and pulled out some clothes. "I expected the digestive tract to be positive—he almost certainly didn't take the narcotics intravenously. It's the one thing that doesn't fit. But I don't think it's really worth investigating—*hey!*"

Plato had snatched her up into his arms. He carried her across the carpet and tossed her on the bed. "Then why bother getting dressed?"

"I thought you were hungry."

"Mmm-hmm." He kissed her neck, nibbled her ear. "I *am* hungry."

"Plato." She watched him unwrap the towel. "I hate to break it to you, but—"

He paused suddenly, lifted his head and crinkled his nose. "Something smells wonderful! Is that our lunch?"

"I can see where *your* priorities are." Grinning, she grabbed her clothes and squirmed away.

He left her on the bed, followed the scent to the balcony door and slid it open. "I can almost taste it."

"The kitchen vent's just outside our window—see?" Behind him, she struggled into a flowered shirt, white knit pants, and a clean pair of hi-tops. "And out there, straight ahead—you can see the tennis courts."

"Uh-huh." The empty courts were just visible through the trees. Across the river, Plato glimpsed the green hills and valleys of Chippewa Creek's private golf course. He caught a flicker of movement below. One floor down and to the right, Evelyn Baker stood on a balcony of her own. She looked like an avenging Mother Nature, white hair blowing straight out from her face in the stiff breeze. She waved. Plato waved back.

The kitchen was below and to the left; its steep shale roof sloped quickly from eye level down to the base of the balcony. A stainless-steel exhaust fan poked up through the shale and blew tantalizing vapors into Plato's face. "Lasagna, maybe."

"Nope," Cal called from inside.

He stepped back, slid the door shut behind him. "How do *you* know?"

"I looked at the menu." She brushed her hair and

patted a trace of rouge onto her cheeks. "It doesn't matter. We've got to—"

"Spaghetti? Some kind of pasta, I'm sure of it."

"Not spaghetti. Not any kind of pasta." She smirked impishly. "But it's something you'll really like. *And* it's good for you."

"I'll bet." He eyed her suspiciously. "Fish, right? You're always trying to get me to eat fish."

"It's not fish," she assured him.

"Then I'll probably like it." He headed for the door. "Let's go—I'm *really* hungry."

"There's just one problem," she began, following him into the hallway. "I've been trying to tell you—Miguel rescheduled the first editors' meeting. It's starting now, over in the library."

"*Before* lunch?" Plato complained, taking one last sniff before the door closed.

"Don't worry—it'll be a meal worth waiting for."

They stepped down the winding turret stairs, through the main hall and a narrow corridor leading to the other guest rooms, and up again to the top of the opposite tower. The library was spectacular: tall stained-glass windows facing north, south, east, and west, according to the ornate compass tiled into the floor; an octagonal cupola crowning the high peaked roof; an eight-sided parquet table set in alternating blocks of oak, cherry, maple, and rosewood; glass-fronted shelves holding hundreds of volumes, many of which looked older than the mansion itself.

"This heat is unbearable," Harlow Fairfax complained. He stood at the open door to the balcony, patting his neck and forehead with a frilly linen handkerchief. "In heaven's name, who suggested that we stay in this old mansion, anyway?"

Plato decided not to answer.

"You think *this* is hot?" Gates's three-piece silk suit had damp stains across the back and beneath the arms.

"How would you like to have to *sleep* in a room like this?"

He leaned out the door and pointed at the opposite tower, to the balcony above Plato and Cal's. "My room's on the top floor of the other turret—just like this one. Hottest place in the whole damn mansion, and the air conditioner's broken. I left my sliding door open for air last night and now the carpet's soaked. The whole room smells like a pet shop."

Fairfax wrinkled his huge purple nose. "Perhaps we could hold our meeting downstairs. Undoubtedly, it would be much cooler."

Jessica Novak spoke up, startling Plato; he hadn't realized she was there. "Miguel said the only other place with a large enough table is the dining room. They're setting it up for lunch right now. He asked me to make sure all the windows were open up here."

"Where is he?" Gates snapped.

Novak shrugged, her left upper lip twitching nervously. Her tiny face and coal-black eyes retreated behind a puff of frizzled hair.

"Despite the heat, Judith and I are enjoying our stay tremendously," Kelvin Lorantz declared. He held a tall glass of iced lemonade; the others eyed it longingly. He gestured past Fairfax's bulk at the balcony. "She's out golfing right now. It's supposed to be an excellent course."

"I hate golf," Gates replied. "Silly game—chasing a ball around with a stick. Why not just go for a good long hike instead?"

"Too bad for you." Dean Fairfax clapped Gates's shoulder and chuckled. "Miguel has us all signed up for a golf outing tomorrow. I think you're in my foursome."

"Too bad for *you*, then. Tennis is my game. I haven't been golfing in years, and I don't plan on starting now." He moved closer to the balcony and gazed out at the course. "I'd rather die than humiliate myself out there tomorrow."

"I see." Fairfax flashed a curious smile and deftly changed the subject. "With your interest in exercise, I assume you've read this month's article in *JAGS*—the one about osteoporosis and physical activity?"

Something tapped Plato's arm and a quiet voice whispered, "Is this place spinning around, or is it just me?"

Miguel was standing behind him. His copper skin had tarnished to a ghastly shade of green. One hand was braced on a rack of books, the other hovered in the air for balance. His eyelids drooped like gobs of wet clay.

Plato frowned critically. "You're standing still, Miguel. I think your clothes just create an *illusion* of motion."

"What do you mean?" he asked, looking down. His red plaid tie seemed to dance against the deep blue background of his checkered shirt. The buttons of his beige blazer were misaligned; one tail was tucked into his gray polyester pants. At least his shoes matched. "Don't I look okay?"

Cal saw him and gasped. She straightened his tie, fussed with his jacket, and stepped back. "That doesn't help, does it?"

"He looks like a pattern book in a wallpaper store," Plato replied.

"I got dressed in the dark." Miguel blinked. "It's awfully bright in here, isn't it?"

Evelyn Baker detached herself from the cluster near the balcony and walked over. She reached out and squeezed Miguel's arm. "Hung over, are we?"

"Me?" He swallowed heavily. "I think I'm coming down with something—there's a flu virus going around."

"Yeah," Plato agreed. "*Penguin* flu. Sort of like swine flu, but worse."

Cal elbowed him.

Baker nodded. "Uh-huh. Let's head down to the kitchen before anyone else sees you." She passed her arm through Miguel's and guided him quickly toward the door. "I've got just the cure for penguin flu. Orange juice, tomato juice, salt, a little dry vermouth. And lots of water."

Out on the balcony, Harlow Fairfax was arguing with Eldon Gates. Their debate had reached a fever pitch.

"The research is unanimous." Gates stood with his back to the rail, arms folded across his chest, speaking in the same calm, patient tone he'd used with Mrs. Clemens that morning. "Stimulant laxatives are clearly more effective than fiber preparations. Show me one piece of research that says otherwise."

"*Journal of Contemporary Geriatrics,* November 1994." Fairfax crowded Gates against the railing and poked his adversary's chest with a plump finger. "Penfeld's group found that bulk fiber laxatives had similar efficacy, with far less potential for abuse and addiction!"

"*Laxative* addiction?" Cal murmured.

Plato nodded.

She sighed. "Now I've heard everything."

"I read Penfeld's article," Gates replied coolly, his lips curving into a faint smile. "Wasn't that study underwritten by Medicon—the same company that makes Fibrosol?"

Fairfax's face purpled. He blinked once, twice, opened his mouth to speak, but nothing came out. He finally exhaled, a hissing sound like a fat beach ball bouncing on a shard of glass. He turned away and stormed back inside.

Plato turned to Cal. "And you thought geriatrics wasn't exciting."

Evelyn Baker returned with Miguel just a few minutes later. His eyes were clear and focused, the green tint had faded, and he'd gotten rid of the tie and jacket.

"If it's okay with everyone, I'd like to get started now." His voice quavered slightly. "Sorry I'm late; I had to take care of some urgent business."

Once everyone was seated, he gazed around the table. "I spoke with the publisher this morning. He's formally approved our working title—*Handbook of Practical Geriatric Medicine*—as well as our basic outline."

He flipped open a notebook and studied it closely. "By the way, I'd like to dedicate the book to the memory of Victor Godwin."

"I think that's a wonderful idea," Evelyn Baker declared. "I'm sure Victor would have been honored."

Around the table, most of the others nodded agreement.

"And I've chosen an epigraph for the book." He was still looking down at his notes. "It's a passage from *Paradise Lost* that I think is especially appropriate:

"Far off from these a slow and silent stream,
  Lethe the river of oblivion rolls."

"Lethe—the waters of forgetfulness," Cal noted.

"Always the poet, our Miguel." Gates's upper lip curled slightly. "River of oblivion? Sounds like the Cuyahoga here. Who picked this godforsaken place for a conference, anyway?"

Lorantz ignored him. "I think dedicating the book to Victor is a good idea. And I like the quote, don't get me wrong. But I thought we were shooting for a more positive, constructive tone."

"Sounds somewhat ageist to me," Fairfax added.

Jessica Novak's voice was almost a whisper. "I think it sounds nice—peaceful."

"Exactly," Miguel agreed. "Acceptance. Our readers—doctor and nurses—need to realize that they can't do everything. Until there's a cure for some of these problems—like dementia—the best we can do is help people learn to live with them. Anyway, this is an open forum; I'm open to suggestions."

"I think it's excellent," Evelyn Baker announced. Plato and Cal nodded their agreement.

"We can discuss it again later. For now, I thought you should know that the publisher has moved our deadline back a few months. Victor was working on several chapters covering the geriatric assessment, and he was handling some of my executive editor chores." He held his hands out, palms open. "The publisher was very understanding. But he also reminded me that we have some competition."

Plato frowned. "Competition?"

"I guess another group—Doctor Rice and associates—is also putting together a practical geriatrics textbook. Aimed at the same readership: residents, medical students, and nurses."

"Trying to steal our thunder," Lorantz muttered. "Nobody's going to buy *both* textbooks. If theirs is released first . . ."

"I would remind you that none of us are being paid for this project anyway," Fairfax interjected. "Marketing the book is hardly our concern."

"Still, we want to have an audience, don't we?" Baker asked.

"I wouldn't sweat it," Plato said. "Rice's group puts out a whole line of cheap, low-quality textbooks, mostly aimed at medical students cramming for board exams. It's a different league altogether."

"He's a textbook mill," Fairfax rumbled. "Self publisher. A dabbler in everything and an expert in nothing. He's put out texts on every subject from vascular surgery to psychiatry."

Miguel sighed. "All the same, he's recruited some of the nation's top geriatricians as contributing editors."

"Empty titles." Fairfax slapped the table with an open palm. "He hires medical journalists to ghostwrite the chapters, then pays some famous physicians to give him their blessing and their names. Half the time, they don't even read the chapters they've supposedly authored."

"I warned you about this, Miguel. But you wouldn't listen." Eldon Gates leaned back in his heavy, ornately carved chair, fingers steepled before his face. "I said you needed big names for a textbook like this. But you chose your *friends* to be contributing editors. Few of them have connections or national reputations. And some have entirely the wrong kind of reputation. Right, Kelvin?"

Lorantz's face reddened. "I have no idea what you're talking about."

"Perhaps you could tell us why you left a prestigious position in New York to teach at a forgotten medical college in Cleveland?"

"*Doctor* Gates!" Miguel's voice snapped across the table like a whip. "Apparently you aren't aware that Doctor Lorantz is one of the nation's leading infectious disease specialists, or you wouldn't have made such a witless remark. His publication list is longer than yours, and his latest paper was just accepted by the *New England Journal*. He came to Siegel Medical College to take charge of a floundering research program, and he's turned it completely around. Not that it's any of your business."

"I see." Gates still wore a faintly mocking smile. The room fell silent for a moment. Plato could hear the wind in the trees outside, the muted rush of the Cuyahoga flowing down its rocky bed, the clatter of dishes in the dining room far below. And a faint ticking: Gates's pocket watch. The sound reminded him of the interview with Mrs. Clemens that morning.

"Good." Miguel took several deep breaths, then glanced around the table. "Maybe I should review the purpose of these meetings again. I had hoped that by gathering all the contributing editors together and discussing our plans for the various sections of the book, we could make this more of a collaborative process. We all have our own contacts, sources of information that extend beyond the particular topic we're working on. Our jobs will be much easier if we can help each other out."

"I agree completely." Evelyn Baker was nodding. "Just yesterday, I was telling Jessica—Doctor Novak— that one of my authors had backed out of his commitment. She gave me the telephone number of a physician at Harvard; I called her this morning and she fits the bill perfectly."

Jessica was blushing.

"Might I suggest that we all introduce ourselves again, and say a few words about our particular sections of the book?" Baker rearranged her papers. "How about if I go first? As most of you know, my principal area of interest is cultural anthropology. But I'm handling several chapters dealing with practical, administrative matters—a hodgepodge covering health policy, Medicare reimbursement, common legal issues, and so on. . . ."

As Baker rambled on, Plato grew more impressed. She had deftly stepped into a tense situation, followed Miguel's lead and doused the smoldering argument with a constant stream of distraction. Even Gates and Lorantz seemed relaxed and attentive as Baker described her progress with the textbook.

"I'm also writing a chapter on cross-cultural perceptions of aging," she concluded. "Believe it or not, I studied anthropology before I went into medicine, so I'm intimately acquainted with the subject."

Gradually the discussion worked its way around the table. Fairfax related his experience as a cardiologist, his research on cardiovascular disorders, and his chapters on stroke, heart attack, and circulation problems. Novak admitted to holding a doctorate in physiology as well as a medical degree. Her chapters would explore the biology and medical significance of the aging process. Miguel was writing and editing several chapters on dementia and memory loss. Lorantz discussed the latest antibiotic therapies, and Gates spoke at length about geriatric psychiatry.

While they talked, Plato filled in the details of a drawing—a rough sketch of the library with its octagonal table and the figures clustered around it. In his days at Kent State, he had drawn political cartoons for the college newspaper, even taken a few art classes. But the intensity of the art majors had turned him off. They all took everything so *seriously*, looked for meaning in everything.

He gazed around the room, realizing that this group was even more zealous than the art majors. Fairfax and Gates had nearly started a brawl with their laxative debate.

He had sketched the tableau pretty well, if he did say so himself: Harlow Fairfax leaning back, eyes half closed, hands folded across his vast middle; Evelyn Baker's smiling interest as she perched her chin on her hand and listened to the others' stories; Kelvin Lorantz thoughtfully contemplating the ceiling as though profound thoughts were coursing through his mind; Eldon Gates scratching his chin and glaring at his notebook.

Sitting in the corner behind Gates, a childlike figure was smirking, sipping a glass of milk.

"Pretty good," Cal whispered. She pointed at the apparition behind Gates. "But who's that?"

"Doctor Godwin." He frowned at his drawing. "His eyes aren't quite right, are they?"

"No."

Plato's college notebooks were filled with doodlings from his classes; at Siegel, he had finally quit taking notes at all. He'd found that by staring at sketches and caricatures from a given class, he could recall most of the important details.

Miguel had moved around to their end of the table. "As a pathologist, Cal Marley has a great deal of laboratory experience. She's agreed to author a chapter on common laboratory errors among elderly patients. And Plato's specialty is nursing home care."

Plato described his section of the book—several chapters devoted to the art of medicine in the nursing home, unique problems and diagnostic twists, preventive care, and monthly patient evaluations. His stomach muttered counterpoint while he spoke; the meeting was lasting far longer than he'd expected.

"I think that wraps it up, until tomorrow." Miguel rose to his feet and grinned. "I'll see you all in the dining room for lunch—I understand our chef has prepared quite an unusual meal for us."

"I hope he's quick about it," Gates grumbled, glowering at his pocket watch. "I want to get some sun—it's brightest in the early afternoon."

"It's also the most dangerous then, isn't it?" Lorantz muttered softly.

Miguel lagged behind and collected his papers. He smiled sadly at his friends once the others had left. "Too bad you never made it to the Joie de Vivre."

"We still had a great dinner." Cal shook her head and grinned. "Besides, it was free."

"Well, happy anniversary anyway. You folks planning anything today?"

Plato thought for a moment, then shrugged. "It was going to be a surprise, but I might as well admit it. I canceled my workshop tonight—told them I was sick. I made reservations for six-thirty."

"Oh, Plato!" Cal dropped her notebook and gave him a hug. "You didn't have to—"

"I was only one of several panelists. It's going to be pretty boring—a workshop on incontinence."

"Ah, l'amour." Miguel sighed. "Skipping an incontinence workshop, a chance at fame and fortune, a national reputation, all for the sake of love."

Plato growled at him.

Miguel grinned and led them to the door. The hall outside was flooded with a delicate aroma. They headed down the long winding stairway, across the parlor and great hall, and into the dining room. The others were already arranging themselves around a long table. Fine crystal glittered beneath the low chandelier, silver shone deep and bright, delicate bone china rested on spotless white linen. Several bottles of white wine were chilling at intervals along the table. Plato saw trays piled high with twice-baked potatoes, sweet corn on the cob, cinnamon apple tarts for dessert.

He sniffed the air again and turned to Cal. "Southern-fried chicken?"

She shook her head. "Not even close."

Mitch, the chef who had brought them yesterday's splendid lunch, stood proudly at the center of the table, one hand resting on the lid of an enormous metal roasting pan. His long brown hair was tucked up under his tall chef's hat; his pale gray eyes glittered with anticipation. "Is everyone here? Yes? Then *voilà!*"

The other guests clapped appreciatively.

"Wonderful!" someone exclaimed.

The tray held dozens of long, tube-shaped blobs with wormlike appendages at one end. Fairfax lifted one onto his plate, drowned it in a very dark gravy, sliced an appendage and forked it into his mouth. "A sumptuous treat—I commend the chef."

"The Japanese do the most *wonderful* things with squid," Evelyn Baker noted.

"Squid?" Plato let Cal guide him to a chair. Dumbly, he watched as she sat down beside him and spooned a blob onto his plate.

"Stuffed squid with ink sauce," she corrected. She ladled the bluish-black sauce over the tentacles. "Collecting the ink without bursting the sac can be a real accomplishment—our chef must be awfully good."

"Awfully." Slowly, painfully, his fantasies of pizza, lasagna, fried chicken were squelched beneath the reality of stuffed squid. With ink sauce. "You *said* we weren't having fish for lunch."

"A squid is not a fish. It's a mollusk." She sucked a tentacle into her mouth and licked her lips. "Specifically, a cephalopod."

"A cephalopod." He regarded his plate sadly. "I don't know if I can eat this. Aren't cephalopods supposed to be intelligent or something?"

"You're probably thinking of cetaceans—whales. Of course, squids *are* pretty highly developed, for invertebrates. Their eyes are said to look almost human." She poked his cephalopod with her fork. It quivered. "Dig in."

CHAPTER NINE

"I noticed that you brought a tennis racket, Cal." Evelyn Baker fell into step with them as they left the dining room.

"We both did," Cal replied. "But I promised Plato we'd go for a walk after lunch—a hike through the woods."

Plato had only planned a short hike, along the driveway and up to the lodge for some real food. He was still ravenously hungry. After just half a tentacle, he'd set down his fork in defeat. The lodge's restaurant was open all day to serve those conference-goers who missed meals.

He turned to Cal, smiling graciously. "That's okay. I don't mind going by myself."

"All three of us can play," Evelyn countered. "We'll just hit the ball around, maybe play a little cutthroat."

"Really, I—"

"C'mon. It'll be *fun*." Cal grabbed his arm and dragged him toward the stairs. She turned to Baker and waved. "We'll both be right down."

Back in the room, Plato grumbled as he pulled on his shorts and tennis shoes. "Don't *I* have a voice in these decisions?"

"You did have a voice. But you were overruled. You need to socialize more." She pinned her hair back with a pink ribbon, then turned and squeezed his bicep appraisingly. "Besides, the exercise will be good for you."

"An exercise in humiliation." He rooted around the closet for their rackets: the oversized graphite Prince he'd bought her last Christmas, the dented aluminum Wilson he'd had since high school.

"What are you worried about?" she asked as they walked out the door. "You've been playing a lot better lately. You're much more accurate; you hardly ever hit it over the fence anymore."

He stood there, arms folded across his chest, and glared at her. "Unlike you, I wasn't born with a tennis racket in one hand and a ski pole in the other."

"Ouch." Cal frowned thoughtfully. "Mom didn't mention that."

She made a silly face at him and grinned. He tried to hide a smile but couldn't. She grabbed his hand and pulled him toward the stairs. "Hey—it's not a matter of life and death, you know? It'll just be a friendly game."

"I guess so."

"Surely you don't find Evelyn Baker intimidating . . . she's like a cross between Carole King and somebody's grandmother."

"And Jackie Joyner-Kersee. Did you see the muscles on that woman?"

Outside on the veranda, Eldon Gates was perched on the porch rail. He was wearing white shorts, a light cotton sport shirt, and tennis shoes. "I bumped into Evelyn and she suggested a foursome. I hope you don't mind."

"No." Cal forced a brittle smile and avoided Plato's eyes. "Not at all."

Gates brandished his racket like a sword—newly strung tight as a hangman's noose, shock foam near the handle, wicked-looking boron/graphite frame unmarred by a single scratch. "Ordinarily, I'd rather die than play with anyone but the pro at my tennis club. But Evelyn says you're both rather good."

"Oh, we don't have time for more than a half-dozen tournaments a year," Cal said nonchalantly. She spun her racket in the air and caught it, backhanded, between her left thumb and forefinger.

"That's wonderful," he replied, rising from his seat. "Playing with amateurs really contaminates my style."

Plato touched his wife's arm and edged toward the door. "Cally, I—"

She dragged him back outside. "I know *just* what you mean, Eldon. Novices are such parasites."

Gates reached into his backpack and popped the plastic lid off a can of tennis balls.

Cal sneered. "Surely we're going to open a *fresh* can, aren't we?"

"But I just opened this yesterday—"

She grabbed one of the balls and squeezed it in her hand. "Flabby and bald." She squinted at him narrowly. "How can you play with these?"

"But I—"

Cal tossed it back to him. Gates fumbled it, nearly dropping the can. She snapped her fingers and Plato sighed, unzipped the bag, and tossed a fresh can into her open hand. She waved it beneath Gates's nose, pulled the ring and popped the seal. "Smell that? Fresh *Penn*'s—nothing like it in the world."

"I—I see." Gates sniffed tentatively and blinked several times. He stared at Cal with wide-eyed respect and a nervous smile, like a zookeeper locked in the tiger pen.

"That's the first lesson my pro taught me—consistency. Your game can't be consistent unless you—" she pounded her strings with each word, *"always—use—fresh—balls."*

Her gaze flicked over to Plato. "Isn't that what Sven always says?"

"Sven?" Plato frowned at Cal. The corner of her mouth turned up slightly. "Oh, *Sven.* Yes, yes. He's very insistent about that. Kind of a fanatic, Sven is."

"Er—of course. I agree entirely." Gates tossed the rejected balls into a trash can at the foot of the steps. "My pro says just the same thing."

Evelyn Baker popped through the door in a tennis skirt and pink shirt and chirped, "Are we all ready?"

"Certainly," Cal replied brightly. She patted Gates's shoulder. "We were just exchanging tips. Eldon claims to be quite a tennis player."

Gates backed away nervously. "No. Really, I—"

"Nonsense, Eldon," Baker chided. "You said the same thing to me on our hike this morning. About how we all would learn something from you."

She and Cal strolled on ahead.

Walking beside Plato, Gates was silent most of the way to the tennis courts. Finally, he sighed. "Quite an interesting woman, your wife."

"I think so." Plato glanced over at his companion. He didn't look much like Sean Connery anymore. He looked old, shrunken. "I'm surprised you're not at the conference today."

"It's pretty dead this afternoon. Three sessions on caregiver burnout—can you believe it?"

"It's a pretty important topic," Plato noted soberly.

"I suppose so. One of my partners practically worked himself to death, years ago." He stared off into space and chuckled softly. "Some people just don't know how to keep their perspective, keep their distance."

Gates made it sound so easy. It probably *was* easy, for him. Plato decided to change the subject. "Giving any more lectures?"

"Two more. The big one is tonight." Gates lifted his chin again, straightened his shoulders, and bounced the heel of one hand against his racket. "I'm receiving an award from Marcal Pharmaceuticals—I'm their Researcher of the Year. Several thousand dollars. I just need to give an acceptance speech and make a few product endorsements."

"Congratulations."

Gates didn't hear. He seemed to have recovered his confidence. His eyes were half closed, and he swung the racket slowly through space—forehand-backhand-forehand-backhand-*smash*. He glanced at Plato and smiled apologetically.

"My pro taught me to do this before each match. Tennis is very psychological, you know."

"Very." At Plato's skill level, psychology played a very minor role. Most of Plato's attention centered on hitting the ball with the racket. All else was secondary.

They walked through the gate; Cal and Evelyn were already volleying on the clay court. Gates called out to them. "How about some mixed doubles, to keep things fair? Plato, you can go down and join your little woman."

He and Gates dropped their racket covers, keys, and watches beside the water fountain near the center of the court. Gates unslung his backpack from his shoulders, grabbed a bottle of tanning lotion, and daubed his forehead, neck, arms, and nose. Turning to join Baker, he frowned back at Plato. "Your wife—she's not really all *that* good, is she?"

He grinned. "Look at it this way, Eldon—maybe the little woman will teach you something."

Over the next hour or so, Plato certainly learned something. He learned that he played even worse on clay than on hardcourt. The ball bounced lower and faster. His feet, when they didn't slip, needed more time to speed up and slow down. And when he finally did make it in time, planted his feet perfectly and swung through just like Cal had taught him, the ball would hit a lump of clay or gravel and take a quirky

bounce, slamming into the edge of his racket and sail-
ing through the air like a wounded quail. If he was
lucky, it landed somewhere inside the fence.

Not that it mattered. When Cal played the net, the
ball rarely reached him at all. She'd spring from one
side of the court to the other, skating artfully through
the dust, timing each leap, each dodge, each pirouette,
with the skill and grace of a ballerina or a gazelle. And
from the baseline, she'd slice her shots left or right,
over or under, adding shifty spins that set the ball
bouncing grotesquely and twisted her opponents into
pretzels.

Gates called a truce after the first set. As they walked
to the net, he glared at his partner and panted, "I think
it's time to change teams."

Baker beat him to the punch. "How about boys
against girls? That would be fun."

He raised his hands and shook his head. "That's
hardly fair to you two. I wouldn't want to—"

"Sounds like a fine idea to me," Cal mused. She
gestured to Baker. "Evelyn?"

The older woman hurried around the net and joined
her. Plato followed Gates over to the fence. While he
drank from the water fountain, his teammate snatched
a bottle of Evian from his backpack and swigged lust-
ily. Gates replaced the bottle, pulled his shirt off, and
grabbed the tanning lotion again. Slathering it over his
shoulders and back, he complained, "Baker's not very
good, you know. Doubles tennis is a fine art—mostly
knowing where to stand and reading your teammate's
signals."

From Plato's point of view, Gates and Baker had
similar skill levels: he hit the ball harder and she em-
ployed more finesse.

"Not only that, but I've got a damned headache."
Still shirtless, he walked onto the court, stretching the

heavy muscles of his arms and back. "My game is really off today, as you can see."

"My game is never *on*," Plato joked.

"It had better be." Gates turned and glared at him. "I don't plan on losing to a couple of *women*."

"We won't lose," Plato muttered softly. "We'll get slaughtered."

But it wasn't quite as bad as he'd expected. He was getting used to the clay surface; his timing was better, and he learned to anticipate the bounces more closely. Baker had lost her consistency, and Cal seemed to be easing up on them.

Gates wasn't much help, though. When Plato played the net, his partner would break to the front and push him back. Then Gates would backpedal to the baseline again, calling for shots that were clearly out of his range. By the middle of the set, he was panting heavily, clutching at his chest for breath—when he wasn't wincing and holding his head.

His constant stream of commentary and coaching didn't help either. He even adjusted Plato's grip between serves. "No—put your thumb *down*, more to the inside—that's it. Now toss the ball higher. Arch your back before you swing."

Going after sideline shots, Plato would hear Gates shout, "Slide with your left foot—*left* foot, damn it!"

Still, the set was pretty close; at six games apiece, they had to play a tiebreaker. When they switched sides of the court, Plato heard Gates wheezing. His tongue lolled, and his eyes were glazed. Even the coaching had died down.

"Are you all right, Eldon? Do you want to take a break for a while?"

He shook his head. "What? . . . Lose our . . . momentum? I'm . . . okay. Just a headache."

It was Plato's serve; they were losing the tiebreaker 6–5. If they lost the point, they would lose the set as well. Gates was standing ahead and to his right—leaning over, really. Trying to catch his breath.

If only Gates weren't wearing that damned pocket watch; the ticking was driving him crazy . . .

And then, tossing the ball into the air, Plato remembered how his partner had left his watch on the sideline, in his bag—before they ever started playing. Yet the ticking had persisted, coming from Gates throughout the entire set.

The ball fell, clunked off the rim of his racket, and rocketed over the fence. Plato tried to put the noise out of his mind; he didn't want to lose the match on a double fault. Tossing the ball up again, he tried to forget Gates's suggestions as well, just tried to swing naturally, willing the ball over the net and into that little square right in front of Cal, easy as pie, nothing simpler—and there it went, over the net and down inside the line—*Thwick!*—Cal returned it, a lazy looping spinner that spat dust in front of Gates's feet; he slipped his racket down just in time—*Thwock!*—over to Baker, she hit a simple line drive back to Plato—*Thwick!*—back to Cal, then to Gates, then a slow arc back to Baker again; she had plenty of time to line it up in her sights so when it came she was poised, ready with a fully premeditated stroke—artful, crafty, and deadly—she fired it down the line and Gates was running, running back, calling Plato off, shoulders flailing ahead, legs pinwheeling to catch up, swinging too soon, much too soon—*Thwunk!*—he hit it, unbelievably, the ball careened off the racket frame and sailed up, up, into the sun, Gates still pounding along helplessly, slamming into the fence and turning to watch it fall.

Out of bounds, apparently—Baker just stood back, let it bounce in front of her, bounce again and die as she called, "Long! We win!"

"On the line, damn it!" Gates cried.

Plato didn't expect much sportsmanship from his partner; still, he was surprised when Gates ran across the court, cursing, and knelt in front of Baker to check for the ball mark. So Plato jogged over to join the crowd, ready to intervene if it came to blows.

But Gates was gasping for air, clutching his chest. He slumped back into the clay.

"Doctor Gates—are you all right?" Plato knelt beside him.

"Damned headache—" On his side, he peered down at the countless scuffs in the red clay, as though *his* mark might have made a lasting impact. He scrabbled at his chest again and froze, a tortured statue, a sculptor's study in pain.

The ticking had stopped. The sudden silence was filled by the wind in the leaves, the scuffle of knees in the clay, the rush of the river from somewhere far away. Plato checked the neck for a pulse, but couldn't feel a thing.

CHAPTER TEN

"Coffee, Jeremy?"

Cal was playing the perfect little hostess, hanging their guest's coat in the closet, seeing that his chair was comfortable, brewing a fresh carafe of coffee in the kitchenette. It might have been a quiet evening at home, with Jeremy Ames dropping by for their traditional Friday night pinochle match. Except that Cal was still wearing her blue surgical cap and blood-stained Keds, Lieutenant Ames had his notebook out, and they were sitting in the physicians' lounge at Riverside General Hospital.

"Sounds great." Ames propped his feet on the heavy oak coffee table scattered with back issues of the *Wall Street Journal, Business Week, Fortune,* and a few *JAMA*s and *New England Journal*s. A hole was starting in the sole of his left shoe, and his navy polyester slacks were puckered with several aborted cigarette burns.

Jeremy Ames always made Plato a little tense—like watching a lion pace the length of his cage, back and forth, back and forth. When he wasn't trying to set himself on fire, the detective constantly fidgeted, drumming his fingers on his knees, tapping his heels on the floor, flicking his gaze around the room. His energy was legendary; rumor had it that he only slept on weekends. Ames worked sixty hours a week for the Cuyahoga County Sheriff's Department, volunteered at

the Boys' Club, and taught an evening police proce-
dural course at the community college. He'd been di-
vorced three times, and each new wife was a little
younger. He seemed to wear them out.

Maybe Ames was hyperthyroid; his eyes bulged
with permanent surprise, his hands trembled sometimes, and he hardly ever blinked. But Plato doubted
that he'd be interested in a cure.

Ames glanced at him and flashed a quick grin. "Cal
says you two are going to the Joie de Vivre tonight."

"We're *supposed* to," he replied, glancing at his
watch. Past eight-fifteen. "Actually, our reservations
were for five minutes ago."

"Great place." He grabbed a *New England Journal*
and flipped through the pages. "Took Nina there a couple of weeks back. Six-month anniversary."

"Congratulations."

Cal poured coffee for herself and Ames, and opened
a can of juice for Plato. Sitting beside him, she took a
sip and sank back into the plush overstuffed sofa. Unlike most of the hospital, the physicians' lounge had
comfortable furniture, deep pile carpeting, and table
lamps instead of the ubiquitous fluorescent lights. It
didn't see much use, though. For most attending physicians, it was just a place to hang their coats on their
way up to the floors. But Plato had slept in the rolla-
way bed here a couple of months ago when caring for
a particularly sick patient in the Intensive Care Unit.
The kitchen, television, and private bath were a far cry
from the shabby residents' lounge upstairs.

"Sheriff Davis asked me to come out for a chat,"
Ames explained after downing half his coffee. "This
thing happening out by the Cuyahoga Reserve like this,
the jurisdiction's kind of mixed up. The lodge is in the
City of Brecksville, but part of the lands are on the
Cuyahoga Reserve, and so we've got Brecksville police and the forest rangers getting curious. And then

there's the connection with Cleveland, through the medical college."

"Sounds complicated," Plato sympathized.

"It is. And since all the pieces are in Cuyahoga County, the sheriff's been called in to kind of sort things out." He stared at his shoes. "Not that we suspect anything. But somebody already leaked the story to Channel Five. Tomorrow the *Plain Dealer* will probably be all over it—asking questions, poking around. Probably trying to make all of us look like a bunch of idiots. So we've got to be ready with some answers. Like maybe that the deaths were entirely natural."

Cal shrugged vaguely.

Ames finished the rest of his coffee, and his spring wound down a little. He brushed a hand over his silvery crew cut—a relic of his years in the Marines. "You've got to admit, it looks pretty suspicious. Two doctors dying in the same hotel within a day of each other. Got to be coincidence, though. This Godwin guy was pretty old, right?"

"Seventy-three," Cal replied noncommittally.

"Good. Probably a heart attack or something." He crossed and recrossed his legs. "Let's just tidy up the books and then we can go home. Nina's parents are visiting from Italy. She made *saltimbocca alla romana*—veal stuffed with prosciutto and mozzarella."

"Maybe we *all* can have dinner at your place tonight," Plato suggested. His stomach growled and he looked at his watch again. Eight-thirty.

"That would be some anniversary—the two of you, me and Nina, and her eighty-year-old parents. You're a real Rudolph Valentino, Plato."

"Do Nina's parents speak English?" Cal asked.

"No. And I don't speak Italian." Ames chuckled dryly. "A few words from when I played piano—

andante, allegro, things like that. They think I'm a traffic cop."

"I wouldn't mind learning some Italian," Plato mused. "*Saltimbocca alla romana*. What a beautiful language. It just kind of rolls off your tongue, you know?"

"It sure does. And we're playing pinochle afterward." Ames was able to sit still for pinochle; sometimes he relaxed enough to blink once or twice. "So let's just wrap this up. You folks can head on out to your restaurant and I'll make it home before my inlaws go to bed."

While Cal was reviewing the details of Godwin's autopsy, one of the surgeons trudged through the door and scowled at them. A grizzled old curmudgeon; Plato had rotated on his service during residency, but he'd forgotten his name. The surgeon crossed to the dictaphones in the far corner of the room and slammed a briefcase onto the table; a pile of charts spewed out. Muttering darkly, he snatched up a microphone and started sifting through the records.

Plato couldn't blame him for being cross; Sunday evening dictation was particularly grueling torture. But there was no way around it; every Monday morning, some nine-to-five executive pushed a little button on a computer in the administration's penthouse and it cranked out the names of all the physicians who were behind on their records. The machine spat out yellow slips that looked like parking tickets and sent them to the offending doctors. If a physician fell too far behind or generated too many yellow slips, his or her admitting privileges could be suspended. The hospital supposedly lost a million dollars a year from tardy dictation and billing, but no one ever calculated how much the hospital would lose if physicians only worked forty-hour weeks.

Ames was frowning at Cal. "You're calling the Godwin case a Class *Four?*"

Plato groaned softly. A Class Four cause of death meant there were no clear anatomical, toxicological, or histological findings—in other words, no discernible cause of death. Cal probably designated more of her cases as Class Four than most pathologists did. Patient, meticulous, and thorough, she admitted when she wasn't sure about her findings; her methods drove some police detectives to distraction. In the end, though, she had probably unearthed more than her share of buried secrets.

"For now, yes," Cal replied. "Once some more tests come back, I may be able to—"

"For God's sake, Cal. Victor Godwin was seventy-what?" The detective looked down at his notes. "Seventy-three years old. You're telling me you can't find a cause of death? What about a heart attack, or a stroke, or something?"

"Old people aren't immune to murder, Jeremy," Cal said softly.

"*Murder?* Who said anything about murder?" Ames was almost shouting; the surgeon dropped his dictaphone and glared across the room at them. Ames lowered his voice again. "Cal, don't kid around—it's not funny. If the press heard you talking like that, they'd be on my department like a pack of leeches. Not to mention what that kind of story would do to the convention trade around here. Cleveland's still not exactly a boom town—we don't need a bunch of rumors getting started."

"I'm just saying that I don't have all the answers yet. That maybe we need to check a little further, start a little informal investigation."

"For what? Some vague suspicions and a blood test with traces of narcotic?" Ames's jaw stiffened. "Anyway, there's no such thing as an informal *homicide* investigation, Cal. It's like being 'sort of' pregnant."

"Or sort of dead," Plato added dryly.

"I haven't told you about Gates's autopsy yet."

Ames fumbled in the breast pocket of his jacket, pulled out a pack of Marlboros and fiddled with the unopened wrapper. With a trembling hand, he slipped them back into his pocket. Finally, he looked up at Cal and shook his head. "You owe me some saltimbocca."

Plato didn't quite grasp the logic behind this, but Cal nodded. "How about a sub from Luigi's instead? Next time I have to eat lunch at the courthouse, I'll bring one around."

"Deal." The detective settled back and listened.

It was ten minutes to nine; meals at the Joie de Vivre took so long that they didn't accept any new diners after nine o'clock. Plato glanced at his wife. She was wearing a pair of faded blue jeans and an old Chicago Bears football jersey; her dress and shoes were hanging in the specimen closet down in the morgue. If she hurried, they still had a slim chance.

"Gates was in excellent health, as far as I could tell," Cal began. "That's what makes it seem so strange. A fitness nut—into running and hiking and weightlifting and all that. And tennis, of course. Very vain about his body. Quite healthy, aside from the heart valve."

"Heart valve?" Plato and Ames asked together.

"Starr-Edwards valve, aortic." She glanced at the yellow legal pad on her lap. "Looks like he had rheumatic fever a long time ago; there are some calcifications on the other valves."

"Rheumatic fever?" Ames's face was still blank.

"Hah!" Plato snapped his fingers and chuckled. "That explains it!"

"Explains *what*?" Cal asked.

"The clicking noise—remember how Gates was always wearing that pocket watch?"

"Mmm-hmm." She considered for a moment. "Yeah—it fits. I told you he was vain."

"I heard the clicking on the tennis court; it practically drove me crazy." Plato chuckled. "Especially when I noticed he wasn't wearing his pocket watch."

"Will somebody *please* tell me what you two are talking about?" the detective demanded. "What do valves and pocket watches have to do with anything?"

"Sorry, Jeremy." Cal leaned over to pat his hand. "I found a Starr-Edwards heart valve when I did Gates's autopsy. From the changes in his other valves, I'm pretty sure he had rheumatic fever years ago—it's a nasty side effect of strep infections that can damage the heart valves. If the injury is severe, a damaged valve might have to be replaced with an artificial heart valve, like the Starr-Edwards."

"It's a pretty amazing contraption, really—shaped sort of like a Ping-Pong ball in a wire cage," Plato added. He grabbed the legal pad and drew a picture for Ames. "When the heart pumps the blood *out,* the ball moves up—like this. When the heart relaxes, the pressure in the aorta pushes the ball back down, blocking the opening and keeping the blood from spilling back into the heart again."

"Okay." He scratched his head. "So where does the pocket watch come in?"

"Gates had this big gold pocket watch—wore it everywhere," Plato explained. "I *thought* he was wearing it out on the tennis court. By the way, Cal, I would have aced that last serve if I hadn't been distracted."

"Uh-huh." She rolled her eyes and turned to Jeremy. "Anyway, the Starr-Edwards valve makes a sharp *click* each time the ball is forced up into the cage. Gates wore a pocket watch so everyone would assume the clicking was coming from his watch. That way, no one would know about his illness."

"I still have trouble believing it." Ames shook his head. "You're saying this valve was noisy enough that it clicked with every single heartbeat—loud enough that people could hear it across a room, or even out-doors?"

"Right," Cal agreed. But she flashed a dubious glance at her husband. "I'm not sure about the tennis court, though."

"Things got awfully quiet during that last set," Plato insisted.

"I don't think I could stand that." The detective shuddered. "Hearing every single heartbeat. Like Chinese water torture or something. And what if it stopped?"

Plato grinned. "Call 9-1-1."

"Most people get used to the sound after a while," Cal said. "Many of the newer artificial valves aren't so noisy. And they're getting better at using natural valves—pig valves."

"Pig valves. I hope I never need heart surgery." Ames snapped his notebook shut and dropped it in his pocket. "Well, all this is pretty interesting, but I don't see that it's very relevant to the case. I'll just call the sheriff and—"

"I haven't told you about the nitroglycerin yet."

"Nitroglycerin, huh?" He frowned. "Now you're going to say someone planted a bomb in Gates's pocket watch."

"The *medicine,* Jeremy. It relaxes the heart and blood vessels. High levels of nitroglycerin cause the blood to turn a chocolate color."

Food again, Plato thought. Why couldn't they just say "brown" or "tan"?

"I noticed the odd color right when we started working on Gates. I ran a test, and his blood is definitely.

positive for nitroglycerin by-products. We don't have a level yet, but I'm sure it's quite high."

"Come on, Cally." Plato was getting annoyed. "I can think of a dozen reasons why he'd be taking nitroglycerin. It's a common enough drug, even among people with heart valves."

"Blood doesn't turn that color unless there are very high levels of nitroglycerin. *Toxic* levels."

Plato was skeptical but Ames nodded soberly. He scribbled something in his notebook. "Got anything else on this?"

"We'll have the blood levels later on this evening. That should tell us for sure whether he died of an overdose."

"Good." For the first time that evening, Ames's hands were resting calmly in his lap. His heels weren't tapping the floor. He even blinked once or twice, fishlike eyes staring blankly into space, then turning back to Cal. "Call me with the results—I'll wait to hear from you before I talk with the sheriff."

Plato's pager beeped. He checked the display; it was the number of the Joie de Vivre. He walked over to the telephone in the kitchenette to call and apologize. It took longer than he'd expected. By the time he was finished, Cal and Ames were wrapping things up.

"Tell Nina hello for us," she was saying. "I'll call you later on tonight."

"Great." The detective glanced over at Plato. "Enjoy your dinner—I hope you folks can make it."

Cal glanced at her watch. "Oh—look at the time! I'm sorry, Plato."

He shrugged.

"Too late, huh?" Ames thought for a minute, then clapped his hands. "Hey, I've got the perfect spot for you two. There's this new place up on Murray Hill—they've got a salad bar and some great appetizers. All kinds of wine. A jazz band, too, but I don't know if they're playing on Sunday nights."

"I've heard this somewhere before." Cal sighed. She glanced at Plato. "Maybe we'll give it a try."

After Ames left, she turned to her husband and gave him a hug. "Sorry, dear."

"Relax," he told her. "It's not your fault. Anyway, I just remembered another place we can go and have a nice, quiet, private dinner. No salad bar, no jazz band, but it's still pretty nice."

She grinned. "I bet I know just where it is."

"I bet you don't." Holding her shoulders, he turned her around and pointed her toward the door. "Put your dress on and I'll get the car, okay?"

She met him outside the main entrance, cap and Keds removed, hair tied back in a short ponytail, still wearing the blue jeans and jersey. The dress was still on its hanger, wrapped in plastic and slung over her shoulder.

"Going casual tonight, are we?" he asked as she climbed in the car.

"Get real. You didn't think I'd put on all that lace and taffeta for a meal at the Rusted Penguin, did you?"

He shrugged. "Suit yourself."

While Plato drove, Cal reviewed the meeting with Ames. "He sure was in a hurry to finish up."

"He's always that way when he gets a new wife."

"He's never been *that* anxious to get home before. I always thought he was a workaholic."

"I think he's been cured." Plato stared out the window as they crossed the Veterans Memorial Bridge. Far below, the waters of the Cuyahoga were bottomless and black. Out on the lake, the lights of a small freighter burned holes in the night.

They passed Public Square and followed Ontario back down toward the river. "Besides, you haven't met Nina yet, have you?"

"Not yet." She tugged his arm over her shoulders and nestled in.

"Twenty-six or twenty-seven. Comes from northern Italy—tall and blond, high cheekbones. Looks like some Nordic goddess. Or the figurehead of a ship."

A hint of wistfulness slipped into his voice. Cal sat up and let his arm drop behind her. "You've got a problem with *short* and blond?"

"Don't be ridiculous," he soothed. She slid beside him again. "You know I don't go for big women. Too pushy and domineering. Just give me a short, blond, meek, humble, quiet, shy slip of a thing any day."

"Yeah, sure."

"But I *am* a little jealous about the saltimbocca," he confessed.

She elbowed his ribs.

He grunted. "Of course, eating out is always nice."

As if on cue, they turned onto Canal Road and pulled up in front of the Joie de Vivre. The pink neon sign was dark, the windows were shuttered, and the CLOSED sign hung from the door. Even the tricolor flag had been taken down from beside the doorway.

"Plato—what are we doing here?" Cal asked.

"Georges asked me to stop by." He stepped out of the car, opened her door and escorted her to the restaurant entrance. He knocked loudly.

"Is his father sick again?" She looked around nervously. The street was deserted and dark. In an alley nearby, a pair of cats were fighting, or making love, or singing at the moon. Something clattered, and Cal jumped. "I wish he could come to the office like the rest of your patients. Sometimes I think you go a little too far—"

A shadow approached the doorway, a key fumbled in the lock. The door opened, and Georges D'Armand, owner of the Joie de Vivre, grinned at them.

"Madame, monsieur! So good to see you. Come inside, *s'il vous plait*." He led them past the small bar in front, through the main dining room, to a small candlelit table near a window at the back of the restaurant. A bottle of wine and two glasses glowed red in the flickering light. Through the window, the Cuyahoga River was visible just below, mirroring the streetlights and the stars.

Plato watched comprehension dawning in her eyes as she stood motionless, staring at the table, the window, the stars. He slipped his hand around hers; it suddenly felt very small. "Happy anniversary, dear."

Georges suddenly remembered he had urgent business in the kitchen.

CHAPTER ELEVEN

"I must confess a tragedy—the duck could not be saved. It grows bitter this late," Georges clucked later, once they were seated. Though the Joie de Vivre was closed and all the employees and guests had left, the tall thin restaurant owner still wore his black tuxedo. Gold cufflinks sparkled at his wrists, and the sommelier's chain dangled from his neck. "But the lamb, it will be perfect, I think."

"That sounds wonderful, Georges," Plato assured him. He glanced over at Cal. She still looked slightly bewildered; she was holding his hand across the table and staring into the sputtering candle flame.

"And the wine—I hope you will approve. I chose our 1983 Echézeaux." He lifted a bottle and showed it to Plato. "*Domaine de la Romanée-Conti.* One of the best producers in France. And 1983 was a very good year for Burgundy."

"I hope it wasn't *too* good a year," Plato hinted. Even with three credit cards in his pocket, he didn't want to risk another Cindy Brunelli fiasco.

"It can never be too good a year, my friend. You know that." He lifted the cork and placed it on the table.

Plato ignored it, as Georges had taught him to do. Instead, he plucked a piece of bread from his plate and nibbled casually, clearing his palate. Georges poured a bit into one of the glasses. Gripping it by the stem,

Plato first held the glass against the white tablecloth to judge its color. He slowly lifted it to his lips and held it there for a moment, breathing through his nose with a thoughtful expression. Don't *sniff,* Georges had told him once. Breathe, as though tasting the wine with your mind. He tasted the wine with his mind, or tried to, then tasted it with his mouth. Setting it down, he contemplated the candle flame, then the window. He calmly lifted it to his lips, tasted it again, then finally turned to Georges. "I agree. An excellent choice. Violets with the slightest hint of cedar. And the finish is splendid."

The owner clapped his hands and laughed. *"Très magnifique,* Plato. You are progressing very well. But one thing—do not tell the sommelier about the bouquet or finish—address those comments to your lady. The wine captain is a servant, a piece of furniture. You would not seek approval from this candlestick, would you?"

"Not unless I was a candle."

"Certainement! Then if you are pleased with the wine, simply nod for the server to pour out." Georges grinned and squeezed Plato's shoulder. "Otherwise, your performance was splendid—the timing, the thoughtful pauses. Truly you seemed to be tasting the wine with your mind."

"Except for that bit about violets and cedar," Cal interjected. "He says that every time."

"Exactly," Georges agreed. His gray eyebrows knitted together. "You must add some variety—black currants, vanilla, even nutmeg or ginger."

"But what if I'm wrong?" Plato asked.

"Ah—that is the beauty of it!" He waved extravagantly. "You say you taste black currants; who can say otherwise? All will be impressed."

They laughed together, and Georges darted back to the kitchen.

"A 1983 Echézeaux," Cal said, looking down at her Chicago Bears jersey. "Somehow, I feel a little bit underdressed."

"Take it easy." He gestured around the empty restaurant. "There's no one else here to see you."

"*You're* here," she replied, rising to her feet. "And Georges. And that bottle of wine. I feel like a schoolkid crashing her parents' dinner party."

Cal turned and darted back to the front entrance. She returned a moment later with her dress and shoes, winked at Plato, then headed off to the ladies' room.

While she was gone, Plato contemplated the bewildering array of forks, knives, spoons, and dishes scattered around the table. Thanks to Georges, he now knew the difference between a salad fork and a dessert fork, knew how to fold a napkin in his lap, how to hold a wineglass and a teacup. His father the cop would have scoffed at such extravagances, but then Jack Marley had lost his appetite for polite society shortly after Plato's mother left them. He even seemed vaguely disappointed and distant when his son graduated from medical school, as though a medical degree conferred class and breeding and taste, like the touch of the king's sword on the shoulder of a knight errant. As though Plato, too, would suddenly see his father as she had—tasteless, common, and mundane.

Jack Marley hadn't lived long enough to meet Cal, to see how much she resembled Plato's classy, aristocratic mother in that yellowing family picture taken when Plato was just five, just before she left. Maybe it was just as well.

Cal emerged from the gloom again, and Plato's heart gave a little lurch. The black off-shouldered dress casually exposed her pale skin, the lace and taffeta barely hid the shapes and curves at the plunging neckline and upswept hem. Like glimpsing the moon behind a veil of clouds or the sparkle of a diamond in the earth.

"I'm kind of glad it worked out this way," she said breathlessly. "I hadn't worn this dress in public before—it's a little more, uhh, *revealing* than I realized."

"Don't worry about it, Cal." Plato reassured her. "It looks perfectly decent from here."

"Just ask Georges not to turn on any more lights, or he may lose his liquor license," she joked. Sitting down, she frowned. "Speaking of Georges, I'm a little worried about something."

"What?"

She sipped the wine. "About whether we'll be able to make next month's mortgage payment."

"Cal, I know it's a great wine. But Georges wouldn't steer us wrong—he knows our price range." Aside from his lessons in etiquette, Georges often chose the wine for them. The cellar at Joie de Vivre held a number of buried treasures, and the owner passed the secrets on to a few of his friends.

"And Georges's father is one of your patients." She took another sip. "This *is* good. But he's keeping the restaurant open just for us. How much is all this going to cost?"

"No more than it would during regular hours, according to Georges."

"But why would he—"

Plato settled back, steepled his fingers. "Remember that time a couple of months ago, when I spent the night at Riverside General because that patient was crashing in the ICU?"

"Yeah. We had tickets to the Indians doubleheader against the Yankees."

"Uh-huh. And you went without me."

She grinned. "I thought of you when Albert Belle knocked the winning home run into the center field bleachers."

"You're so kind. Anyway, it was Georges's father who was in the ICU."

"Oh."

"When I called to cancel tonight—*again*—he insisted that we come anyway."

Georges arrived with a tray. "To kindle the appetite, I saved some of our excellent pâté maison. Our chef's recipe is quite mild, so it will provide a reasonable prelude to the lamb. A seafood dish would be better, but of course Plato has—mmm—*limited* tastes. Eh, Cal?"

"Violets and cedar," she replied with a grin.

Plato sulked.

"*Au juste.* A typical American palate. But I respect *your* judgment, my dear." He carved a piece of French bread and added a spread of pâté, then served it to Cal.

"Delicious! Even Plato will like it, I think. What's in it—tarragon? Madeira?"

"That, and chervil, nutmeg, and allspice. Delicately, though; otherwise the palate may be overwhelmed."

"This *is* good," Plato agreed after trying some. "Just scrumptious. Georges, have you ever thought about canning it? This stuff would be great on sandwiches. A little Grey Poupon mustard, maybe a pickle or two . . ."

Georges frowned at him, then chuckled. "For a moment, I almost thought you were serious."

Watching him walk away, Plato muttered, "I *was* serious."

It wasn't until the main course arrived that he remembered the ring in his pocket. The ring he hadn't been able to afford when they got engaged; the ring Cal had spotted in an antique store and cast broad hints about. They had even checked the price after the wedding, taken it to an independent appraiser, thought about buying it. Back before they bought the house.

Over the past year, Plato had squirreled away enough for a hefty down payment, and the credit limit on their MasterCard had provided the rest. Counting next month's slated raise, he figured to have it paid off in just under a year.

It made him nervous, carrying the tiny box in his pocket. As much as he looked forward to giving it to Cal, seeing her eyes light up, he was just as anxious to have it someplace safe and secure, where it couldn't slip through a hole in his pocket or get stuck between the sofa cushions. Someplace like her left ring finger.

He set his fork down and reached for her hand. "Callie, I—"

She was preoccupied. "Isn't the lamb *wonderful*? And these little potatoes, and the vegetables. I don't know how Georges does it, but everything just tastes so *perfect* together."

"I just wanted to ask you . . . to *tell* you . . . to say that—"

Her pager shattered the stillness of the empty restaurant. Freeing her hand from his, she reached down to switch it off, held it beside the candle and read the display. "Oh, good. It's just the lab—they probably have those nitroglycerin levels for me."

She fished in her purse for some change and hurried off. While he waited, Plato finished his lamb and had Georges bring the dessert—a grand marnier soufflé dusted with powdered sugar. And some of the restaurant's famous mint chocolate coffee, to clear their heads from the wine. Plato had two cups while waiting for Cal; he didn't plan on sleeping much tonight anyway.

When she returned, she was breathing hard and her eyes slid away from Plato's gaze.

"What's wrong?"

She glanced up at him and bit her lip. "Remind me to call Jeremy after we get back to the hotel."

"Something interesting?"

"The nitroglycerin level—it was way above normal." Cal suddenly switched to Cafeteria Mode, down-

ing the lamb as though it were Thursday night goulash
at Riverside General. She swigged her wine like a lusty
sailor. "And given Gates's heart condition, it was probably high enough to have killed him."

Plato nodded. "It wouldn't take much, being out in
the sun like he was."

"And playing tennis." She stabbed a potato and the
last bit of lamb, forked them into her mouth. "All that
exertion put him at risk. But even if he were taking nitro for his heart, I don't understand why the blood
level was so *high.*"

"Maybe he had some pain during the tennis match
and took too many sublingual nitro pills," Plato suggested. But he was almost certain Gates didn't.

Cal sighed, moved her empty plate away and dove
into the soufflé. "You're right. I suppose it might even
have been suicide—but it's a pretty unusual technique."

"That's for sure."

"The thing I don't get," she said with a frown, "is
why he didn't have a headache. Even at normal dosages, nitroglycerin often causes headaches. With a
blood level this high, it should have felt like a migraine, or worse."

"He *did* have a headache," Plato replied, remembering the afternoon match. "He complained about it all
through the last set. He looked pretty awful there, toward the end. I even asked him if he wanted to stop,
but he said he didn't want us to lose our *momentum.*"

"Momentum, huh?" Cal grinned slightly, then sobered. "I remember now—he said something about a
headache just after he fell down, didn't he?"

Georges appeared at Plato's elbow. "May I get you
some more coffee? No?"

"Thank you. Just the check is fine." When it came,
Plato noticed that the wine wasn't listed on the bill.

"No, it is not a mistake." Georges shook his head

sadly. "The Echézeaux has reached its peak; it is a short-lived wine. Another month or two and it might begin to sour. You have done me a favor by enjoying it here, on your anniversary."

Cal stood and gave him a hug. "It was a wonderful meal—something we'll always remember."

Georges, the suave, sophisticated Frenchman, blushed and scuffed his feet shyly. "*De rien,* Madame."

He hurried off to call a cab.

Back at the hotel, the light was flashing on their bedside telephone. Cal dialed the front desk and found that Jeremy Ames had phoned three times that evening.

"Why don't you start the fire and warm things up— how would Georges put it? 'Kindle the appetite,' " she said, winking at Plato. "I've got to call Jeremy and give him the results—it'll just take a minute or two."

While the hotel operator put the call through, Cal watched her husband undress, tie on his robe, and start the fire. He glanced over at her, smiled that crooked little-boy smile of his, and winked. She grinned back.

Plato was handsome in a rugged sort of way, and he had a nice body—even if he was a little clumsy with a tennis racket. But it was his *eyes* that had made her do a double-take the first time she'd met him three years ago, when she bumped into him outside the morgue at Riverside. He'd been lost, of course. She'd looked into those pale green eyes and felt her breath catch, felt her heart give a little lurch. All silliness, of course. But there it was.

She'd gotten his name from the medical society directory, found out he wasn't married, figured out what floor he worked on, and contrived to bump into him a few more times—mostly in the cafeteria. She built up his confidence enough so that he finally asked her out. It took a couple of months, though. He didn't have a lot of self-confidence—she could see that.

You could see everything in his eyes. Some people wore their hearts on their sleeves. Plato's heart lay at the bottom of those clear green depths, every emotion, every thought. Honest eyes.

She watched him slump into a chair beside the fireplace and drag out another Rex Stout novel. He loved the old classics. Plato would read an author's works from start to finish, and if he liked it, run through the whole series twice. He'd collected a stack of Nero Wolfe novels and was reading them all over again.

Too bad real life wasn't like that. Once you finished the series, you'd have all the answers.

Ames's voice was gravelly with sleep. "Cal? That you?"

"What's the matter, Jeremy? Couldn't wait for me to call you back?"

"I wish." He sighed mournfully. Cal wondered if he had lost the pinochle match, or learned a few more Italian phrases. "It's the sheriff—he's been on my back all evening. I told him what you said, and he just about hit the roof. Gave me a long talk about the local economy, the mayor's five-year plan, the works. I think he'd just as soon push this all under the rug and forget it ever happened. He says unless you've found anything new, that's what we should do."

"Sorry, Jeremy." She took a deep breath. "We found something new."

Ames was silent for a long minute. Cal looked over at Plato. He hadn't turned a page in several minutes; he was just squinting at the fire. She wondered what he was thinking about. Probably what a lousy anniversary it had been. Probably dreading the months and years ahead, wondering why he'd ever married a "professional" woman instead of a happy little housewife who could sew her own clothes, cook like Georges, stay awake for romantic evenings, and be around for anniversaries and birthdays and holidays.

"I don't think I'm ready for this," the detective muttered.

"The blood tests on Gates showed very high levels of nitroglycerin," Cal said bluntly.

"High enough to kill him?"

She considered, then decided on the truth. The report would find its way to Davis's office tomorrow morning anyway. "Probably. With the heart valve, and the strain of the tennis match, and the sun—I'd have to say yes."

"Hold on a minute, Cal." Ames was still hunting for an angle. "You're saying his heart condition might have contributed to this? Then even if someone tried to poison him with nitroglycerin—not that I believe it for a minute—his heart problem's what really killed him. Right?"

"Wrong." She slumped onto the bed and stared at the ceiling. "In the first place, the heart valve was just a factor in his death. In my opinion, the proximate cause of death was still the nitroglycerin overdose."

"Damn. I thought I was onto something."

"You weren't. Even if the nitroglycerin overdose had only been one percent responsible for his death, even if the *cause* of death was a failure of his heart valve or something, it could still be ruled a homicide or suicide."

The detective sounded disgusted. "You're kidding."

Cal searched her memory for a good example. "Remember that smash-and-grab case last year—the car robbery? That old guy struggled a little and the muggers let him go. He collapsed from a heart attack trying to run for help. The *cause* of death was a heart attack, but the *manner* of death was homicide."

"Those kids got convicted, too," Ames mused. "*Accidental* homicide, but still . . ."

"Right." She sat up. "So you're going to call Davis?"

He sighed again. "I guess I have to."

"Anyway, tell him I doubt it's anything. But I think someone ought to look into it, poke around a little."

"An *informal* investigation, huh? You really know how to hurt a guy, Cal." Ames sighed and hung up.

Cal set the phone on the nightstand and stretched. It was late, but she still felt oddly awake and alert. And content. Even with the decaffeinated coffee. Hanging the dress up in the closet she smiled, remembering the way he had looked at her at the restaurant, the candlelight reflecting in his eyes. She slipped into the other negligee, the cream one with the scratchy ruffles and lace. The huge Mickey Mouse T-shirt would be more comfortable, but she doubted it would make his eyes shine like the dress had.

She padded across the thick carpet to the back of the chair and rested her hands on his shoulders. "Okay, lover. Come on to bed."

He didn't move; he was still looking down at that dumb novel. Last thirty pages. Cal sidled around the chair and snatched his book away, then slipped into his lap. Sliding her arms around his neck, she swept her lips across his cheeks and blew in his ear.

Nothing.

His head slumped forward onto her shoulder. He snored in her hair.

"Plato. Wake up." Sitting on his lap, she shook his arms, slapped his hands, twisted his head back and forth.

The 1983 Echézeaux was evidently more potent than they realized. Plato had drunk more than two-thirds of the bottle. And he had gotten up early for rounds this morning.

And she didn't tell him that the coffee was decaffeinated.

She stood, hung his arms over her shoulders, and dragged him to his feet. It was touch-and-go by the fireplace for a moment, until she recovered her balance. Then across the floor, lurching, careening into the wall, finally collapsing on the bed in a tangled heap of arms and legs, lace and chiffon. She slipped his robe off, sighed wistfully, then tucked the covers under his chin.

"Good night, lover boy." She kissed the back of his neck and snuggled in, trying to remember what their honeymoon had been like.

CHAPTER TWELVE

"Go 'way." A hairbrush was tickling Cal's cheeks. A hairbrush with lips. She swatted at it and felt a jarring impact as her hand smacked into something hard. She opened her eyes. "Oh. Sorry, Plato."

He was fully dressed, tie and all, sitting up and rubbing his bearded chin. He opened his mouth and worked his jaw back and forth. "I'd heard the *first* year of marriage was rough; looks like the second year is even worse."

"I thought you were a hairbrush."

"Oh."

"With lips."

"Sweet talker." He sat up and tightened his tie.

"Where you going—one of the lectures?" She hooked a finger under the knot and pulled him back down. "Maybe you should skip it. This tie doesn't look very comfortable. Here, let me loosen it for you. And that shirt—"

"Hey!" He stood quickly, buttoning his shirt again and tucking it back in.

She pouted. "Must be *some* meeting you're going to."

"It's not a meeting." He leaned over again and kissed her nose. "Office hours, remember? I'm putting in a half day today. Should be back in time for the golf outing at three."

"Too bad." She sighed, slipping her legs from between the sheets and stretching languidly. "I was hoping we'd have a little time *alone* today."

"Me, too. But I've got a full schedule this morning."

"And we can't miss the golf trip, either." She folded the sheets back and perched on the edge of the bed. "I think Miguel's counting on everyone to show up."

"He's trying to keep things as normal as possible, to keep this whole project from falling apart," Plato agreed. He forced his gaze away from her and contemplated the fake watercolors hanging over the bed. "What are *you* doing today? Besides sleeping in. And snooping around for Jeremy."

"That about covers it." She glanced over at the clock and sat up. "Actually, *I'm* going to a lecture—I've got to get up anyway."

"Who's giving it?" He grabbed his briefcase and headed for the door.

"Evelyn Baker. She's talking about cultural attitudes toward death."

He grinned. "Sounds like you two really *do* have some common interests. Maybe you can ask her if Gates was murdered or not."

Half an hour later, Cal squeezed into a seat near the back of Room E at the Chippewa Creek Conference Annex. Baker's lecture was being held in the smallest of the five conference rooms—the planners hadn't expected it to be very popular. But death was a hot topic at any geriatrics conference and always would be. New technologies, procedures, and functional assessment scales might come and go, but death was inevitable. Especially in geriatrics.

Cal was sandwiched between an obese physician spread across two of the puny linking chairs and a nurse who kept talking about hepatitis B and AIDS. Sitting in front of her was one of the Beautiful People—tall, blond, broad-shouldered, with a Dudley

Dooright chin and a smile to match. Somehow, he managed to flex his muscles and ripple his shoulders for even the slightest activity—opening a notebook, fingering his hair, chasing a speck of lint from his spotless lapel. Cal saw dozens just like him every day in beer commercials and cigarette ads, bold plasticene symbols of the New Youth. Shiny, spotless, and utterly sanitized.

Before the lights went down, he flashed a few casual glances back her way. Sizing her up, probably wondering if she'd had her blood tests and shots.

Evelyn Baker walked to the podium without fanfare, adjusted the microphone and began to speak.

" 'Whoever has lived long enough to find out what life is, knows how deep a debt of gratitude we owe to Adam, the first great benefactor of our race. He brought death into the world.' " She looked up from her notes. "Mark Twain wrote those words over a hundred years ago, and they're more relevant now than ever before."

Baker launched the main body of her lecture with examples from prehistory, the Bible and Koran, Eastern teachings and the rituals of the Hopi. Funeral rites and religious beliefs, philosophy and archaeology. Fascinating stuff, but Cal couldn't keep her mind from wandering back to one death in particular.

So far, they had no evidence that Gates's overdose was anything but an accident. Jeremy had called this morning, saying they had a warrant to search Gates's belongings. If the researcher was taking nitroglycerin—as Plato had suggested—any allegation of murder would look pretty ridiculous.

But a little voice in the back of her mind spoke up, reminding her that the stomach and small bowel contents were negative for the drug.

That didn't mean anything, since nitroglycerin was absorbed quite rapidly. Many people took sublingual nitro for angina—placing the pills under the tongue, where it was readily absorbed. Even the longer-acting swallowed forms disappeared into the bloodstream very quickly.

If Gates *was* taking nitroglycerin, the mystery was solved. She'd write "probable accidental nitroglycerin overdose" on the death certificate and put the case to rest. She nodded to herself and tried to concentrate on Baker's lecture.

In front of her, Dooright hitched an elbow up on the back of his chair. He half turned and graced her with a faint smile. Baker's face was eclipsed by the tip of his chin; Cal had to squirm sideways to see the podium. Another photo flashed on the screen—a Hopi village baking in the sand. A field of corn withering beneath the desert sun. In the foreground, a dry old woman baked piki bread over an open fire.

Cal's little voice hadn't put the case to rest yet. Even if Gates was taking nitroglycerin, the murderer might have known that and used it to his advantage. Nitroglycerin helps diseased hearts at normal dosages, but hinders their function at higher levels. If Gates was already taking the drug, an intentional overdose would seem like an accident. A lot of drug addicts died from "accidental" overdoses that might have really been homicides.

Ridiculous. If it was murder, how was the nitroglycerin administered?

Maybe at lunch—maybe with a longer-acting form of the drug. Maybe the murderer was counting on Gates taking a hike, or swimming, or something. Working out in the hot sun so the nitroglycerin overdose could have its deadly effect.

Cal chuckled softly. Too many maybes. The murderer couldn't count on Gates exercising. What if, instead, he had gone back to his room for a nap after lunch? Besides, the idea of a murderer slipping that much nitroglycerin onto Gates's stuffed squid was laughable.

"As you might expect, water played a prominent role in the religious rites of the desert-dwelling Hopi," Baker was saying. "Upon death, the breath-body, or soul, journeyed to the underworld. Breath-bodies could rise to the earthly sky and become clouds, showering essential rain on the crops of the living."

That tennis court had certainly felt like a desert yesterday, with no rain clouds in sight.

That was it! the voice shouted triumphantly. Gates's bottle of Evian! By poisoning his water, the murderer could be sure the nitroglycerin would be taken when Gates was exercising. Hiding the taste might be a problem, but it was a possibility.

Cal told the voice to stop gloating, and reluctantly decided to ask Ames to save the water bottle for testing.

"Contact with the dead was not uncommon among the Hopi," Baker continued. She pressed a button, and a kachina doll appeared on the screen. "Some had dreams or visions of recently deceased relatives, and dying persons often had more involved contacts with family and friends from the underworld. Such experiences helped them accept their own impending deaths."

Victor had certainly seemed aware of his own impending death. By the way, where did *his* death fit in? Was it just a coincidence, or—

Damn! Cal cursed herself for a fool. She should have had Victor's blood tested for nitroglycerin the moment she learned about Gates's positive results. She was sure Victor wasn't taking nitroglycerin—their talk with Miguel had confirmed that. If nitro by-products showed up in *Victor's* blood, the two deaths would be linked, and murder was a much stronger possibility.

Maybe deep down, she didn't want to know

Cal shook her head—she wouldn't cover her eyes like Ames and Davis. Victor's body was still down in the morgue, along with blood samples. She'd call the lab and have them run a quick test. Cal stood, but found her passage to the aisle blocked by the fat man. He was fast asleep. He didn't even stir when she kneed his thigh.

Ahead of her, Dooright came to the rescue. He stood and one-handed his chair into the air, then squeezed past the woman beside him. He gestured for Cal to leave through his row.

She had no choice but to follow. "Thank you."

He sketched a clumsy bow with his chair and leered. "You're quite welcome, Miss—"

"Doctor Cal Marley. I'm a forensic pathologist. My husband's a geriatrician." She wondered if that was a clear enough hint.

"Pleased to meet you, Cal. I'm Doctor Charles Rice." He escorted her up the aisle, held the door open and followed her into the bright atrium, still holding his chair. Finally, he set it down and shook her hand. "Perhaps you've heard of me—I edit a line of textbooks."

"I'm afraid I haven't," Cal lied. She was shocked at how young Rice appeared. From the comments at yesterday's meeting, Cal had pictured the editor as positively ancient. Then again, the careful evenness of his tan, the telltale tightness of skin at cheekbones and jaw, the perfect regularity of his hair, told her Rice probably wasn't as young as he looked.

"A forensic pathologist—how *fascinating*." He leaned against the doorjamb and smiled easily. At least his teeth looked real. Except for the gold-capped canine glinting at the corner of his mouth. "I'll be doing a textbook on forensic science soon—right now it's just in the planning stages. We could discuss it over breakfast."

"Sorry." Cal shrugged and turned away. "I just got paged out for an urgent autopsy."

By the time she returned from her phone call, Baker was taking questions from the audience. Cal stood in back and listened to the wrap-up, applauded with the others as Evelyn strode down the aisle toward the exit.

The older physician saw Cal and stopped. "You didn't have to stand here the whole time, did you?"

"No—it's kind of a long story."

Most of the audience was streaming toward the exit for the next lecture; Cal and Baker were pushed and jostled by the press of bodies. They broke through the doorway and found a quiet spot in a corner.

"Your lecture was excellent, Evelyn. I really enjoyed it."

"You weren't bored?" She pursed her lips. "I heard someone snoring up near the front row. And on my way out, I saw that I had put more than one person to sleep."

"They're probably leftovers from the *last* lecture." They laughed together. "Anyway, I thought the cross-cultural perspective made for a fascinating discussion. I didn't realize that attitudes toward death were so varied. And so—*arbitrary*."

"Yes—that's *exactly* the point I was trying to get across." She nodded vigorously. "The chronic warfare of the Yanomamö, the infanticide of the Netsilik, the geronticide of the Ugandan Ik. Attitudes have to be viewed in a cultural context—I hoped these extreme examples would help doctors understand that their patients' thoughts and beliefs can be just as diverse." She paused and seemed embarrassed at her sudden outburst. "Anyway, I'm glad you enjoyed it."

"I really did."

Baker paused outside the door to one of the other conference rooms. The orderly rows of chairs had been cleared and a buffet was set up. The rest of the room was filled with a dozen huge round tables. "Have you had breakfast yet?"

"Actually, no. I'm famished. That rumbling noise you heard during your lecture wasn't snoring—it was my stomach."

"Great." She hovered in the doorway, frowning thoughtfully, then turned to Cal. "Only problem is, I'm getting a little tired of these institutional meals. Especially after you've just given a lecture—twenty people sitting around a table smiling politely at you and trying to think of something nice to say."

Cal had never looked at it that way; she always assumed that lecturing at a national conference would be fun and rather flattering. But Baker made it sound tiresome and mundane. "We could try the lodge's main restaurant, overlooking the pool. We'd have to pay for it, but I don't mind. The buffet doesn't exactly look promising."

Baker glanced over at the main buffet's serving tables. "Bran muffins and glazed doughnuts and stale coffee. And *networking*. God, I hate that word." She sighed and nudged Cal's elbow. "Come on, let's go."

The restaurant was in the older part of the lodge—a vast room with a cathedral ceiling webbed by hammered beams and darkly stained joists. Heavy oak braces stood at intervals along the rough plaster walls. The fireplace across the flagstone floor was large enough for a committee meeting.

They found a table near one of the tall windows. Children splashed in the pool below while their parents—mostly spouses of conference attendees, Cal suspected—sat in loungers and caught the first rays of morning sun trickling through the trees. The restaurant itself was all but empty; most of the lodge's guests were either attending presentations or breakfasting on bran muffins and stale coffee.

Baker ordered eggs Benedict and Cal had a fresh

fruit platter. She was still full from last night's feast. Cal leaned forward and whispered confidentially, "You know, I feel almost like a truant out from school."

The older woman chortled. "I used to feel that way. Come to enough of these conferences and you'll get over it. Where's Plato?"

"Office hours."

Baker tilted her head curiously.

"Their practice is one doctor short," Cal explained. "He and his partner are splitting the office work this week so they both can come to the conference. But I think I'm seeing more lectures than he is."

"Poor Plato." She clucked sympathetically. "Sounds a little like my first practice, up in the Northwest Territories—near the Arctic Circle. No partner, no other doctor within a hundred miles or so. Almost never could break away."

"You're from Canada?" Cal asked.

"I hide it well, don't I?" Baker grinned. "Toronto, actually. Wealthy society family, so naturally I had to break the mold and go live with a bunch of Eskimos."

"And *that's* how you got interested in anthropology."

"The other way around, actually." Their food arrived. She stabbed an egg yolk, watching the fluid spill onto her plate. "Anthropology came first, but then I saw how things were. On my first field expedition up north, I couldn't maintain that scientific detachment that the old farts wanted me to—don't touch, don't interfere, don't feed the starving babies. So I got a medical degree and went back."

Baker had lived the fantasy Cal had always dreamed about—until a hundred thousand dollars in school loans woke her up. "What was it like?"

"Brutal—absolutely brutal at first. This was decades ago, remember. The Department of Northern Affairs had just gotten set up in the region, but Pelly Bay was still very much an Eskimo village. The men didn't want me; they didn't think much of women. Actually tried to get me to leave." She flashed a knowing smile. "But they finally came around."

"How?" Cal pictured Baker harpooning polar bears, wrestling sea lions, proving herself in some tribal ritual.

"The clan leader's son came down with meningitis. The Catholic missionary there convinced the leader to send the boy to me." Baker grimaced. "Thank goodness it wasn't a girl, or they'd have just let her die. They left me alone after that, even accepted me."

Cal glanced out the window at the sunny summer morning, carefree children playing in the pool. The contrast shocked her briefly. "So how did you end up in the States?"

Baker chuckled again. "A geriatrics conference, would you believe it? In Toronto—that's where I met Bob."

"Bob?"

"My husband."

Cal grinned. "I never thought of geriatrics conferences as very romantic." So far, this one certainly wasn't.

"They're not—believe me." Her gray eyes lost their focus; she stared unseeing at the window. "Geriatrics wasn't even my primary interest then. But I was going stir-crazy, and another physician had finally been sent up to help me out. One of my friends was attending the conference in Toronto, so I flew down and tagged along. I was waiting for her at a club after the first day of meetings when this fellow came along and asked if he could buy me a drink. Can you believe it? Me pushing forty and a happy old maid."

"Life plays some funny tricks sometimes," Cal said. Baker had probably been quite attractive at forty; even now her fine features showed through the wrinkles and gray hair.

"That's the truth. Of course, I recognized Bob from the conference—he was one of the presenters. Doctor Robert Halley, renowned expert in geriatric medicine. It was a new field back then, you know. Anyway, I decided to play a trick on *him*." The older woman grinned mischievously. "He didn't place me as a medical type at all—he thought I was a secretary or something. I played along the whole evening."

"And the next day . . ."

"I was sitting in the front row at his final presentation. With my 'M.D.' on my badge, plain as day." Baker's giggle was as easy and natural as the laughter of the children in the pool below. "Don't get me wrong—he'd been a perfect gentleman. Still, he *had* been rather patronizing. Never asked me anything that first evening, just went on and on about his research and faculty position."

The older woman closed her eyes and remembered. "He was pretty surprised when I agreed to visit him in New York. Even more surprised when I asked him to marry me."

"You asked *him*?"

"I was thirty-eight years old—he was probably my last chance." She laughed again. "Not that I didn't miss working with the Eskimos. I *still* go up there on hunting trips now and then. But six years of nothing but fish and the occasional caribou was a bit much. And I loved Bob dearly . . ."

A hint of sadness had crept into her voice. Cal didn't ask the obvious question; Baker answered it for her.

"Just eight years—happy ones, though." Her voice roughened with the memory. "He died seventeen years ago this fall."

"I'm sorry."

"So am I, Cal. So am I." She turned away from the

window and smiled. Her eyes shone and she brushed them with the back of her hand.

Cal handed her a Kleenex, but she had no idea what to say. At times like this, she knew why pathology had been so appealing. Cal was awful at counseling, at talking to people. She always came on too strong, or said the wrong thing. Her bedside manner made patients recoil—people seemed to get sicker just from talking to her. Eventually, she gave up. Dead patients were past hurting or crying or looking to their doctor for sympathy or intelligent answers. In pathology, all the answers were there, etched in flesh and blood and clay. All you had to do was find them.

Evelyn Baker seemed capable of finding her own answers. She snapped the Kleenex into her purse, along with the sadness and hurt, and suddenly brightened. She glanced out the window again. "This pool's pretty big—almost Olympic-size. The one over at Cliff House is about three hundred lengths to the mile. Maybe I should swim here instead."

"You'd have to steer a lot," Cal noted. "It looks like an obstacle course down there."

"I don't mind children, really." She sounded almost wistful. "You and Plato don't have any yet, do you?"

"No. We wanted to wait at least a year, just be ourselves for a while." She rolled her eyes. "Not that it's meant much. With Plato's practice and my duties with the coroner's office, we're lucky to have dinner together every other night."

"It'll get easier," Baker assured her. She propped her elbows on the table and cradled her chin in her hands. "Though I'm sure the last couple of nights haven't seemed that way. An amazing and awful coincidence—we're still kind of dazed about the whole thing. Miguel's very upset, and I don't blame him."

"I'm surprised that he's going on with the project, as though nothing happened." Cal frowned. "If it were me, I'd have probably canceled the rest of the meetings and sent everyone home."

"I think he'd rather not—I think he's trying to distract himself from Victor's death." The check came, and Baker nimbly snatched it off the plate. "My treat."

"Thanks."

"What good would it do to send everyone home?" she continued, putting some money on the plate. "We're all here; we might as well get some work done."

"I suppose so." Cal's beeper buzzed and startled her; it was still set on silent mode. The sudden vibration felt a little like an electric shock. She glanced at the display: Jeremy's office.

"Duty calls?" Baker stood and smiled. "Good timing, anyway."

The older woman headed off to another lecture while Cal searched for a pay phone. Ames answered immediately, sounding even more tense than usual.

"I've got some bad news, Cally," he muttered. "You're not going to like this. You're not going to like it at all."

CHAPTER THIRTEEN

The message was taped to the brass lamp on Plato's desk. Like all of Hilda's notes, it was written on "I Love My Dachshund" paper and took some deciphering. He could barely make out Cal's name, and something about migration. No—"migraine"? Cal got migraines sometimes; that must be it.

Plato looked closer. His nurse didn't use German in her notes anymore, but she still tended to capitalize her nouns and salted her vowels with umlauts. *"Migüel,"* Plato finally decided. Cal had called about Miguel—he probably wanted to reschedule the next book meeting.

"Doctor Marley." Hilda burst into the doorway—panting, holding a plump trembling hand out to him. "Come quickly . . . it's Mr. Perovsky."

She darted away and Plato followed her down the hall to an examination room. Inside, Henry Perovsky—Plato's nine o'clock appointment—was hunched over on the green vinyl exam table. Enormous bony hands clutched his bare chest, and his breaths came fast and shallow. His usually ruddy face was nearly as white as his hair. He grin-grimaced at Plato. "Don't feel . . . so good."

"Try not to talk now, Henry." Hilda eased him back onto the table and squeezed his hand. She looked up. "I called a crash team first—they should be here soon."

Henry was shaking his head vigorously. Plato

slipped a stethoscope onto his patient's chest and listened. Irregularly irregular rhythm—the heart seemed to be beating at random. He was probably going into fibrillation already, the chaotic fluttering that heralded complete cardiac arrest. Henry was muttering something; Plato had trouble hearing the heart sounds.

The stethoscope was suddenly jerked away. Mr. Perovsky was holding it in his hand. Amazingly, he was still conscious, still shaking his head. "No, Doctor Marley. No—remember?"

He passed out. His pulse disappeared completely. Plato lowered the exam table and placed his hands in the proper position—near the base of the sternum, two fingers up from the xiphoid process. He looked up at Hilda. "What was he talking about?"

She counted his five compressions, then delivered a breath and lifted her head again. Her bright red lipstick was smeared. "Something about not bringing back. But he doesn't have a DNR order."

DNR order. "Do Not Resuscitate"—a legal request that the physician or emergency team make no extraordinary lifesaving efforts, like cardiopulmonary resuscitation.

"Damn!"

Plato stopped the compressions and waved Hilda away. Just last week, Mr. Perovsky had come to the office, very upset about the death of his sister. A massive heart attack; they had brought her back and she languished for a week as a helpless vegetable from a massive stroke that had destroyed most of her brain. Plato usually recommended DNR certificates to his older, less healthy patients. But Perovsky had insisted. Hilda had been on vacation last week; she didn't know about the change.

The team arrived: a resident, two interns, a medical student (panting), and a crash cart. They stared at the doctor and nurse flanking the dying patient and doing absolutely nothing at all.

"Sorry, folks," Plato told them while they caught their breath. "This one's a DNR."

"Okay, Doctor Marley." The interns and resident simply nodded and turned away; they had seen the procedure before and understood the odds. Apparently the medical student hadn't; he flashed a telling glance over his shoulder as he walked out the door—a look of betrayal, even accusation.

Plato wondered if Mrs. Perovsky would feel the same way.

The morning slid downhill from there. A summons to appear in a malpractice case—not his own, at least. A lab report showing new cancer in a patient who'd been in remission for years; they both thought she had beaten the odds. A long, frustrating conference with a pair of sons who wanted their mother committed and didn't want to believe that she was perfectly sane. Money did strange things to people; Plato would probably appear in court for that one, too. And the telephone call to Henry's wife. Hilda had trouble tracking her down; Mrs. Perovsky was out most of the morning making plans for their fiftieth wedding anniversary.

Still, she took it surprisingly well. A long, long silence, a lot of tears, but no anger or recriminations. Sometimes Plato's patients seemed to trust him more than he trusted himself. She promised to call him back with the date and time of the funeral.

He didn't bother to ask her about an autopsy. Henry had been under Plato's regular care for angina and several small heart attacks. He'd turned down bypass surgery, knowing his number would eventually come up. Because of his condition, and because he'd died in his doctor's office, Henry had spared his wife the added pain of a coroner's investigation.

Plato forgot all about Cal's message until she paged him later that morning.

"How's it going?" she asked him cheerfully.

"You don't want to know."

"That bad, huh?"

"I don't have much time. What did you want?"

"That bad." She made an angry noise in the receiver, a little chuffing sound like she'd swallowed a feather. "It's nothing important. Why don't you call me back when you can talk?"

"Sorry." He sighed, leaned back until his cheap desk chair was propped against the windowsill. "It's been a particularly lousy day. Remember Mr. Perovsky?"

"The cabinetmaker, right?"

"Right." A craftsman. Plato remembered the wedding present Henry had made for them—a solid cherry end table fashioned entirely by hand, doweled and mitered flawlessly, invisible joints and seams, a finish like melted glass. The only truly valuable piece of furniture in that great barn of a house. Plato imagined those enormous hands cutting, shaping, sanding, finishing, clutching at his chest, pulling his doctor's stethoscope away. *Listen to me.*

"Plato?"

"He died today—this morning. Heart attack, probably."

"Oh." Her voice softened. "I'm sorry."

"In my office."

"Oh."

The sharp intake of breath; it hit her just the same way. More than the hospital, far more, the doctor's office seemed a safe haven, a sanctuary against death. Nonsense, of course. Patients were just as likely to die there as anywhere else, maybe more so. But still it felt like a violation.

"He was a DNR; we just talked about it last week. So Hilda and I just had to stand there. And watch." It was one thing to advise patients against resuscitation, discuss the odds, the potential pain and suffering, the expense, the burden on the family. Statistics, numbers, paper. The reality was harder.

"That must have been pretty tough on you."

"I don't think Henry enjoyed it much, either."

She considered. "Maybe we should go somewhere for lunch."

"Can't. I'm too far behind already. There are two more patients waiting in the exam rooms. If they're still alive," he concluded bitterly.

"What if I brought some take-out? We could eat it in your office. That way, you wouldn't have to walk across to the cafeteria for lunch."

"I'll just send Hilda over for something." Actually, food was the last thing on his mind. But Plato hadn't had any breakfast, and he would hit the wall around three o'clock if he skipped lunch, too. "She'll rustle up a stale hamburger, maybe. Or some cookies."

"How about Player's? A pesto pizza, maybe with sausage this time, and that weird goat cheese of theirs—"

"You don't even have a car—I took the Chevette this morning, remember?" He grimaced. "Anyway, I'm not sure we can *afford* a pizza, now. Just bring some old shoe leather."

"I'll take the bus. What do you want on your shoe leather? Sausage? Chicken?"

"Both. And ham and double cheese. And onions."

"That's more like it."

"What *did* you call for, anyway?"

"Oh, just to talk about the case." Something strange had crept into her voice—forced breeziness, a fake smile. "Gates's gastrointestinal tract is negative for nitroglycerin. He did have nitro pills in his backpack, though."

"Just like I said. Sublingual?"

"Yes, but—"

"Then his GI tract *should* be negative. You know that, Cal. The pills are meant to dissolve under the tongue, right?"

"It was a bottle of thirty pills, and none were missing." She sighed. "It doesn't make any sense."

"I guess not." Wasn't there something else in Hilda's note? He glanced around the morass of his office—stacks of papers, files, books, letters, and lab reports—looking for the message. It was hopeless now, an exercise in archaeology.

"How about if I show up around twelve-thirty?" she asked. "That'll give you another hour to get caught up."

"Fat chance." He closed his eyes. "Still, you might as well. I've got a feeling things aren't going to improve anytime soon."

But the rest of the morning wasn't as bad as he'd expected. His next patient turned out to be a simple blood pressure check. No new complaints, no problems with his medications, no trouble at home. He'd brought seven bottles of pills and when Plato counted them, they all tallied up correctly. An amazing feat, since most of the drugs had different dosage schedules.

His last patient, Mrs. Andreas, had brought baklava.

"Happy anniversary, Doctor Marley." She knew the dates of Plato's birthday, Cal's birthday, their anniversary, the first day she'd visited his office, the day Plato had passed his board exam and certifying exam for geriatrics, the day he'd graduated from medical school. Each event was commemorated with a familiar foil-wrapped package.

Plato acted surprised. "Thank you very much, Mrs. Andreas. You didn't have to, you know."

"I know—that's what makes it special." Sitting in her underwear on the exam table, she beamed. It was hard to believe Henry Perovsky had died on the same table just two hours ago. The room's gloomy air had dissipated; Mrs. Andreas tended to create her own atmosphere.

"I remember my first anniversary with Nikolas, back in the Old Country, Eddie was—let's see—he was just a month old then or so, always crying he was, my Eddie, one doctor said he needed coconut milk, can you believe it?—wait—wait—" She held one hand across her plump Aunt Bee chest, another out palm-forward to stop any interruption. Mrs. Andreas's greatest frustration in life was the need to take a breath while speaking. A hundred pack-years of smoking hadn't helped much. "Anyway, we took him to see a specialist in the city, we lived not far outside Athens; you'll never believe what this doctor told us to do: he tells us to hold Eddie upside-down by his feet for three minutes every night. And did we do it? No—maybe the doctor thinks Gina Andreas was stuck behind the door when God passed out the brains, wait—wait—"

It took another fifteen minutes before Plato realized that all Mrs. Andreas needed was a refill for her nitroglycerin paste.

"No more angina pain, Doctor Marley. You are wonderful, yes. I keep telling my son he should come see you, but Eddie doesn't listen. Better we should have hung him upside-down by his toes like that doctor said, maybe his brain would have grown a little more, right?" She grinned her sly little Greek woman grin, the one that showed who was the real boss of the family. "I have no more pain, just a little headache now and then, like you said. Much better than the pills."

And only then did Plato realize he'd had the answer all along.

CHAPTER FOURTEEN

"The pizza cutter's in the top drawer of my desk," Plato told Cal as she entered his office. "Next to the prescription pad."

"Any idea where I can put this down?" Holding the pizza box, she glanced around the cluttered room. Every inch of flat surface area—the desk, three file cabinets, the credenza, all hospital-issue sheet metal and fake wood—were paved with a thick layer of paperwork, mail, and charts. So was most of the floor. Plato was wedged in a corner, a medical record propped on the narrow windowsill, portable Dictaphone balanced on his knee. "You look like a prisoner."

"I *feel* like a prisoner." Plato picked up the microphone again. "Assessment: Urinary tract infection. Plan: Bactrim DS one tablet q twelve hours times seven days with follow-up in ten days."

He set the machine on the floor and picked his way across the room to Cal. She was wearing vacation clothes: her Cleveland Indians baseball cap, a clean pair of hi-tops, and a cutoff Allman Brothers T-shirt that didn't quite reach the top of her faded denim shorts. Cal's hospital wardrobe was generally quite prim: slacks and blouses and the occasional skirt. She'd probably snuck in the back door. He gave her a kiss and patted the pizza fondly. "Hold on a minute."

He dashed out into the hallway and returned with a tall, stainless steel procedure tray, the kind used to hold medical instruments during minor office surgeries. "I was hoping for something in teak, but this'll have to do."

Cal raised her eyebrows, but propped the box on the tray and retrieved the pizza cutter. While she served, Plato stole some paper plates and napkins from the employees' lounge. He staked out the battered swivel chair and she bulldozed a corner of the desk for herself.

"It's the crust that makes Player's different," he commented after the first slice.

"How can you tell?" She squinted at the pizza—a thick blanket of cheese and meat and onions covering a crispy piece of dough and a dash of sauce. "There's so much stuff on this, I can't even *taste* the crust."

"That's how I like it." He downed another slice, wondering whether pizza had ever been tested for clinical depression. It probably beat conventional psychotherapy. "Thanks for bringing lunch."

"No problem." Cal tossed her plate away after the first slice; she had remarkable self-control. "Sounds like your day's going a little better."

"A little. Hey, I've got some news for you."

"Yeah?" She checked to make sure the door was closed, then sat down on his knee. Hungry eyes followed every bite.

"Can I help you?" he finally asked.

"Well, *someone* has to watch your diet." She opened her mouth and pointed inside.

"I didn't know you took it so literally." He held the pizza up for her and watched her take a monstrous bite. "How noble of you, to just have one slice."

She shrugged. "So what's your news?"

"I figured it out," he announced. "Gates wasn't murdered. In fact, I'm pretty sure he—"

She covered his mouth. "Before you embarrass

yourself, I'd better tell you what we found. I'm afraid Gates really *was* murdered. And Victor, too."

He pulled her hand away. "You sound pretty certain."

"I am, for once." She shivered and hugged herself, then stared at the floor. "I had the bright idea of checking Victor's blood for nitroglycerin."

"And?"

"And he was positive. His blood level wasn't as high as Gates's, or his blood would have been chocolate colored, too."

Plato frowned. "High enough to kill?"

"A young, healthy person?" She shook her head. "Probably not. But Victor was seventy-three. Besides, I bet the narcotic played a big part."

"I don't know, Cal—"

"And Victor's autopsy findings make sense now," she continued. "The discoloration of the kidneys— tubular necrosis. The way his blood pressure apparently took a nose dive for no reason at all. Everything fits in with nitroglycerin poisoning."

Her face fell. "Only problem is, we don't know how it was given. I thought maybe Gates got it in his bottled water, but it tested negative."

"That wouldn't explain Victor's death, anyway." Reluctantly, Plato closed the pizza box. "*He* sure wasn't into bottled water. Was Victor taking nitroglycerin?"

"No. Miguel said his heart was healthy. Ames checked through his belongings and only found the Motrin and DiaBeta." She shrugged. "So what was your bright idea?"

"It doesn't sound so bright, now." He sighed. "But I was wondering whether Gates might have been using a topical nitroglycerin paste, so the drug was delivered through the skin. A lot of my patients are on the paste now—that's how I thought of it. Gates could have been using the nitro pills as well, but just for emergencies.

Anyway, maybe he applied too much nitroglycerin paste Sunday, or the exercise and sun made him absorb it too quickly. The police could have overlooked his nitroglycerin paste when they went through his belongings. Since topical nitroglycerin comes in a tube, it would have been easy to overlook."

"They didn't overlook it; I went over the entire list." Her eyebrows dipped together. "Still, it's a good thought."

"Except it wouldn't explain *Victor's* death," Plato noted. "He wasn't taking nitroglycerin, so it couldn't have been an accidental overdose."

"Right. And we still have to account for the narcotics in Victor's blood." She pursed her lips. "His digestive tract was negative for narcotics, and he almost certainly didn't get it intravenously. Topical nitroglycerin paste is a good idea. It's just too bad there aren't any topical narcotics."

Somewhere in the room, the telephone rang. It was buried; the ringer echoed faintly from the rubble. Cal saw the baffled look on Plato's face and giggled.

"Shh-h-h." He held up a hand and stood. Second ring. "Now, let's not panic. I've done this before; it just takes a little concentration."

Third ring. He localized it to the right side of the room, away from the door. Another ring and he had its quadrant, started lifting stacks of papers, files, books. He almost gave up hope before he spotted the wire trailing across the floor, up over the credenza, into one of the file drawers. Plato slid it open and found his prize. He remembered putting it in there last time, so he would never lose it again.

"Doctor Plato Marley," he answered.

It was Hilda. His one o'clock had just arrived, would be ready in about ten minutes. He thanked her and hung up, grabbed the box again and snagged another slice of pizza.

He glanced over at Cal. "What's so funny?"

"Nothing." She was perched on the edge of his desk, carefully braiding her hair. "Nothing at all. But if any of your patients ever get lost—"

"Don't say it." He sat in his chair again. "Now, what were we talking about?"

"Topical nitroglycerin," she prompted. "I was thinking, it's too bad there aren't any topical narcotics. Otherwise we might have an explanation for both deaths."

"Actually . . ." Plato stood and bit a thumbnail. He tiptoed back to the credenza, to the third pile from the left, lifted three inches of papers and mail and sifted until he found the latest *Pharmaceutical Reports* about halfway down. He handed it to Cal. "Euphecin and Vixerin. Two topical narcotics. The FDA approved them last year, but not many people know about them yet."

Cal glanced at the title page. She looked up at him, eyes wide. "I'm impressed."

He gave a self-deprecating shrug. "Well, my medical knowledge *is* pretty extensive; I actually did quite well on the pharmacology section of my National Boards—"

"*That's* not what impressed me." She spread her hands and gestured around the room. "I'm just amazed you were able to *find* this thing in here. Among thousands of sheets of paper, you found this in less than a minute. Have you ever thought about a career in library science? Or maybe secretarial work? Of course, you'd need a shorter telephone cord—"

He snatched the newsletter away and swatted it at her.

She ducked neatly, grabbed it back and scanned over the articles while Plato fidgeted. "Here it is: 'Euphecin and Vixerin, two topical narcotic drugs, were released within one week of each other by separate pharmaceutical companies. Both drugs have half-lives of four to six hours and are available as pastes, allowing precise dosing. Their primary recommendation is for analgesia in situations where morphine and oral medications cannot be used or are poorly tolerated, as among terminally ill patients cared for outside the institutional setting.' "

While she was reading, Plato stood by the window and glanced out at the roof of the nurses' dorm across the street. Dan Homewood, his partner and a bachelor, relished late afternoon dictation on hot summer days, sitting in his office next door and watching the young ladies gather sun from their beach towels and lawn chairs. The roof was so far away that the nursing students looked like tiny albino ants in the springtime, tiny brown ants now, in late summer. Not that Plato ever looked.

"I wonder what they smell like," Cal mused.

"What?"

"Euphecin and Vixerin—I wonder what they smell like." She peered at him suspiciously and studied the view from the window. "What did you *think* I meant?"

He shrugged. Thankfully, the dorm roof was still empty of ants. "Does it matter what they smell like?"

"Of *course* it does—just think about it." She wrinkled her nose. "If Euphecin smelled like skunk spray, for instance, you couldn't exactly sneak it onto someone's skin. Right?"

He tried to think, to empty his head of those ants with their towels and lounge chairs and suntan lotion. Then it came to him. He spoke casually, as though the explanation were childishly simple. "I don't think it matters. Unless the drug smelled really awful, the murderer didn't have to worry."

"What do you mean? Of course he did; how would he get it onto—"

"He didn't. Gates and Godwin put it on themselves."

She curled her lip contemptuously. "I think you've had a little too much pizza."

"Think back. They were hot days, remember?" She still looked puzzled, so he continued. "Hot, *sunny* days."

Cal snapped her fingers. "Tanning lotion!"

"Right. The perfume would drown out the smell of the medications." Plato grinned. "I *know* nitro has a slight odor, but the cocoa butter in Godwin's tanning lotion almost knocked me over."

"And Gates put on some suntan lotion between games yesterday, didn't he?"

"A ton of it." He glanced at her appraisingly. "So you *do* notice some things."

"How could I miss?" She grimaced. "Every time I came to the net, he flexed his pecs at me, like he was an ostrich or something. I'm just glad you didn't take *your* shirt off."

"Thanks a lot."

"Not that I would have minded." She winked grotesquely. "But with Evelyn there, well . . . We wouldn't have wanted *two* heart attacks on our hands."

"Right." He cocked his head. " 'Evelyn,' is it?"

"She and I had a wonderful morning together—we met for breakfast after her lecture. She's quite an interesting person. I'll have to tell you about her sometime."

"Sometime." He glanced at his watch.

"Now that I've buttered you up, how about doing me a favor?"

His eyes narrowed. "I *knew* you had a reason for coming."

"Believe it or not, I was going to take care of it myself." Her eyes glittered. "But I've got to run down to the lab, order a few tests."

"Dressed like that?"

She looked down at her bare legs, bobby socks and

tennis shoes. She tried tucking the T-shirt into the shorts, but it popped out again as soon as she took a breath. "*Damn*. Stop laughing."

"You could take the Chevette back to the hotel—"

"There isn't time." She glanced around the office and pointed to the coat tree behind the door. "Here—lend me your lab coat."

He helped her into it. The "Doctor Marley" printed above the lapel was right, but the size was all wrong. It didn't quite drag on the floor, but the hems brushed the tops of her shoelaces.

"You look like a monk or something," Plato told her.

"Or something." She rolled the sleeves up until her hands were visible again. "Like a flasher, maybe."

"So what's this favor you want me to do?" He was still grinning.

She furled the sleeves a little higher, reached inside the coat and slipped a piece of paper from the back pocket of her shorts. "Jeremy wants some background information about Gates and Godwin—he thought there might be a link between someone at the conference and the two victims, but he didn't know where to start."

"So?"

"So I tried to tell him about the state boards and medical societies, how they all work, who to call, what to ask, and he kind of got lost. He asked me to do it, since I've got a medical background and I'd know what to look for."

"That's nice."

"But since I have to do those tests across the street, I thought you might . . ." She sidled close and slipped her arms around his waist.

Plato glanced down at her. "Hey! What're you doing?"

She had slipped the list into his back pocket. He pulled it out. The phone numbers of the New York,

Connecticut, and California medical boards were printed on it, along with the state and county medical societies.

"Cally, *I* don't have a free minute this afternoon." Plato was thinking about the pile of delinquent charts across the street, waiting to be dictated. The prospects of making it to Miguel's golf outing were growing bleaker by the minute. "Besides, it's a waste of time."

She frowned. "Why?"

"Over three hundred people are at the conference. Even if I find records of Gates and Godwin's associates, how am I supposed to know if any of them are at the conference?"

She walked to the window and muttered something. "What?"

"Jeremy thinks it's someone at Cliff House— someone in our group of editors."

"Great." He scowled. Things weren't bad enough; now Jeremy would be following them everywhere, questioning everyone, sitting in on their meetings. Miguel was under a ton of pressure already. "Anybody in particular?"

"Well, yes. I wasn't sure if I should tell you—"

"Doctor Marley!" Hilda barked from the doorway. She loved doing that; Plato wondered if she stood in the hallway sometimes, waiting for a quiet moment she could shatter.

He waited for his heart to slow a little. "Yes, Hilda?"

"Your one o'clock has been waiting in the exam room for ten minutes now. Mr. Wilson." She tapped the face of her watch.

"You're a tyrant, Hilda."

Her jowls stretched into a smile, as though he'd given her a compliment. "That's why your patients love you."

She was probably right, Plato reflected. "Okay, I'll be there in a minute."

Hilda hurried away. Cal turned from the window. "Just remember that we're going golfing today."

He kissed her and helped her back toward the doorway. "How could I forget?"

"Oh, I don't know. I just thought you might get a little *distracted*." She jerked her head at the window and grinned.

After she left, Plato crept back to the window and peered out. Sure enough, a dozen brown ants were now clustered on the roof of the nurses' dorm. They must have had a short day today.

Far below on the sidewalk, a familiar white-coated ant was getting ready to cross the street. A face turned up; a tiny hand waved. Plato waved back.

CHAPTER FIFTEEN

The secretary at the American Grants Monitoring Commission was indignant.

"That information is *strictly* confidential," she replied when Plato asked about Godwin's current and past investigations. She might have used the same offended tone with an obscene phone caller. "We simply *cannot* release that information without a subpoena. And even if you succeeded in *obtaining* one, I *seriously doubt* that we would allow such a breach—"

"But one of your most important reviewers may have been *murdered*," Plato protested. Her officious lilt was contagious. "Very possibly as a result of his *investigation,* or some disciplinary measures he *recommended.* Doesn't that *bother* you?"

"Sir, my *feelings* on this matter are completely beside the point." She spoke through clenched teeth, as though her jaw were wired shut. A hiss of static fuzzed over the line. "I simply *cannot* release the information."

And that was that. The commission's records were locked in a vault somewhere in Washington, D.C. Getting them subpoenaed could take days; by then, the conference might be over. Or another editor might be dead.

Plato pushed the phone away, stared at the charts spread across his desk in the physicians' lounge, and sighed. He'd been dictating discharge summaries between phone calls, to avoid having his privileges suspended. Three yellow slips had ambushed him when he opened his mailbox this morning, and he'd already finished two of the tardy records. But the third and last chart lurked at the bottom of the pile like a sunken ore freighter.

Mrs. Sara Levin's manila file chronicled a hospital nightmare. The record was over two inches thick, flabby with hundreds of pages of physicians' notes, nurses' notes, lab slips, radiology reports, consent forms, and order sheets. Plato had procrastinated as long as he could, and now he had trouble remembering why she was hospitalized in the first place.

He picked up the Dictaphone and frowned through the chart. Sara Levin had bounced from the Intensive Care Unit to the regular floor and back for over a month. Her hospital course was a poorly marked trail through a jungle of fevers, infections, gastric bleeds, transfusions, a minor stroke, and a final bout of pneumonia that had nearly sent her to an appointment with Cal in the basement.

He scribbled a full page of notes, then pushed the button and began. "The patient, a seventy-seven-year-old woman with a history of Type II diabetes mellitus, a recent duodenal ulcer, and osteoarthritis, presented at the attending physician's office complaining of a cough and mild shortness of breath . . ."

Twenty minutes later, he finally rested the Dictaphone in its cradle. It had taken less time than he'd expected, mainly because the sheer scope of Sara's illness defied any realistic attempt at a detailed summary.

He proudly hefted the chart onto the pile of completed records, then dialed the California State Medical Board. Victor's record there was squeaky clean. No charges brought, no cases pending. He'd served in several offices of the California Medical Association, and had received the Silas Fenweather Award for Distinguished Medical Research in 1989.

Plato decided to try Victor's office at Ashbury Medical Center. A soft voice answered the telephone.

"I'm sorry." She sighed. "Doctor Godwin isn't in. He passed away last Friday."

"I realize that," Plato replied. "I was asking if you were Doctor's Godwin's secretary."

"Yes. I mean, I *was*." Her voice was flat, listless.

"I'm sorry about what happened." He spoke gently, and glanced around the room. The lounge was still empty. "My name is Plato Marley; I was there at the conference when he died."

"You *were*?"

"Yes. I'm calling from Cleveland, Ohio. I wonder if you could answer a few questions for me." He picked up a pen and slid his notebook closer.

"That depends." Suddenly her guard was up; an icy draught of brisk secretarial efficiency chilled her voice.

"I'm a friend of Miguel Velasquez—we went to medical school together," Plato explained. "I met Victor at the conference. My wife and I are helping out with the textbook."

"I see." She thawed a little. "I remember Doctor Velasquez from when he did his fellowship here. Tell him Barbara says hello."

"You've been there a while, then."

"It hasn't been *that* long. He only graduated two years ago." She sighed again. "But you're right, I've been here a while. Ever since Doctor Godwin came to Ashbury, back in, let's see . . . 1968."

Her voice sounded a lot younger than that—Plato would have guessed she was in her late twenties. He put his pen down and leaned back in his chair. "I liked him. We gave Victor and Miguel a lift to the conference, and we all had lunch together Friday afternoon. He was an interesting character."

"*Character* is right." Barbara laughed. "E.G. used to drive me nuts sometimes. You wouldn't believe—"

"E.G.?" Plato asked, confused. "I thought his first name was Victor."

She chuckled sadly. "He went by Victor, signed all his letters 'E. Victor Godwin,' but nobody knew what the E. stood for. Except me—you can't hide much from a secretary."

"Edward?" Plato guessed. "Eric?"

"You'd never get it in a million years." She paused, then announced with some relish, "Egbert."

"Egbert?" Plato smiled to himself, remembering Victor's speech about names last Friday afternoon. A fellow sufferer. "No wonder he used his middle name."

"He swore me to silence. But I used to tease him sometimes, calling him E.G., talking about our little secret, especially when he started getting out of line." Barbara sighed. "He was always picking fights with the administration or the other doctors, putting things off and making me work like crazy so he could catch up, running around the office ranting about his little pet peeve of the day.

"But he was a *kind* man, you know? And that made all the difference. Sent me a dozen roses every Secretary's Day."

Plato had let Nurse's Day slip by last year. Hilda would never let him live it down.

"But you didn't call to hear me reminisce about E.G., did you?"

"That's okay, Barbara. But I did have a few questions for you." He coughed. "Victor wasn't the only person who passed away at the conference this weekend. Another one of the editors—Doctor Gates—also died suddenly."

She sucked in a breath.

"What's wrong?"

"I *should* say I'm sorry to hear about it, but I can't."

"Why not?"

"That man had been calling practically every day for the past two weeks. E.G. asked me to say he wasn't in." Her voice sharpened to a shrill edge. "So Doctor Gates started in on me—said he knew I was lying, covering for him, that sort of thing. I've been a secretary for thirty years now and, mister, I've never *heard* such language. As if I had anything to do with the investigation."

"I understand he and Doctor Godwin weren't on the best of terms."

"Like two wet cats in a sack."

"That was my impression, too." Plato glanced around the room again. "Anyway, we're putting out feelers, checking for any connection between Gates and Victor and anyone else at the conference. I thought I might run through a few other names with you, see if they sound familiar."

She considered. "Do you mind if I ask why? I mean, I don't really see why you should be interested—"

"We think the two deaths might be connected, somehow."

"But E.G. died of a heart attack or something, didn't he?"

"We're not entirely sure of that, Barbara."

"Oh. I see." She gave a thoughtful pause, but didn't ask for details. "Then go right ahead. I'll help in any way I can."

He reviewed the list with her. At first, Gates's was the only name Barbara recognized. Plato went over the list again, and she stopped him when he mentioned Kelvin Lorantz.

"That sounds a little familiar," she decided. "I might have typed a letter to him."

Plato's pulse quickened. "Did Victor ever speak about Doctor Lorantz?"

"No—not that I recall." She sighed. "E.G. had been

so busy lately, we hadn't had time for much more than hello and good-bye."

"I see." Her voice was getting misty again, but Plato pressed a little further. "Do you have copies of his letters, in case the police need them?"

"Who knows? I always made Xeroxes, but E.G.'s office always looks like a tornado just hit it. I'll be sorting through his papers for the next week. He was a sweetheart, but he wasn't very organized. Some people are like that."

"I know just what you mean," Plato replied, picturing his own office. "Could you keep an eye out for any correspondence to those people we talked about?"

"I sure will—I wrote the names down already." She took a deep breath. "Believe me, Doctor Marley. If there's anything else I can do to help, anything at all, just let me know."

He said he would, and hung up. His pager went off just as he was about to make another call. An in-house line.

He dialed the number, and Cal answered on the first ring. "Guess what?"

"I know, it's two-thirty," he grumped. "I'd be done by now if I didn't have to make all these phone calls. I've been billing them to *my* office—when do I get reimbursed?"

She ducked the question. "I'm still down at the lab. And I've got the skin test results already."

"Hooray." Plato closed his eyes and let his chin slump onto his chest. Somehow, he'd nursed a flickering hope that their theory was wrong. That Godwin and Gates had died natural deaths, that no one had been murdered, that he could put the telephone down and go back to the hotel, maybe take a nap before Miguel dragged them out golfing. But Cal sounded too certain for that.

"You were right, Plato," she announced. "The skin

washings were positive for nitroglycerin. Hundred to
one it was in the tanning lotion, but we won't know
until we test the bottles. Jeremy's rounding them up
now."

"Huh."

"By the way, the forensics lab couldn't ID the narcotic in Victor's blood."

"No?" Plato lifted his head hopefully. Maybe it was
all a mistake. The mystery drug would turn out to be
aspirin or something.

"But our mass spec system doesn't have Euphecin
or Vixerin in its computer files yet—the drugs are too
new. So we're sending a blood sample down to the
state lab in Columbus."

"Oh." His head drooped again.

"And one more thing—Jeremy said they found one
of those threatening letters when they went through
Victor's luggage. He thinks maybe the person who
wrote them was at the conference."

"Goody."

"I know. I'm not exactly thrilled about it, either. But
at least we're sure now."

"Uh-huh," he agreed. "We're sure that Miguel's
book will never be finished, that Jeremy'll be tagging
after all of us for the rest of the conference, that you'll
be off doing God knows what for the investigation, and
that I'll be making phone calls until my tongue turns
blue. And getting nowhere, incidentally. Oh—and
don't forget, we're pretty sure that one of our shrinking
little group of editors is a murderer."

"I detect a hint of sarcasm."

He leaned farther forward, pillowed his head on the
stack of charts and talked through the side of his
mouth. "I'm sorry. It's been a long day. I just finished
dictating three horrific charts. I think some of that
Echézeaux is still running around my head. And having one's first patient in a Monday morning schedule

croak on one doesn't exactly foster a spirit of brother-
hood and goodwill."

"Our phone calls aren't going well?"

He growled.

"A simple 'no' would suffice."

"No. Our phone calls are not going well. We got our
ear chewed off by some officious secretary in Washington. Godwin's secretary was okay, but she couldn't
remember anything helpful. And I've drawn a blank
everywhere else."

"Poor dear," she murmured. "Why don't you just
call it a day? We can drive to the hotel and change
clothes before we go golfing."

He squinted at his list. "I've just got a couple of
more calls to make. Start walking up; I should be done
by the time you get here."

He tried Gates's office, but there was no answer. He
reached Miguel's secretary and introduced himself.
She recognized his name and explained that both offices were in an uproar over some surprise investigation. Most of the clerical help was busy pulling files
and Gates's former secretary probably wouldn't be
available until tomorrow.

The woman at the Connecticut Medical Board was
very sympathetic. She *tsk*'d apologetically at the news
of Gates's death, as though each and every physician in
the state were part of a big, happy family. She took
several minutes to locate Gates's name in the computer. Apparently, he had no malpractice suits or other
complaints pending; no charges had ever been brought
against him, and he had no history of any threats to his
license. "His record is completely clean. Exemplary,
I'd say."

Plato had thanked her and hung up. Cradling the
phone again, he remembered Miguel saying that Gates
had practiced in New York before moving to Hartman
in Connecticut.

He called the New York State Medical Board and introduced himself. "Would you have any information on a Doctor Eldon Gates? A geriatric psychiatrist. I believe he practiced in New York several years ago."

"Eldon Gates? G-A-T-E-S?" The clerk was very efficient. Her keyboard clicked in the background like a shower of bullets. "Yes, his license here is still valid. But we show no pending cases under that name, sir."

"No complaints? He wasn't named in any lawsuits?"

"You're referring to previous complaints?" She hesitated. "Our records go back for several years, sir. Twenty years on-line, and there are a lot of physicians in New York. A full search could take several minutes."

"I'll wait."

"I'll have to put you on hold." She clicked off.

Trying to ignore the telephone Muzak, Plato glanced over his notes. Nothing new, unless you counted the possible letter from Godwin to Lorantz. From their conversation in the A-V room last Friday, he already knew that Victor was suspending Kelvin's funding. But if Barbara came through with a letter, Jeremy Ames might be interested.

"Doctor Marley?" Mercifully, the clerk cut in just as the tape started recycling. "I'm not sure if this is what you're looking for, but the computer did find a case. Let's see—yes. Doctor Gates was named as a co-defendant in a malpractice suit once. But that was seventeen years ago. Apparently, he was practicing general internal medicine at the time as well. He's double-boarded, in medicine and psychiatry. The plaintiff's name was Anderson."

"And the verdict?" It was probably too far in the past to have anything to do with the murder, but it didn't hurt to be thorough.

"Interesting. Doctor Gates's name was struck from the case. Technically, this shouldn't even be on the record, then," the secretary mused. "The court ruled against the other defendant—his partner. The settlement was quite substantial."

"I see. What was the other defendant's name?" She told him. It didn't fit with anyone he knew at the conference. And anyway, the partner had died shortly after that. The trail had played out to a dead end. Plato sketched a fitting picture in his book—a collection of circles and a long, sweeping ellipse. Maybe the case would be solved in another sixty-six years or so. "Thank you very much."

CHAPTER SIXTEEN

Chippewa Creek Country Club was a desert. Saturday's rains had boiled away already, leaving the ground parched and petrified. The dusty fairways were a mottled sandy brown, the tall stands of maple and oak drooped weary auburn leaves in surrender to an early fall, and even the greens looked bleached and barren in the shimmering afternoon sun.

Up on the first tee, Kelvin Lorantz surveyed the lay of the land like a feudal lord inspecting his fief. The heat didn't seem to bother him despite his checkered polyester pants, monogrammed sports shirt, tweed cap, and heavy spiked golf shoes.

Standing below in his shorts and tennis shoes, Plato felt the sweat trickling down his temples, jawline, and onto his neck. His T-shirt was soaked through. Across the river and through the trees, he could see the lodge's main swimming pool, the high diving board, children and lucky adults plunging into the water with extravagant splashes.

He sighed wistfully. As if the heat weren't bad enough, the cart path behind him was lined with a dozen golfers, all waiting to tee off. They would all witness the humiliation of his first shot.

Plato pulled a towel from his bag and mopped the sweat away.

Lorantz unsheathed his driver and tossed the cover to his wife. Judith handled it like the Holy Grail, carrying it to the cart and gingerly folding it into a golf bag that wasn't quite large enough to swim in. Her mouth was cast in a stern frown, nearly as rigid as her anthracite hair. Her twill walking shorts and silk campshirt looked carefully casual and suited the occasion perfectly. She selected a driver from a more modest set and hovered at the back edge of the tee, practicing her swings.

"How'd we get paired up with *them*?" Plato whispered to Cal.

"I asked Miguel to," she explained, glancing back at the next foursome clustered beside their golf carts. Miguel, Evelyn, Jessica Novak, and Harlow Fairfax would tee off next. Behind them, more conference attendees were joining the line. "I thought we should get to know some of the suspects a little better."

"Yeah, right." Plato still found the whole murder thing a little hard to believe. On the other hand, he hadn't used any sunscreen today. "Hey, did Ames find the tanning lotion yet?"

"He found Victor's bottle wrapped up in his beach towel; I had him send it down to the lab." She frowned. "They couldn't find Gates's, though."

After mashing his tee into the hard ground, Kelvin Lorantz was ready. All conversation in the area hushed. Judith crouched several paces back from her husband to track the shot.

A practice swing or two, then Lorantz set his sights on the ball. The driver made contact at the precise midpoint of his swing, sending the ball aloft with the ghostly *whoosh* of an arrow in flight. Some trick of the eye made it seem to accelerate as it rose, hooking ever so slightly to follow the dogleg left. It finally touched down again and rolled to the center of the fairway, a chip shot from the green.

A few onlookers in the small audience actually clapped.

Lorantz ignored them as he stepped off the tee, shaking his head and grinning ruefully at Plato and Cal. "Nearly hooked that one right into the trees."

"Wish I had that problem," Plato sighed. "My main concern is getting the ball into the air. Everything else is trivial."

"Don't put yourself down," Lorantz replied. He stood beside them, watching his wife's practice swings. "I'm sure you're better than that."

"No, he's not." Cal was grinning. "Wormburner City. And you should see his putting."

"Thanks, dear."

"Judith had a lot of trouble, too," Lorantz noted. "Until we started golfing together. I coached her quite a bit, and it's really paid off. She's dropped nine strokes from her handicap."

His wife's shot sketched a perfect line down the midpoint of the fairway and trickled to a stop twenty or thirty yards behind Lorantz's ball.

"You just have to pay attention to the fundamentals," he added.

Cal was next; she bravely dropped the three-wood back into her bag and dragged out the driver. Her shot sliced a little, landing even with Judith's but just off the fairway.

As he set the ball on the tee, Plato tried to imagine away the rest of the foursome, Miguel's group behind them, the long line of golfers expectant and silent, all waiting for him to shoot. Just him and the tee and the golf ball. Like he was practicing on a driving range.

The club face smacked the ground and then the ball with the sound and feel and clumsiness of a baseball bat hitting a brick. Topspin ripped the ball along the grass for twenty yards or so, then dragged it through the deep turf like a jet plane crashing in a forest. Plato retrieved his tee, smiled nonchalantly as though he'd planned it that way, and slipped his club back into his bag.

"How about if Plato and I ride together?" Lorantz suggested generously. "I think I know what he's doing wrong."

It happened every time Plato went golfing; some friend or acquaintance adopted his cause with the same instinct that led people to nurse wounded animals back to health. Except his case was hopeless. All the coaching just crippled his game further with each successive hole.

He smiled at Lorantz as though delighted with the idea. "Sure, Kelvin. That sounds great."

They switched golf bags and piled into the carts. Cal and Judith raced on ahead and parked beside the fairway near their balls. Kelvin helped Plato dig for his shot in the rough. He carefully adjusted Plato's grip, his stance, his backswing, reminded him to keep his left arm straight, move his hips, flex his knees and keep his head down, and swing slowly through the ball. Plato pretended he hadn't heard it all before.

This time, the shot caromed off the side of his three-wood, slicing into the forest at a right angle to the fairway, then taking an incredibly lucky bounce off a tree trunk and plonking into a tuft of deep grass. The third, fourth, fifth, and sixth shots weren't much different, but Plato gradually worked his way up to the others.

Cal welcomed him like a lost explorer. "Doctor Marley, I presume? So *good* to see you again! And Doctor Lorantz. I trust you didn't find the jungle too trying?"

"Some yellow fever, and a spot of malaria," Plato replied.

"And some restless natives," Kelvin added, pointing back at the tee. The line of carts and people now stretched almost to the clubhouse. Dean Fairfax was taking practice swings. "Don't worry about Harlow hitting you. I've been out with him before—he never takes it more than a hundred yards."

"Let's stop talking and get moving!" Judith Lorantz snapped. The corners of her mouth drooped even lower. She glared back at the crowd and grabbed an eight-iron. "This is all so *embarrassing*."

Cal glanced at Plato and rolled her eyes. Kelvin looked away and sighed. Judith punched her shot onto the green, about four inches from the pin, and stormed back to her cart.

After they finished the hole, Lorantz sat on a bench and tallied the scores. "How about if we just stop counting at ten, Plato?"

"Great," he replied. "Then I can't score more than 180."

"You might have a personal best today," Cal noted.

By the ninth hole, Plato's coach was ready to admit defeat. "Know what? We might be trying to change too many things at once. Maybe if you just use your own swing, I can give you a few pointers."

"Sounds good." Plato's other erstwhile coaches usually reached that conclusion sooner, but Lorantz had a lot of patience.

By sheer luck, Plato's ball screamed over the pond and landed on the far shore, then trickled down the fairway beyond. Lorantz whistled appreciatively. Cruising along the banks and over a bridge, Kelvin casually broached another subject.

"That police detective came by this afternoon, you know." His jaw was set, expression unreadable as he stared straight ahead and piloted the cart. "You were at your office, right?"

"Yeah. My partner and I are splitting the coverage this week."

"Then he'll probably want to talk to you, too." He glanced over at Plato. His eyes held something unread able. Fear? Anger? Or just curiosity? "He tried to act casual, but he seemed pretty suspicious about Gates's death. And Godwin's, too."

Plato met his gaze, uncertain how to respond. Exactly what had Ames said? "I heard the police were getting involved, but I wasn't sure why."

"He said something about drugs—that there was a slim chance Victor and Ernest were poisoned," Lorantz explained. He parked the cart near Plato's ball. As usual, Cal and Judith were farther up the fairway. He handed Plato one of his own clubs, a steel three-wood. "Here, try this."

Plato's next shot glided all the way to the edge of the green. Cal's applause floated back to him on the breeze. Maybe the right club *did* make a difference.

"Great shot!" his partner exclaimed. Once they were back in the cart, he shifted tacks again. "Your wife did both autopsies, didn't she?"

Plato nodded.

"Then she must have come up with *something* the police found suspicious." Still the set jaw, the constant forward stare, except for brief looks flicked over at Plato. "She didn't say anything?"

Plato shrugged. "As far as I know, everything was pretty normal. She seemed to have trouble finding a cause of death at all."

"Strange," Lorantz mused. "Godwin was old, but Gates seemed so *healthy*."

They met the others at the green. Cal was down in a bunker, practically invisible. Judith was surveying for a long putt. Plato walked over to watch his wife's effort.

"I've just *got* to get close with this one," she was muttering. "Can't afford to two-putt."

"Why not?" He sat on the edge of the bunker and dangled his legs. It was a deep one; his feet didn't reach the sand. "Don't tell me you're keeping score."

"I was one stroke ahead until this hole, and I had to land in the damned sand trap." She grabbed a pitching wedge and stormed the bunker.

"Temper, temper."

"She's just so incredibly *patronizing*." Cal swung, lifting the ball and a pound or two of sand up over the high rim of the bunker and onto the green. The ball rolled past the pin and down a small hill, stopping near the edge of the green about twenty feet from the hole. "Damn!"

Judith Lorantz smirked.

Plato helped his wife out of the bunker and raked the sand flat. "Women can be so competitive."

While Cal was lining up her shot, Judith reminisced. "Back in New York, I sank a similar putt to win the Selma Buckingham Amateur Open. On the eighteenth hole. Remember that, Kelvin?"

Lorantz gave a tired nod.

Cal barely missed; the ball curved along the crown of the hill and perched on the rim of the hole. Judith bit her lip and two-putted, scowling and muttering under her breath. Kelvin and Plato finished putting and replaced the flag, and the group wandered off to their carts.

"I'm awfully thirsty," Kelvin announced. "How about a truce before we hit the back nine?"

"Sounds reasonable," Cal replied. "Okay with you, Judith?"

The champion of the Selma Buckingham Amateur Open shrugged. "If you need a break, that's fine with me."

On the patio outside the clubhouse, Lorantz tallied up the scores. "Cal and Judith are tied, I see."

Judith patted Cal's hand. "You're doing so *well,* dear. I've never met anyone who could keep up with me. Maybe we should play together again sometime."

"Maybe," Cal replied coolly.

"Of course, I don't come to Ohio very often."

"I thought you lived here," Plato said. "With Kelvin working at Siegel—"

"When he got the job, we didn't really move." Judith smiled with her nose. "I still live in New York. We have our own brownstone, just off Park in the upper seventies, and we couldn't *bear* to leave it. Could we, Kelvin?"

Kelvin shook his head.

"He spends most weekends at home with me, and stays in Cleveland during the week," she explained. "I don't see how he does it, really. Whenever I come here, it seems a little like *camping,* you know. Once you're accustomed to life in the City, you can't *imagine* living anywhere else."

"Judith's in advertising," her husband explained. He swirled the ice in his glass and drained the last few drops of Coke. "Couldn't find a job out here."

Her laughter was high-pitched and jagged, like the tinkle of shattered glass. "I couldn't picture it, really. Moving from Madison Avenue to . . . to *this.*"

Plato and Cal exchanged uncomfortable glances.

Judith sipped her Bloody Mary and set it down, dabbing at the corners of her mouth with a napkin. She glanced at her husband. "Of course, Kelvin is coming back to New York. He's already interviewed for a couple of jobs, but everything's tied to the research money he can bring along. Lucky he just got that big National Institutes of Health grant. Cornell should snatch you up now, right, Kelvin?"

He shrugged noncommittally, then glanced over at the ninth green. "There's Miguel's group. We'd better get started on the back nine."

Riding over to the tenth tee, Plato decided to ask Lorantz for more details about his NIH grant. He mulled over the stormy confrontation between Godwin and Lorantz in the audiovisual room Friday afternoon.

It seemed like a month had gone by since then. "So you have a research project underway?"

"A little one," he replied. "Judith tends to blow things out of proportion."

Plato doubted that was true; NIH grants were status symbols, even among the heavy hitters. Attracting federal research dollars to a small medical college like Siegel was quite an accomplishment. "What are you studying?"

"Mechanisms of resistance. The way bacteria become immune to certain antibiotics. Mutations, plasmids, that sort of thing." His careful indifference dropped away as he warmed to the topic. "It's an important new area of research—maybe the biggest question in the field of infectious disease."

Plato nodded encouragingly.

"Think of it. All the billions of dollars spent discovering and testing new antibiotics, just so bacteria can become resistant in a few years, or a decade." His face flushed with excitement. "But finding a way around their resistance mechanisms, halting bacterial communication—that's the magic bullet for all antimicrobial therapy. It could change the entire face of medicine."

He continued his monologue while Cal and Judith teed off; Plato had to remind him when it was his turn. Lorantz flubbed the shot and sliced badly, but he didn't seem concerned. He just droned on about the latest discoveries: chemical messengers and genetic coding and bacterial reproduction. Plato listened patiently over the next several holes, half wishing he had such a passion for research. But the field of geriatrics had no magic bullets.

Despite his ongoing lecture, Lorantz was reluctant to share any details about his NIH funding.

"It's a small grant, really," he repeated. "One-year renewable."

"I've heard they can be really particular about details," Plato hinted.

The researcher frowned blankly. "What do you mean?"

"The NIH. I've heard they're real fussy about issues like informed consent, hospital review board approval, things like that."

Plato wondered whether he was too obvious with the hint about informed consent—the reason Lorantz's grant was pulled. But the researcher just shrugged. "Not really. No more than you'd expect with other grants."

They were jarred back to reality on the sixteenth hole. Plato had sliced his ball into the rough near the river, and Lorantz was helping him hunt through the tall grass. For once, Judith had badly hooked her tee shot, driving it deep into the woods. Cal's shot had traveled much farther; she had left Judith near the trees and piloted the cart down a small gravel path between the fairway and the river's edge. Lorantz found Plato's ball just as a dull *thwock!* rang out farther up the fairway. Plato looked up to see Cal pull her cart off the path and scramble out.

They hopped in their cart and sped up the roadway.

"Did you hear that?" Cal asked as they approached. "I think someone hit my cart with a golf ball."

"Over here." Lorantz pointed at the back left corner of the vehicle, near the wheel well. "Made a pretty big dent."

Plato crouched down and inspected it. The grapefruit-size dimple in the fiberglass was perfectly round. He felt the little black gouge at the center. "It made a hole, I think."

"Funny, I don't see any golf ball around." Cal was inspecting the area. "I can't imagine why anyone would be shooting this way. No matter *how* bad they were."

She glanced at Plato.

He glared back. "I'm getting better. Really."

Judith Lorantz puffed across the fairway and grunted at the damage. "Well, *I* certainly don't intend to pay for it."

Kelvin thumbed the dent and frowned at his wife. "It's a good thing Cal didn't get hurt."

Judith flashed him a strange look, then dropped her bag into the cart. "Come on, let's finish the round. And then I'm going to register a complaint."

Another unpleasant surprise was waiting for them as they stepped off the eighteenth green. A blue Ford LTD was parked near the clubhouse, with Jeremy Ames pacing beside it like a caged tiger. A cloud of blue cigarette smoke hovered in the still air above his head. His crewcut was limp with sweat and his gray polyester suit looked damp.

Kelvin parked the cart beside the clubhouse. While the others tallied up their scores, Plato glanced back at the detective again. Jeremy had stubbed his cigarette out and was watching the next foursome cruise up the fairway. Fairfax and Novak were in the first cart, Miguel and Baker were in the second. Ames waited patiently until the group finished putting, replaced the flag, and started up the path toward the clubhouse. As Miguel dismounted from his cart, Jeremy approached and tapped his shoulder, flashed a badge. "Doctor Velasquez? Would you mind coming with me, please?"

Plato quickly strode over to Miguel's side. "What's going on, Jeremy?"

Ames shrugged nonchalantly. "We just need to bring Doctor Velasquez in for some questioning."

"Questioning about what? Why can't you just question him here?"

Miguel sighed. "Plato—"

"Are you appointing yourself as his legal counsel or something?" The detective's eyes bore into Plato's.

"Gentlemen, *please*." Cal had appeared at Plato's elbow. She tugged Jeremy's sleeve and led the group over to the privacy of the parking lot. Then she turned to Ames. "Why *aren't* you just questioning him here?"

"We don't want to call attention to the case, Cal. You know that."

"Come on, Jeremy. It's not a secret anymore. You've talked to all the other editors already."

Ames pulled out another cigarette and shrugged. "You might as well know. Sheriff Davis wants to talk to him."

Cal sucked in a breath. "I thought you said he wasn't—"

"Why is he so interested in Miguel?" Plato interrupted.

Miguel coughed. "I think I can explain that."

Ames shot him a surprised glance.

"I got a call from the president of Hartman University Hospitals this morning," Miguel continued. "Apparently Eldon Gates sent a memo to the hospital's chief of staff last week. Gates claimed to have found some inconsistencies in my research accounts, said he was suspicious and wanted a full investigation. The hospital has started a check of Eldon's records—and mine—to find out where the money went."

"So how did the police—" Plato began, confused.

"I knew you had some suspicions about Victor's death—and Eldon's," Miguel replied. "So I advised Hartman's president to contact the sheriff's office and tell them the whole story."

Ames slowly shook his head. "It doesn't make any sense."

"It makes *perfect* sense," Miguel argued. "Since I'm innocent anyway. Let's go and get this over with, Officer."

But the detective wasn't listening now—he was staring back at Cal's golf cart. He stepped closer to the fender and the others followed. Judith Lorantz hurried over when she saw him crouch beside the wheel well.

"Can you believe it?" she asked him.

"No," said Ames. He ran a finger over the dent. "When did this happen?"

"On the sixteenth hole," Judith Lorantz answered. "Someone must have made an awful shot. Didn't even yell 'fore.' Reckless behavior. I'd like to give the management a piece of my mind."

"Don't bother." Ames pulled out a Swiss Army knife. He poked and pried at the black gouge near the center of the dimple. The fiberglass crumbled and fell away. A small black object dropped into his hand. He held it up.

"Wh-what's that?" Judith Lorantz asked. But she seemed to know already; she held a trembling hand over her mouth.

"Small-caliber bullet," Ames answered casually. "Maybe from a hunting rifle, but it's hard to say."

Still studying the bullet, he stretched out his other hand and caught Judith Lorantz just as she collapsed.

CHAPTER SEVENTEEN

"Obviously, someone doesn't want us to finish the book," Kelvin Lorantz reasoned.

The huge octagonal parlor was silent; no one was paying any attention. A storm had swirled in just as they returned from the golf course, a bold chorus of thunderbolts followed by a halfhearted drizzle and a dismal fog that seemed to permeate the room. Evelyn Baker stood near one of the windows, watching raindrops dance on the swimming pool. Harlow Fairfax was spread across a sofa, eyes closed, feet propped on a coffee table. As usual, wispy Jessica Novak was nearly invisible, hovering motionless near the fireplace like a frightened rabbit.

Plato and Cal were standing near the snacks, talking in low voices.

Fairfax finally opened his eyes and sat up. "And who might that be?"

Lorantz was sitting across from him in an overstuffed wing chair, brooding over his Manhattan. "Charles Rice."

"The book publisher?"

Lorantz nodded sagely.

"You're joking, right?" Plato asked. "You can't really believe that someone would commit murder because of a *textbook*."

"Got any better ideas?" Lorantz challenged. "First Godwin, then Gates. And now they're shooting at us."

He glared over at Cal. "Do the police know about Rice?"

She sighed. "I'm not sure. But I don't think it really—"

"The textbook has nothing to do with it," Fairfax pronounced. He slapped his hands on his knees. "Godwin served on the Grants Monitoring Commission. A simple check of his records would undoubtedly reveal a number of people with grudges against him."

Plato sighed. Unfortunately, a records check was not very simple at all.

"That might explain Godwin's death, but what about Gates?" Lorantz asked. "And the shooting today?"

"A hunting accident," the dean replied. "Like that detective said. The golf course runs beside Cuyahoga Reserve land there, and it's mourning dove season."

"Hunting is illegal in the reserve," Plato pointed out.

Fairfax shrugged. "So?"

"That's what I've been trying to tell Judith." Kelvin Lorantz jerked his head at the ceiling, up toward their room. He'd already explained that his wife didn't feel well enough for dinner. "But I'm not buying it. I think someone's trying to scare us off."

"We're not making any money from our book—just a few fringe benefits like this meeting," Fairfax reminded him. "I doubt that even Rice makes more than a modest sum from his textbooks—hardly enough to justify murder."

Lorantz sniffed.

"The whole idea is utterly preposterous," Evelyn Baker declared. She turned away from the window and smirked at Lorantz. "Have you ever met Charles Rice? No? I assure you he's far more interested in face-lifts and hair dye than the success of his textbooks."

Cal smiled to herself.

"On the other hand, even if we assume Rice is innocent, that doesn't rule out foul play," the dean noted.

He wrinkled his wide forehead at Cal. "I must confess, I've worried that someone might be trying to hinder the investigation, by silencing the coroner assigned to the case."

She shrugged. "Inspector Ames says it came from a low-power rifle at long range—that's why we didn't hear the shot. He said at that range, no one would be crazy enough to try to hit a moving golf cart, let alone a person."

Just then, the chef poked his head through the door and announced that dinner was being served.

Baker joined Plato and Cal as they left the room. Wearing an anxious frown, she bent her head and spoke in a low whisper. "Please do be careful, Cal. You're not necessarily dealing with a *sane* person."

Holding Cal's hand, Plato felt her tremble.

She shrugged and flashed a nervous grin. "You're right—anyone who hunts mourning doves has *got* to be crazy."

The staff at Cliff House had outdone themselves for tonight's dinner. The huge Waterford chandelier glowed low and bright over the table, delicious aromas and soft music filled the air, and a cheery blaze crackled in the fireplace. But the room still felt gloomy and cold. The table was far too big, even though its leaves had been removed. The guests stared at one another like strangers at a funeral.

Mitch the chef wore his usual merry smile and a tall white hat. "I know Doctor Velasquez had a cookout planned for this evening, but I assumed you all would rather be *inside*."

He gestured through the tall windows at the downpour outside, then lifted the lid from the silver tray at the center of the table. "Still, we managed to get the grill lit. Filet mignon, charbroiled shrimp, and lobster tails. I hope you folks don't mind a little honest rainwater."

The meal was splendid, far better than the conversation. Kelvin Lorantz stared at his plate most of the time, hardly touching his food. Together, he and Jessica Novak spoke less than a dozen words during dinner. Harlow Fairfax devoted all of his energy to his meal. Plato watched Cal eating, drinking, breathing, doing the usual things people do when they're alive. Hunting accident or not, the bullet might have easily struck three feet higher. What if the marksman had coughed, or sneezed?

Maybe he had—maybe that was why he missed.

When dessert arrived, crepes filled with vanilla ice cream and topped with a brandy sauce Georges would have been proud of, Evelyn Baker finally broke the silence. "All this brooding isn't doing a bit of good, you know."

The others looked up; even Harlow Fairfax set his fork down and listened.

"Miguel had planned tonight's dinner as a brainstorming session. Remember? We were going to rough out a format for the clinical problems and case studies." She frowned around the table, a stern mother clucking over unfinished chores. "Tomorrow's our last planning session, and the conference ends on Wednesday. If we're ever going to finish the book—"

"We're not," Lorantz interrupted. "We're not going to finish the book."

"Oh?" Baker raised an eyebrow.

"Look, we've lost two of our biggest names already. Gates and Godwin had national reputations—you can bet that's part of why the publishers signed on. And unless our executive editor can get hold of a word processor in jail—"

"He's not in jail—he's just being held for questioning." Baker nodded briskly. "Until he's released, we may as well get some work done without him."

Fairfax dabbed at his mouth with a napkin and suppressed a belch. "I'm afraid I must agree with Kelvin. At best, the entire fabric of the book will need to be altered, and Miguel must be consulted before we take any steps. At worst, the book may be canceled, and any further efforts would be wasted."

"You—you're all ignoring the most important thing!" Jessica Novak exclaimed.

The provost and dean leveled his eyes on the young geriatrics fellow. "And what is that, my dear?"

"Miguel—Doctor Velasquez—is being accused of murder. While we sit around eating lobster tails and steaks and wondering what to do next." Her upper lip twitched frantically as her gaze met his. But she held her ground, pushed her frizzy hair back over her shoulder and continued. "Do any of you think he killed them? Doctor Godwin was his best friend."

The others looked away.

"Jessica," Plato began gently. Her eyes were shining; she seemed on the verge of tears. "We all believe Miguel is innocent. But what can we do about it?"

Plato felt guilty enough already; he had tried to see Miguel just before dinner, but the sheriff's secretary claimed he was still being questioned. Plato had wanted to boycott the dinner and camp out in Ames's office, but Cal insisted that they should come.

"Maybe we can find out who the *real* murderer was," Jessica suggested. She smiled sadly. "I know it sounds silly, but the police can't have very much evidence. They've hardly talked to anyone but us—it's like they want to keep it a secret. We could talk to people, find out if anybody saw—"

"Despite our proximity to the main lodge, we're surprisingly isolated here," Fairfax said. He wagged his enormous head like a wet Saint Bernard. "Too remote for anyone to have seen anything. Even if we could interview all the conference attendees and staff, I doubt we'd find anything new."

"Doctor Marley?" Jessica looked at Cal.

"Dean Fairfax is probably right," she replied. "Anyway, no one's accusing Miguel of anything, yet. He's just being questioned. And I spoke to Lieutenant Ames just before dinner—he said that Miguel should be released later tonight."

"I'm glad we all agree on *something*." Fairfax nodded and pushed himself away from the table. "If you'll excuse me, I'm delivering a lecture this evening to the cardiology subsection. We're covering the latest drug regimens."

Lorantz also stood. "I think I should see how Judith is doing."

Baker spoke sharply. "We'll all meet tomorrow afternoon, as we agreed?"

Fairfax stopped at the doorway. "Even if Miguel isn't released? I doubt we'll accomplish much, but I have no objection."

Lorantz nodded reluctantly, then hurried from the room.

"I can't believe it," Baker complained. "The publisher puts them up for five days in a luxury hotel, and I have to twist their arms to get them to work."

"Kelvin seemed pretty worried about his wife," Cal noted. "I think the accident really shook her up."

Evelyn nodded. She glanced over at Jessica Novak and frowned. "You don't look very well, either. Are you all right?"

The fellow shrugged.

"You've had a rough time of it," Plato sympathized. "Coming here and losing your fellowship director, then watching them arrest Miguel."

"I suppose you'll miss Doctor Gates; he must have been a very good mentor," Evelyn murmured softly. She didn't sound convinced.

"Not at all," Jessica blurted. Her eyes swept the room, challenging them to disagree. "He was a mean, selfish, egotistical liar. I only came to the fellowship because Miguel was there."

"Miguel is a unique individual," Baker agreed calmly. She didn't seem surprised by the fellow's outburst. "But most people join fellowships because the *director* is popular or well-known in his or her field."

"Not me." Jessica laughed bitterly. "I actually tried to *leave* because of Gates. Miguel almost talked me into staying."

"So you were switching programs anyway?" Plato asked. Most geriatrics fellowships lasted two years, but dissatisfied fellows sometimes switched between their first and second years.

"N-no. Not exactly." Her righteous anger suddenly melted into confusion. She shook her head. "I interviewed at a couple of places, but I couldn't . . ."

She seemed flustered, started to speak again, but caught herself. She shrugged and smiled. The uncertainty disappeared, but her face was still pale. "Just changed my mind, I guess. Things weren't so bad after all."

As she rose to leave, Plato exchanged a dubious glance with his wife. Cal obviously didn't believe Jessica's story, either.

CHAPTER EIGHTEEN

In the shower the next morning, Cal couldn't help peering around the curtain every minute or so, especially while she rinsed her hair. Visions of *Psycho* kept swirling through her memory. The door to the hall was double-bolted and chained, the bathroom door was locked, and she'd propped a fireplace poker up against the sink, within easy reach. But she still showered as quickly as she could; imaginary killers weren't intimidated by chains or locks, or even fireplace pokers.

Plato was gone. Cal had hardly seen him since dinner last night. She'd acted brave, made jokes about the shooting, laughed off his concern about leaving her alone while he went to a committee meeting, urged him not to worry about her when he was called to the emergency room after the meeting, and even feigned sleep when he slumped into bed in the middle of the night. Exhaustion finally claimed her then; but she woke up this morning alone again.

The note on his pillow explained that he was presenting at the poster session in Conference Room C. He was off call today, thank goodness; maybe they could spend a little time together and talk things over. Cal had some ideas, but she had more questions.

At least one good thing had happened last night: the county forensics lab called and told her that Godwin's bottle of tanning lotion was positive for nitroglycerin and an unidentifiable narcotic. The state lab hadn't yet tested the blood sample she sent yesterday, so the lotion, skin washings, and blood sample would all be analyzed together. Hopefully, the same narcotic would be found in all three samples, clearly demonstrating the murder method. Cal had little doubt that the state people would find either Euphecin or Vixerin, the two topical narcotics on the market. Even without them, the finding of nitroglycerin in all three sites was probably proof enough.

She stepped out of the shower and toweled the mist from a patch of mirror. She looked awful: dark circles under red-rimmed eyes, scraggly hair that hadn't been cut in two months, pale and flabby arms and legs, even her *stomach* sagged a little. Before the wedding last year, she'd worked out at the club almost every day for a month, gotten in shape, lost a few pounds, felt better than she had since high school. Then she'd gained it all back on the honeymoon.

Wrapping the towel around her, Cal picked up the poker and crept into the bedroom. The door was still bolted and chained, and the heavy curtain was pulled across the sliding door to the balcony. She flicked on a light and dragged her pink cambric skirt and cream-colored blouse from the closet.

Victor had died early that first afternoon. Struggling into her panty hose, Cal wondered how anyone could have been able to doctor the tanning lotion so soon after their arrival. With all the people on the patio, adding the drugs during or after lunch would have been incredibly risky.

The next murder was probably much easier; the killer had far more time to wait for a good opportunity. And of course, Gates had hosted a small reception in his room Friday night. According to Ames, all the editors had attended, except for Plato and Cal and Evelyn Baker. Gates had invited a few others as well, including Charles Rice.

Like Evelyn, Cal doubted that the textbook entrepreneur ever would have—or could have—pulled off a murder as intricate and subtle as this. He was too shallow and superficial, too impressed with himself. A man like Charles Rice would do something more flamboyant: an Errol Flynn-style murder—run his victim through with a sword, or challenge him to a duel.

Now that she was dressed, Cal felt secure enough to pull back the curtain and peer outside. The rain had finally stopped, but mist still drooped low over the treetops and knolls of the golf course across the river. A few diehards were braving the weather, slogging across the puddled and muddy fairways. Farther off in the distance, a cart zipped along the riverside near the sixteenth fairway and swerved around the hairpin turn where the shooting had occurred.

Suddenly shivering, Cal drew the curtain again. She wondered if Ames really believed his line about a hunting accident. For one thing, didn't bird hunters use shotguns rather than rifles?

Someone was knocking. Cal picked up her fireplace poker and tiptoed over to the doorway. She didn't touch the locks. "Who is it?"

The reply was barely audible, so she unbolted the door and left the chain on. She squinted through the crack and saw Evelyn Baker standing in the hallway.

The older woman smiled. "Mind if I step inside?"

"Of course not." Embarrassed, Cal slipped off the chain and flung the door wide. "Come on in."

"I missed you at breakfast this morning, so I—"

"Breakfast?" Cal frowned, puzzled.

"Remember? After dinner last night, we talked about having breakfast and going to the poster session together."

It all came back in a rush. "Oh, Evelyn—I'm so sorry. I slept in and completely forgot."

"No problem; I had breakfast with Harlow Fairfax

But I still wanted to drop by and see how you were doing. I thought you might have been a little frightened, after the shooting and everything." Setting down her briefcase, she glanced at the poker dangling from Cal's hand. "I guess I was right."

"What, this?" Cal laughed nervously and carried it back to the fireplace. "We had a fire last night—I was just cleaning up."

"You have a gas fireplace, remember?" Baker raised a skeptical eyebrow.

"Okay, okay. Maybe I'm a *little* bit nervous."

Evelyn bit her lip and frowned. "You'd be crazy if you weren't." She perched on the edge of the sofa and Cal sat beside her. "Your safety has to come first."

Cal bristled. "What do you mean?"

Baker squeezed her arm gently. "Only that I'm a little worried about you. Your department has other competent pathologists, doesn't it? People who aren't as close to this case as you are?"

"You don't think it was a hunting accident?"

"I probably have a little more experience with hunting than your Lieutenant Ames." The older woman smiled. "Unless they're incredible shots, most hunters don't go after birds with rifles; they use shotguns."

"That's what I thought." Cal rested her chin in her hands and stared at the cold hearth. "What would you do?"

"I'd be very angry at someone for trying to intimidate me."

"But what would you *do*?" she insisted.

Baker closed her eyes and thought for a moment. Then she shook her head. "I don't know, Cal. I honestly don't know."

"Neither do I," Cal confessed. "But I do know one thing."

"What's that?"

"*Plato*'s going to kill me if I don't go see his poster presentation."

Evelyn grinned and stood. "That's just where I was headed."

As they left the room, she glimpsed Evelyn's face in the mirror. Baker was watching her fondly; the expression reminded Cal of her mother somehow. Worry and concern—the same expression Cal's mother had fifteen years ago, the last time she saw her. The star reporter on her very last story, just before she died.

Cal would never forget that look.

The walls of the three largest conference rooms had been rolled back to form a huge assembly hall. Wide bulletin boards were set up at five-yard intervals, probably close to a hundred of them. At the larger conferences—like the American Geriatrics Society meetings—overall attendance numbered in the thousands, and the poster sessions hummed and buzzed like gigantic beehives.

The drug company booths traditionally occupied the premium spots. Visitors unfamiliar with poster sessions would probably assume they were drug advertising fairs rather than scientific meetings. At front and center, eye-catching multicolored displays, bright lights, gleaming metal and rich fabric backdrops, cozy chairs and literally tons of advertising paraphernalia announced the sponsorship of dozens of pharmaceutical companies. But out near the edges, squeezed against the walls and tucked in the corners, research projects were being presented and discussed by their authors.

En route to the scientific area, Cal and Evelyn were attacked by the drug reps. Cal ended up with a nose-shaped paperweight complete with sinus passages, a talking desk clock, two coffee cups, and a fistful of pens. Baker got an umbrella with a radio in the handle, a solar calculator, and three stacks of notepaper. They carried it all in tote bags branded with the Valdemar Pharmaceuticals logo.

"Not a bad haul," Baker commented after they broke free.

"Plato calls it trick-or-treat for doctors," Cal replied. "Speaking of whom . . ."

His poster was just around the corner. Plato looked awfully good today; the blue pin-striped suit from last Christmas fit him just perfectly. With his full beard and thinning hair just starting to gray at the temples, he looked quite distinguished. And he looked older than he was—a fact which sometimes irritated him, but often helped at times like these. Most people assumed he was senior faculty already, even though he'd only been out of fellowship for two years.

He was talking to a plump little man with a pipe, making grand gestures and occasionally pointing back at the poster for extra emphasis.

" 'Longitudinal Assessment of the Nursing Home Patient: Prognostic Implications,' " Baker read while they waited for Plato to finish. "Sounds interesting."

They stepped closer and Evelyn studied the poster. Cal was familiar with it already; Plato had been working on the study ever since he completed his fellowship two years ago. Like many others at the poster session, this was the first time he was presenting this particular research project. Though somewhat prestigious, poster presentations were usually only a first step. Publication in a journal was the ultimate goal for most researchers, but the posters helped draw attention to a project, encouraged feedback, and sometimes enabled researchers to make changes before completing their study.

The chubby man exchanged business cards with Plato and moved off. They were both smiling.

Plato stepped over to join them. His eyes were

bright. "That was Alfred Hummelman. *The* Alfred Hummelman."

"The guy that makes those cute little ceramic statues?" Cal asked innocently. "I thought he'd be taller, somehow."

Plato sighed.

"One of the premier researchers in nursing home care," Baker explained.

"He's doing a study that's similar to mine," Plato told them. "He wants to make some comparisons between our data sets."

Evelyn was still contemplating Plato's poster. The title was printed in huge 72-point letters across the top. Below, a brief summary of the methods, results, and tentative conclusions was spread in large type across several pages. "Your use of actuarial analysis is very impressive."

"Hummelman said he used a similar technique; he thought it would be very easy to compare the two survival curves," Plato said.

Baker glanced at him. "Did he mention the method he'd like to use?"

"He talked about the Wilcoxan rank-sum test, I think."

She shook her head. "Alfred clings to that test in all his research—I think it's the only one he knows. You'd be much better off using the logrank test—it'll give you odds ratios for different subgroups."

"It will?"

Plato grabbed a notepad and started scribbling. Cal's attention wandered; her statistical understanding didn't extend much beyond the earned-run average. So she moved farther down the aisle, scanning for interesting titles and smiling politely at the presenters.

At the very end, Jessica Novak was sitting alone in front of a tidy display on "Cytochemical Manifestations of the Aging Process; Observations Among Cel lular Organelles." It sounded just as foreign as the Wilcoxan rank-sum test, but Cal couldn't pass it up without saying hello.

Especially after Novak saw her. The geriatrics fellow bounded up from her chair to greet Cal like a death-row inmate meeting the governor. She beamed, grabbed Cal's hand with both of hers, and didn't let go. "Cal! Doctor Marley! Oh, it's so *good* to see you!"

"Thank you, Jessica." She finally retrieved her hand. "It's good to see you, too. Your poster looks very nice."

An older man and woman happened by just then. Novak's manner changed suddenly; her face hardened, and she retreated to her display. She explained the background of the study and pointed to the photographs, which looked like close-ups of the lunar landscape. "Much of the work is cytochemistry, and the changes are very subtle. But we got access to an electron microscope for part of the survey, and documented some dramatic alterations in the cellular organelles. The most obvious changes are apparent among the lysosomes. Take a look at this photo of a neuroglial cell from a seventy-eight-year-old man . . ."

Jessica was right; the photographs *were* the most interesting part of her display. The electron microscope allowed researchers to see intricate details at the subcellular level, to dissect the cell and its organelles in much the same way that Cal explored the human body and its organs at autopsy.

The man and woman moved closer, listened intently to her explanations, then finally drifted off. Once they were gone, Jessica relaxed again. She glanced at her watch. "Just fifteen more minutes."

"Tough day, huh?"

"Not at first." Novak pressed her lips together. Her frizzy hair was bundled in a fancy gold clasp that matched her earrings. She looked sharp in her navy blazer, and she even had a trace of makeup on. But the corners of her thin mouth were turned down in a frown. "Everything was okay for a while. I was nervous—Miguel helped me with the project and he was going to be here today, but . . ."

Cal started. "He hasn't been *released* yet? Are they still holding him for questioning?"

"Oh, no—it's not that." Jessica shook her head. "It's just that he missed a presentation last evening and he had to make it up today."

"Too bad he couldn't be here for you."

"He couldn't help it. Anyway, lots of folks seemed to like the paper. But then one guy put me on the spot, in front of about ten people." She honked into a Kleenex. "Made me feel like a total idiot."

"Don't worry about it, Jessica," Cal consoled. "It happens to everyone."

But Novak was shaking her head. "That's not why I'm upset. I've been thinking about what I said last night and everything. I wasn't completely honest; I wanted to tell you—"

She checked herself when Evelyn Baker approached.

"Am I interrupting something?" the older woman asked.

"N-no. I was just telling Cal about my research project," Jessica replied. Her lip quivered.

"Organelles and cytochemistry," Baker mused, glancing at the title. "My husband . . ."

Her voice trailed off as she approached the display. Evelyn nodded several times while she scanned the text and photos. She finally turned and smiled at Jessica. "An excellent research project. You know, most geriatrics fellows end up covering old ground, but these findings may be quite significant. I think your conclusion is especially well-stated."

"It's *extremely* well-stated," a new voice added from

behind Cal. "But I happen to disagree with it completely."

Charles Rice had joined their group. He was looking very GQ today: the casual loafers, cotton pants and carelessly unbuttoned shirt, hair just slightly mussed, breezy cock-hipped stance with one hand tucked in a pocket. Like a model standing on the sprit of a yacht in a cigarette ad, but not quite young enough. Or handsome enough.

He stepped forward and read the last sentence of Novak's conclusion aloud. " 'Further research may disclose practical applications for this information, including potential interventions for reducing disorientation and memory loss.' That's a crock—everyone tosses out some hopeful nugget about dementia at the end of their papers, and nobody believes it."

Novak paled. Cal and Baker waited for some reply, but Jessica was having trouble swallowing. Her lip twitched wildly. She frowned at her poster like it was a hideous reptile.

"Well, *I* believe it," Evelyn finally declared.

Rice snickered. "A *treatment* for dementia? Come on, Evelyn. I thought you were more sensible. Brain cells don't reproduce, and a lost memory is gone forever."

Baker faltered a moment, but recovered quickly. "The paper makes no claim about recovering lost memories. The conclusion reads 'potential interventions for reducing disorientation and memory loss.' That sounds more like an attempt to arrest or slow the process. Isn't that right, Doctor Novak?"

"Exactly." Jessica beamed gratefully. Her voice slowly recovered its strength as she continued. "We were referring to interventions to *slow* the cellular aging process, not reverse it. Prevention of damage through antioxidant vitamins, for instance . . ."

Baker winked at Cal and they moved away. "She can handle the rest on her own, I think."

"Rice was pretty harsh," Cal noted.

Baker shrugged. "Jessica shouldn't have been caught off guard like that. She ought to be better at thinking on her feet."

The session was nearly over, so they headed outside. Dusky clouds loomed above the mist, but the rain was still holding off. They crossed the road and followed a long winding path beside the river. Far below, the black water rushed and bubbled and churned with the power of yesterday's rains and the promise of more to come.

The path sent a branch toward Cliff House, but Baker continued on the main trail. Cal shrugged and followed her along the edge of the cliff.

"He was wrong, though," Baker added. "To put it that way. If we all listened to the naysayers, no one would make any progress."

Cal nodded, but Baker didn't see her. She was looking across the river. Half hidden in the trees, the ruins of another old mansion were visible. Funny that Cal hadn't noticed it before; the ruin was nearly as big as Cliff House. And it looked even older. A crumbling footbridge spanned the deep ravine here; Cal hoped Baker wouldn't try to cross.

"He was wrong about dementia, too," Evelyn continued. "Scoffing at the idea of recovery, a cure."

She stopped, still staring across the river. Her voice dropped, as though she were talking to herself. "Have you ever known—*loved*—anyone with dementia?"

"No," Cal replied after a moment. "Not really."

"It's a terrible, cruel thing." Baker turned and looked at her. "Taking care of them, I keep telling myself there's somebody in there. A living, feeling human being. Trying to get out. Trying to break free, make contact with the world outside."

She glanced back at the decrepit, abandoned house across the river with its sloping roof, dangling shutters, peeling paint, and empty black windows. "But sometimes, I can't help feeling hopeless. Like Rice. Thinking there's nothing but an empty shell. And nobody home."

CHAPTER NINETEEN

"I'm going to strangle that little weasel," Plato grumbled.

He and Cal were sitting in the library at Cliff House, where the surviving editors of the *Handbook of Practical Geriatric Medicine* had gathered for their final meeting. Miguel and Evelyn hadn't shown up yet. Sitting across the table, Harlow Fairfax had just finished another long tirade about the need for research experience in medical school curricula.

"I'd hardly call Dean Fairfax a 'little weasel,' " Cal observed quietly. "More like an angry hippopotamus."

"I'm talking about Ames," Plato muttered. He leaned back in his chair and stared up at the steely clouds through the cupola. "I've been trying to ask him about Miguel, get some details about this grant money business, and he keeps brushing me off."

"I had lunch with Jeremy today, while you were meeting with Hummelman." She fussed with a stack of papers. "He told me a little more about Miguel."

"I knew they didn't have a case against him. But I started to worry when they didn't release him until midnight last night."

"I guess they didn't have enough evidence to hold him," Cal mused.

"Not *enough* evidence? How could they have any?"

Evelyn Baker arrived just then, and took a seat. She glanced around the room. The eight-sided table had been full at Sunday's meeting; two days later, only six seats were occupied. "Has anyone seen Doctor Velasquez?"

"I saw him in the parlor on my way in," Kelvin Lorantz replied. He sounded tired, and his eyes were framed by dark circles. "I think he was talking to that detective."

Plato shot an anxious glance at Cal. She frowned and shook her head slowly.

"They're questioning him *again*?" Jessica Novak was wearing a gauzy white dress and a hunted look. "Don't they have any other suspects?"

"Perhaps they do," Harlow Fairfax replied. The plump folds of his face almost swallowed his pebbly eyes. "I heard we will *all* be questioned again today."

Baker shrugged. "At any rate, we probably should wait a few minutes and give Miguel a chance to return before we start."

"That would seem reasonable," Fairfax grunted. He folded his chubby little hands on the table, rested his chin on his chest, and closed his eyes.

Lorantz stood and walked over to the balcony. Jessica huddled down in her seat and stared at her notebook. Plato moved his chair closer to Cal's and spoke quietly. "What are you talking about, Cally? What kind of evidence against Miguel?"

"Gates's memo, for one thing." She studied the parquet surface of the table as though a solution to the puzzle were written there, in Mandarin Chinese. "Jeremy told me about it yesterday morning, by the way. I tried calling you at the office—"

"So *that's* what Hilda's note was about." He shook his head. "Anyway, what else? Surely they don't think anyone could get killed over a few missing grant dollars."

"It's more than that, Plato." She forced her gaze up to meet his. "Over the last year or so, a lot of money has gone missing at Hartman. They think Miguel was involved."

"A lot?" To Plato, a lot of grant money was the fifteen hundred dollars he'd gotten from the hospital's Development Fund to buy a computer and run his statistics. "What's a lot?"

She looked away and replied in a flat voice, "About two hundred thousand."

Plato gasped. "That's a lot."

"That's all they *know* about," Cal continued. "Just based on a quick look at this year's records. They think that's only a fraction."

"A fraction." Plato tried to imagine what he would do with two hundred thousand dollars. It would pay off most of their college loans. Tomorrow, not ten years from now. *Poof!* and they'd be gone. It boggled the mind. "What's this got to do with Miguel?"

"He was participating in several of the grants, and he was P.I. on two of the biggest ones."

Principal Investigator—the person responsible for running a research project, including the finances.

"If he wanted to be rich, he wouldn't have gone into geriatrics," Plato growled. "Does Jeremy believe any of this?"

"I really don't know." Cal shrugged. "I think he *wants* to believe Miguel is innocent—like I keep telling him. But with Miguel's name on all those grants, and the inheritance from Victor, and Gates's memo . . ."

The memo. That explained the situation at Hartman yesterday, when Plato had tried to call.

He glanced over at Jessica Novak. Her pale face looked ghostly, ethereal, and the gauzy dress didn't help any. She looked like a puff of steam with eyes, as though the slightest breeze from the balcony might sweep her right out the window. Her gaze flitted anxiously about the room and finally fixed on Plato's. He looked away.

"Gates was scamming, Cal. You heard what Godwin thought of him. Remember how Victor said he was investigating Gates's research grants?"

"Other people have heard it, too—that's part of the problem." Cal shook her head. "The police think maybe Miguel killed both of them, to get Victor's money and derail the investigation of the grants."

Jessica Novak rose and slowly drifted over to them, like a balloon cut loose from its tether. She braced against the table and faced them. The backs of her hands were rough and raw, and her fingernails were chewed to splinters. "I've been meaning to talk to you, Cal. Before I say anything to the police."

"The police? Why—"

"I should have said something last night, when they took Miguel for questioning," she began. Her head bowed, frizzy hair swinging forward to hide her face. "It's about the money—for my research project."

The geriatrics fellow looked up at Cal and Plato and bit her lip. She took a deep breath. "A couple of weeks ago, I was planning to buy some statistics software and equipment for my research project. And I had to pay a fee for using the electron microscope. I have a grant from the hospital—not a very big one, just ten thousand dollars—and most of the money still hadn't been spent. At least, that's what I *thought*."

She spoke slowly, deliberately, as though she'd rehearsed the speech. "The money from each grant is kept in a separate account. I checked mine—last Thursday, just before the conference—and found that most of it had been withdrawn."

She stared at the floor. "I tried talking to Doctor Gates about it here at the conference, but he kept stalling and putting it off. I finally spoke to him alone on Sunday morning."

Plato leaned forward. "And?"

"And he told me some story about how Miguel had access to the money, that he suspected Miguel had been skimming from some of the research accounts." Her mouth tightened to a thin line. "I didn't believe it for a minute—I was shocked that he could even say such a thing. I told him so, but he just laughed in my face. He said for all he knew, *I* was the one who took the money."

"Did you say anything to Miguel?" Cal asked softly.

"Not yet. I wanted to talk to him yesterday, but he didn't have time and then that detective came and took him away, and I didn't know what to do." Jessica shook her head. "I just felt sick—all that money, and no way to prove I hadn't taken it. But since then, I've been thinking, what if Doctor Gates took it? And the more I think about it, the more it makes sense."

"How could anyone transfer the funds without your knowledge?" Plato asked.

"It would be easy enough for him." Novak shrugged. "Doctor Gates was the chairman of clinical research at Hartman—he had signing privileges for all the grant money on everyone's projects. Once I got a grant, I still had to get his approval for each expenditure. It was the same way for the faculty. All the accounting was done through his office. I only found out about my missing money because I mixed up the procedure and called the bank directly."

Then the solution was simple, Plato thought. Gates had killed Victor because of the impending investigation. Exposure would have meant an ignominious end to his career, loss of his license, probably a long jail term.

But then who had killed Gates? Accidental death was out. A check of his medical records had confirmed the search of his belongings: he had no prescriptions for nitroglycerin paste. Gates's tanning lotion bottle was still missing, but the drug had been found all over his back and shoulders—clearly, it had been mixed with the suntan lotion.

It wasn't so simple after all.

Cal looked up at Jessica. "You didn't tell the police about this?"

"How could I?" She pressed her fingers to the corners of her eyes and sniffed. "I was afraid they'd think *I* took the money. And if I told them what Doctor Gates said about Miguel, it could make things even worse for him—" She cast a frightened glance around the room. "But last night I decided I should tell the police anyway. They may already know about the missing money."

"They do," Cal agreed. "A lot of money has disappeared at Hartman. From a lot of grants."

"Then I'm not the only one?" The clouds lifted from Jessica's face for a moment, then rolled in again. "Oh, no—is that why they're questioning Doctor Velasquez? They don't really believe he—"

"Probably not." Cal patted Jessica's hand. "Go ahead and tell Lieutenant Ames when he talks to you, okay?"

The fellow nodded, but glanced at Plato.

"Miguel is home free, Jessica," he reassured her. He nodded firmly, wishing he could believe his words. "The police don't have a shred of evidence against him."

Jessica seemed satisfied. She drifted back to her chair and sat, then flashed them a wan smile.

"Very convincing, Plato," Cal whispered. "But there might be too *much* evidence against him. Jeremy may have to arrest—"

The door opened just then and Miguel swept into the room, clapped his hands loudly and grinned. "Wake up, everyone!"

Harlow Fairfax's head jerked up, and Evelyn Baker laughed aloud. Cal and Plato stared at their friend, and

Jessica sighed with relief. Miguel flashed them all a cheery smile.

"Now that I'm finally here, we've got a book to finish!"

"You must be some smooth talker," Plato told his friend later. They were sitting at a tall table in the lodge's tiny lounge, sipping Dos Equis and chuckling bravely like schoolboys after a horror movie. The dark, dank room with its smoke-stained brick walls and ceiling, dingy furnishings, and reclusive bartender suited their mood perfectly. Plato wondered how many conference attendees even knew about the bar. It was hidden in a forgotten wing of the lodge, halfway down a stairwell that apparently led to the basement. A couple of moth-eaten moose and wild boar heads glared from the walls with beady glass eyes, and a pair of shelves was stocked with moldering hardbound books—Nancy Drew and Tom Swift, mostly. It was that kind of place.

"What—the grant money business? Gates really hadn't covered his tracks very well. Lieutenant Ames told me I'm off the hook." The sandstone planes of Miguel's face looked more jagged than ever. "Yesterday, when the CEO at Hartman heard I was a suspect, he kept the accountants at it all night. They found out Gates has been siphoning research funds for years."

"A true servant of his community."

"You've come to know Eldon Gates as I have. *A vuestra salud.*" He clinked glasses with Plato's, tipped his head back, and drained half of his beer. "That's undoubtedly the best beer I've ever tasted."

"I guess they didn't have much of a selection at the police station."

Miguel sobered. "It was truly awful. Between questioning sessions, they kept me in this fleabag little cell. Your friend—Jeremy Ames—brought me a couple of burgers for dinner. Thank goodness for that."

"We tried to get in to see you, but they kept stone-walling us."

"I know—Jeremy told me." He stared across the room at the fake stained glass windows that led no-where, backed by fluorescent light. He studied his face in the tarnished mirror behind the bar.

Plato watched his friend closely. It had been a rough few days—first Victor's death, then Gates's, then the shock of the arrest. He wished Miguel's wife were here, but little Roberto was sick with the flu, so Carmen had to stay in Connecticut.

"At least it wasn't boring," Miguel continued. "They had this pro wrestler type in the cell next to me. Guy named Mack. Alcoholic withdrawal—DTs. Kept moaning about snakes and giant spiders."

"And you thought *I* was a bad roommate."

"You never did the dishes." His dark eyebrows furrowed. "The other half of the time, they were questioning me. Ames and Sheriff Davis and some guy named Swindberg. Had white hair and a face like a dried apple."

Plato smiled with recognition. "That's the Cuyahoga County Prosecutor."

"Yeah. He stutters a little, but he's pretty smart." He shrugged. "I thought about having my lawyer flown in, but I didn't bother; I don't have anything to hide."

"What did they ask about?"

"Gates's party, mostly." Miguel sighed. "You know, last Friday night? Who was there and when, did I see a bottle of tanning lotion—I gather someone slipped nitroglycerin into his sunscreen?"

Plato nodded. "His and Victor's."

"Sheriff Davis was all excited about that for a while." He smiled slowly. "He had this brilliant idea that maybe Dean Fairfax did it, since he's a cardiologist. I explained that you don't have to be a heart specialist to understand how nitroglycerin works."

"On the other hand, he's probably the only one of us

who would recognize the sound of Gates's artificial heart valve—and know that he'd be especially susceptible to nitroglycerin."

"*I* knew about Gates's valve," Miguel confessed. "I had a patient with the same thing. Used to drive her husband crazy at night."

"I guess the killer knew about it, too."

Miguel nodded and twirled his glass back and forth on the Formica table. "When they got tired of asking about the party, Ames would move on to the shooting. Where was I, where were the other golfers, all that. We went over it about twenty times."

"I thought it was a hunting accident."

"Ames doesn't seem so sure. Anyway, none of our foursome had alibis. We were all looking for our balls—remember the woods by the fifteenth fairway?"

"I lost three balls there myself," Plato admitted. He glared back at the wild boar.

"Hey, at least I found out *some* good news." Miguel signaled for another round. The bartender quickly refilled their glasses and returned to *Days of Our Lives* on the little television tucked under the bar. "Ames said they found out who was threatening Victor. They matched the fingerprints on the note with someone at Ashbury."

Plato was stunned. "So they have the killer?"

"No. It was just some crackpot. A phlebotomist who lost his job when Victor caught him loafing and told the supervisor."

"Oh. Too bad." Plato took a sip and wiped foam from his beard. "Speaking of Ashbury, Barbara says hi."

"Victor's secretary?" Miguel brightened a little. "How's she doing?"

"Not too bad." He frowned at the memory. "But she seemed kind of broken up about Victor. She took me on a little trip down memory lane, told me about some of E.G.'s antics, how he drove her crazy, how much she's going to miss him. I guess Barbara's been with him a long time."

"They were very close," Miguel agreed. "He helped her weather a pretty nasty divorce while I was there. Lent her money, gave her lots of time off, the works. That's just the way he was."

They were silent for a few minutes, listened to somebody accusing somebody else of being a heartless cheat, then somebody threatening to make a scandal in the newspapers, then a mysterious telephone call from a Very Important Somebody, which was suddenly interrupted by a 2,000 Flushes toilet bowl cleaner commercial.

"I had time to do a lot of thinking last evening," Miguel said.

"When you weren't helping Mack battle the giant spiders."

"Right. And when you said E.G., it reminded me. They both had same initials, you know."

"Who did?"

"Gates and Victor. He signed his letters 'E. Victor Godwin.' " Miguel frowned thoughtfully. "I never did find out what the *E* stood for, though. I think Barbara knew."

"She does."

Miguel eyed him curiously, then decided not to ask. "Maybe I'll give her a call sometime."

"I think she'd like that."

"Anyway, I was wondering if Victor's and Gates's initials might have had something to do with the murder."

"Like maybe the killer made a mistake, mixed something up. Is that what you're getting at?"

Miguel nodded.

"But how—why would it matter? Unless they put their initials on the suntan lotion bottles . . ."

"Or maybe something else," Miguel suggested. "All of Victor's luggage had his initials—E.G.—right beside the lock."

"So maybe the killer opened Victor's suitcase by mistake." It was starting to fit together. "That's right—we all had to wait in the parlor while our rooms were being made up. The luggage was stored in a room near the reception desk."

"I'm glad this all makes sense to you." Miguel grinned. "The case should be simple to solve."

"Why?"

"The door to that room was locked, right? So we just have to find out who asked for the key and we'll have the murderer."

"There are two problems with that solution, Miguel." Plato glowered at his empty glass. "First of all, the room wasn't locked, even though the management thought it was."

"What's the second problem?"

"Aside from Gates, I think *I'm* the only person who asked for a key."

CHAPTER TWENTY

"Great night to go for a hike, Cally." Plato had ground the Chevette to a halt after spotting his wife on a path near the river. She'd disappeared from their room while he was in the shower; he had driven to the main lodge looking for her. He held the door open. "Come on. The Osler lecture starts in half an hour."

"Okay, okay." She climbed in.

He slammed the car into gear and swerved through the turnaround. The Osler lecture was being sponsored by Siegel Medical College; many of the area physicians were invited, along with those at the conference. The facilities at Chippewa Creek Lodge couldn't handle the expected attendance, so the lecture was being held in downtown Cleveland.

The Chevette felt like a cheap go-cart as they lurched down the driveway. Every bump and rut in the road was funneled through the shocks, struts, floorboard and seat, directly into the passengers' spinal columns. After replacing half the engine, their mechanic had thrown in a fresh set of shocks for free.

Plato didn't notice Cal's shoes until they were on the freeway heading north into Cleveland. The streetlights' intermittent glow penetrated the gloomy interior of the car. The green reflectors on her Asics Gel running shoes blinked off and on like a pair of cat's eyes.

"At least they're clean," he muttered.

"What?" Cal clutched the folds of her midnight blue

evening gown, lifted one dark-stockinged calf, and inspected the oddity at its end. *"Damn!"*

"You look like a bag lady turned Cinderella. But it's kind of kinky. I like the racing stripes." He grinned at her. "Is there any particular reason—"

"I wanted to check something out—a little theory I had." She grimaced. "I had to walk through the woods, and I didn't want to get mud on my heels."

"So you put on your running shoes and left the other ones in the room."

"I thought I'd have time to change back." She stretched her legs. "But these things are so *damned* comfortable, I completely forgot about them."

"We could go back," Plato offered generously, knowing she would refuse. They were already late; the others had left in the lodge's limo almost an hour ago.

"Don't be ridiculous. We'll be in a dark auditorium anyway. No one will notice."

They rode on in silence for several minutes. Like the Cuyahoga River, Interstate 77 plunges through Cleveland's industrial heart before emerging downtown. Steel mills and factories—many still idle—flank the freeway and river like the mountains of Mordor. The air and water are far cleaner than they were in the '70s, when the river caught fire, but the acrid scent of sulfur and coke still permeates the south side of town, ghosts from the city's past. A couple of miles more, and the freeway swings downtown, leaving the factories and soot behind.

"So how's Miguel?" Cal asked.

"Okay, I guess. A little shaken up." Plato shrugged. "But who wouldn't be, after spending half the night in a holding cell?"

She stretched her legs and contemplated her feet. "He told you about the poison-pen phlebotomist at Ashbury?"

"Yeah. He has his own theory about the murders."
Plato explained Miguel's idea about the luggage.

"Sounds possible." She nodded thoughtfully. "We
were stuck in that parlor for quite a long time Friday
afternoon. Victor could have been an innocent by-
stander, his tanning lotion poisoned by mistake."

"It's worth checking out," Plato agreed. "But I've
got a little theory of my own."

"What's that?"

"I think *Godwin* may have been the intended victim.
That very first afternoon, just before I gave my lecture,
I caught an interesting chat between Victor and Kelvin
Lorantz." He told her about the argument, Godwin's
assertions about informed consent, his claim that a six-
month suspension was a slap on the wrist.

"So you think Kelvin Lorantz might have done it?"
Cal sounded dubious.

"He has an NIH grant, Cal. But a suspension could
ruin his career."

She frowned. "Then why would he kill Gates—*after*
Victor?"

"Maybe Gates found out about the murder and tried
to blackmail Lorantz. After what he did at Hartman, I
wouldn't put it past him." Plato flipped the turn signal
and eased into the right-hand lane.

"I think you're reaching. Still . . ." She drummed her
fingers on the cracked vinyl dashboard, then turned to
him. "I didn't tell you this, okay?"

"You never tell me anything. What didn't you tell
me?"

"Jeremy says Kelvin Lorantz prescribed some
Euphecin for his wife and tried to fill it at Riverside
General's pharmacy."

"Naughty, naughty." Plato clucked softly. It could
mean nothing or it could mean everything. At the very
least, the medical community frowned on prescribing
controlled substances—narcotics, sedatives, and other

addicting drugs—for family members. At Riverside General, such prescriptions simply weren't filled, and the pharmacist recorded the name of the prescribing physician. Another slap on the wrist for Kelvin Lorantz.

But it could be more than that. Lorantz seemed to have a motive, at least for Godwin's murder, and possibly for Gates's as well. The prescription for Euphecin was evidence of the method, though trying to fill it at Riverside General's pharmacy didn't seem terribly clever. As for opportunity, anyone at the conference had access to the suitcases on Friday. After all, the room wasn't locked.

"I spoke with Marcus this evening," Cal added. "He said the state lab called—Victor's skin and tanning lotion bottle were positive for both nitroglycerin and Euphecin." She frowned slightly. "But Gates's skin was only positive for nitroglycerin."

"Jeremy still hasn't found Gates's tanning lotion bottle, right?"

"No," she replied. "The killer may have taken it away, knowing we were getting suspicious. But it doesn't make any sense—why did Gates test negative for Euphecin?"

"Maybe Lorantz ran out of Euphecin. It's a lot harder to get than nitro, as he found out. Or maybe he was afraid it would show up on a tox screen and make you suspicious." He swung the Chevette to the right, whomped onto the 9th Street exit ramp just before the stadium.

"Are you sure you know where we're going?" Cal asked. "Didn't you want to get off at Twenty-fifth Street?"

"It's a lot quicker this way, Cal." He turned left at Huron, beside the Gateway complex. Just below them, the Cuyahoga twisted and turned through a maze of buildings and bridges. Up ahead, Tower City and the

Ritz-Carlton hove into view like clipper ships cresting the horizon. Plato ducked the Chevette in at Third Street and pulled into line near the valet parking entrance.

Cal clutched his arm like she did during tense scenes in horror films. "Plato, where are we going?"

"The Ritz-Carlton. Don't you remember?" He glanced over at his wife. Her mouth was a line from a draftsman's pencil.

"Damn." She looked out the front and side windows; the little Chevette was flanked on all sides by a sudden crush of vehicles. Escape was impossible. "I thought the lecture was at Siegel."

The bellhop who helped her from the car glanced at her shoes without betraying the faintest glimmer of surprise. She ducked her head back inside. "Why didn't you *tell* me it was here?"

"I thought you knew—" His response was cut off as she slammed the door.

Plato waved the carhop off; he'd park it himself. He didn't want to risk having the Chevette scratched so soon after its return from the shop. Besides, Cal probably wanted to be alone.

Fifteen minutes later, he caught up with her in the grand ballroom. Miguel had reserved seats for them near the front, but Cal was waiting at a table in an unlit back corner. Her shoes were off, tucked beneath her chair and swaddled in linen napkins.

Miguel would never notice his friends' absence. Cliff House itself could almost have fit inside the grand ballroom of the Ritz-Carlton. Glittering chandeliers the size of small asteroids floated high overhead. The room was filled to overflowing with dignitaries from Cleveland's medical community. The wealthier ones, at least.

Cal was scowling. "Where *were* you?"

"Parking the car." Plato sat beside her and contemplated the exotic salad at his place. It was shaped like a South Sea island, with a small mountain of spinach and kohlrabi, a stream of vinaigrette, a beach of garbanzos and finely diced mushrooms, and a fringe of palms fashioned from asparagus spears and green peppers.

"Eat up," she urged him. "It's delicious. See? There are little shrimp down there, underneath the palm trees."

He lifted a pepper slice and peeked. "I thought shrimp lived in the water."

"Maybe they're supposed to be coconuts. Anyway, it's just scrumptious."

"Yum." The sight of all those leafy green vegetables upset his stomach. He poked hopefully at the mountain; maybe a burger was hidden beneath it.

"There's grilled shark under there, see?" she cheerfully noted.

He groaned. "When's the main course coming?"

"This was all they had left. We're late, remember? I was lucky to scrounge up anything at all."

"I could do without this kind of luck," Plato grumbled. He pushed his plate away.

She leaned over. "Mind if I—"

"No."

While she explored his island, Plato turned his attention to the podium. Harlow Fairfax had just mounted the low stage to deliver his second impromptu eulogy in three days. Head bowed into a multitude of chins, he lamented the loss of a "dear departed friend," a "fine researcher and able clinician," an example of "what every physician should strive to be." Plato wondered how many people in the audience really felt that way about Gates. Certainly not Jessica Novak. Not many others either, judging by the apathy of the crowd.

Fairfax finally raised his head after a noisy Moment of Silence. "As many of you from our Cleveland community may already know, Doctor Miguel Velasquez is a distinguished graduate of Siegel Medical College. After completing his fellowship at Ashbury Medical Center in San Francisco, Doctor Velasquez accepted a post as assistant director of geriatrics education at Hartman University Hospitals in Connecticut. He has published three excellent books of poetry focusing on such varied themes as childbirth, the diversity of life, and of course, old age. . . ." After summarizing Miguel's various activities, and emphasizing the role of Siegel Medical College in fostering his career, Fairfax finally ended his speech. "Ladies and gentlemen, Doctor Velasquez."

He invited Miguel onto the stage, clapping as enthusiastically as the audience.

"It is a great honor for me to be speaking with you tonight," Miguel began. His soft voice hushed the huge audience. From this distance, he was barely visible; a set of gleaming white teeth in a chestnut blur. "Most especially because of the man after whom this lecture is named—Sir William Osler. In addition to being one of the finest, most meticulous researchers of his day, Doctor Osler was a legendary clinician and a servant of his community. I believe that the future direction of geriatrics—and all of medicine—should embrace those three aspects of the medical profession, placing equal importance on each. Patient care, service, and research. This paradigm has a long history. The Greek physicians—"

Plato's thigh buzzed. He reached into his pocket to acknowledge the page. Dan was taking call tonight, so it was probably just a mistake. He glanced at the illuminated display but didn't recognize the number.

"What is it?" Cal read the display over his shoulder.

"Just a mistake," he whispered. "Dan's on call tonight."

"But shouldn't you check anyway?" she asked worriedly. "They don't know who's on call, and if you don't—"

"I know, I know," he grumbled. He glanced up at the podium. Miguel was just hitting his stride; he was an excellent speaker. And he'd surely ask what Plato thought of the lecture.

"Why don't *I* answer it?" Cal suggested. She reached down, unraveled the shoes from the napkins. "I'll just tell them—"

"That's okay." He stood and glanced at her sneakers. She was offering to make a tremendous sacrifice for him. "If it's one of the nursing homes, I'll probably need to talk to them and get things straightened out. You just remember the high points and tell me later."

"I'll do better than that." Cal extracted a small black object from her purse. "Miguel Velasquez—live!"

It was a microcassette recorder. Cal often recorded her autopsy results while driving home from the hospital. She sent the tapes to transcription the next morning.

"Cally, you're a genius."

"I know."

He kissed her forehead and hurried out to the lobby.

The telephones outside were all occupied by other physicians answering pages, so Plato headed upstairs. Here, the phones were available, but two of the adjacent meeting rooms were bubbling with a class reunion. Revelers had popped through the double doors and streamed across the lobby. They formed a bouncing, slithering parade, a cross between a conga line and a polka. An accordionist and a sax player brought up the rear.

Plato dialed the number on his pager. It was long distance; western Pennsylvania, the operator told him. It was probably a wrong number, but he decided to complete the call anyway.

Just as the call went through, a plump matron in a light blue rayon dress and dark blue hair dragged Plato into the line beside her. He dropped the receiver and struggled to break free. Just as he'd given up hope, the woman tucked her thumbs under her arms to do the bird dance. He broke away and grabbed the dangling receiver.

"Hello? Hello?" A cultivated English accent. Someone's butler, probably.

"Doctor Marley here."

"Doctor *Marley*?" The man sounded positively insulted. "Then of course this isn't Doctor Lorantz."

"Sorry. His number's 6514, and I'm 6511. You must have misdialed." It had happened before. When he wasn't getting Cal's pages, or Lorantz's pages, he got the respiratory technician's calls—she was 6512.

"You're probably right. Terribly sorry." The voice paused, considering. "Then you know Kelvin?"

"Actually, we're collaborating on a book." Close enough to the truth, anyway. Plato watched as a phalanx of rope-shouldered bellhops appeared at the opposite end of the lobby. At a slow march, they drove the dancers back into the ballroom, battened the hatches. The noise died down.

"Then perhaps you could save him the trouble of answering a page. Might you be able to deliver a message for me?"

Plato shrugged. "Certainly."

"We're having a hunting expedition on my estate this coming weekend," the voice explained. "Tell him that Bertie—that's me—tell him I said I wouldn't be there until late Friday afternoon. If he gets there early, the key's in the plaster rock beside the stair."

"No problem," Plato assured him. He thought for a moment. "I didn't know Kelvin hunted."

"Oh, yes," Bertie replied. "But his wife is the real sharpshooter. Judith almost never misses her mark."

"I see."

Plato walked slowly back to the ballroom, a thousand thoughts whirling through his head. He returned in time to see Miguel leaving the podium to thunderous applause. Cal was standing on her chair, whistling and cheering.

She turned to him and grinned, flicking a cigarette lighter in the air. "I still have this from the Springsteen concert—remember?"

"I don't think he's going to do an encore, Cal." He shot her a dubious glance, then sniffed her glass. Just water.

"Great lecture—got it all on tape." She sat down again and passed him the microcassette. "You were gone a long time. Who was it?"

"Just a wrong number," he replied. It was only a suspicion, anyway. A *strong* suspicion, but there was no point in alarming her.

A heap of paper was strewn across their table. He lifted one of the sheets. "What's this?"

"Huh?" She grabbed the sheet from him before he could read it. "Oh—just Gates's CV. I got a copy from Jessica."

"Why?"

"Just checking over the loose ends. Being thorough. You know." She leafed through the papers without meeting his eyes.

"Did you find anything?"

"Hmm? I don't know, really—it's all so mixed up. He had over two hundred published journal articles. I'm having trouble just getting this thing in order." She did some more leafing. "I've got a theory, but I'm not sure whether I like it."

He smiled to himself. "I don't think I'd bother."

"Why?" She glanced up quickly.

"I've got a theory, too." If she could be evasive, so could he. "I want to talk to Jeremy about it, maybe in the morning. But I'm pretty sure everyone will be able to catch their planes tomorrow after all."

CHAPTER TWENTY-ONE

It was a crazy enough idea, but worth checking out. Cresting the ridge high above the river, Cal pictured the scene once again. The dilapidated house hidden in the gloom up ahead stood very close to the site of the shooting. Heavy woods screened the old mansion from the fifteenth and sixteenth fairways, and made it virtually invisible from the lodge. Earlier that evening, in her blue evening gown and running shoes, Cal had timed the walks from the two fairways. After intentionally slicing a tee shot into the woods, the killer had ample time to retrieve a rifle from a golf bag, fire a shot, and hide the weapon somewhere in the house.

Carefully she picked her way down the twisting, turning path as it scaled the ravine toward the old footbridge. Her flashlight traced the tangled tree roots, mossy boulders and muddy patches that could have sent her sprawling into the black water seven stories below.

At least she'd taken the time to change into shorts and a T-shirt. Plato and Miguel were back in the parlor at Cliff House, listening to the lecture on her microcassette, reminiscing, and generally having a great time. They'd hardly looked up when Cal announced that she was going out for a walk.

Someone was coming. Heavy, measured footfalls sounded from the ridge overhead. Cal suddenly wished she'd dragged Plato out with her. Quickly, she flicked off the light and flattened herself against the cliff face.

The footsteps came closer, finally turning down onto the path just above her head. Hard, rapid paces. Heavy breathing. Just what you'd expect from a killer. Cal wondered if she could brain her assailant with the flashlight before she was overcome. She peeked out just as the intruder rounded the last turn.

It wasn't the killer, unless killers wore reflective vests and running shoes.

It was Evelyn Baker. Cal flicked on her flashlight and the older woman stopped suddenly, several paces away.

"Who's there?" Baker's voice was level with caution, not fear or panic.

"Just me," Cal replied. She held the flashlight to her face. "Sorry about that. I was a little scared, so I switched my light off."

Baker grinned, a Cheshire cat panting in the darkness. "I was scared, too."

She sounded breathless, not frightened. Cal peeled herself from the brush and branches and stepped out onto the path. "I'm surprised you don't carry a flashlight."

"Messes up my pace." She was still breathing hard, bent over with her hands on her hips for that last molecule of oxygen. "I've run here during the day. No surprises. Except you."

"And now *I'm* messing up your pace," Cal noted.

"No problem," Baker replied, breathing easier. "I need to rest up, for the hill on the other side. What brings you out tonight?"

"Just taking a little walk."

"Pretty lousy night for a walk—or a run." Evelyn looked up and sniffed the air. "It's going to rain soon. Care to join me?"

Cal peered at the cliff face across the river. It was

even steeper than the one she'd just descended. "Thanks, but I'd rather just watch. I'll be lucky to *walk* up that hill, let alone run."

Baker chuckled and resumed her trot. Cal watched her cross the bridge and bound up the far side, long legs pumping tirelessly as pistons. She paused on the opposite ridge and looked back for a moment, hand raised in a silent salute. Then she disappeared, and Cal was alone again.

She switched her flashlight on and followed the path with more confidence. After all, Evelyn had just crossed the bridge in virtual darkness. But then, half-way across, Cal suddenly wished she didn't have a light, either. Her flashlight beam flicked through a gash in the left side of the bridge and fell across the rocks and cold water far below. Cal hated heights; she fought off a spell of dizzying vertigo and willed her feet around the gap and onward to solid ground.

Climbing was easier than descending, she discovered. For one thing, she didn't have to look *down* all the time. A few minutes later, she topped the ridge and hiked across to the sagging veranda of the ruined mansion. Small animals scurried beneath the floorboards and something brushed against her face. A low muttering came from the hills to the west. She had plenty of time; the thunder still sounded pretty far away.

Getting in was no problem. Though the windows were plastered with the usual orange-and-black BUILD-ING CONDEMNED signs, the door was hanging from a single hinge, balanced on one corner and swaying in the gentle breeze like a ballerina's pirouette.

She stepped across the threshold. Casting her light about the alcove and into the rooms beyond, Cal suddenly realized that her task was hopeless. She had expected an empty shell, a house picked clean of furniture, fixtures, rugs, anything of value. Nothing but bare walls and floors, maybe a beer can here or there, maybe a rifle tucked into one of the closets.

The parlor alone could have been an auctioneer's warehouse, or a room in a museum. Two moldering sofas, an assortment of antique furniture including bookcases, two end tables, a desk, and a china cabinet. All covered with dust and cobwebs, most scratched and battered by vandals and the weather. When she had asked about the ruins this afternoon, the manager explained that the original owners of Cliff House had built this mansion for their son. After he died thirty years ago, Chippewa Creek acquired the property and built the golf course. Apparently, they never bothered to clean out the old furniture.

A sudden flash of lightning revealed some words spray-painted on the far wall. Cal flicked her beam across the room and grinned to herself. PURPLE HAZE— the rebels who'd written that were probably schoolteachers or lawyers or cops by now.

The first floor was vast; the mansion seemed even larger than Cliff House. Cal poked her head in the kitchen, dining room, and the library; all were filled with ancient furniture and trash. An entire arsenal could have been hidden in the old mansion and Cal would never discover it.

Footsteps pattered on the ceiling overhead, and Cal's heart jumped into her throat. Instantly, she switched off her flashlight.

The footsteps slowed, then stopped. Light, airy, rhythmic sounds, like a child playing hopscotch.

Cal had just convinced herself it was nothing—her imagination, the building settling—when the footsteps started again. Quicker now, as though the game must be completed before the storm began.

They faded away just as quickly.

Cal sidled toward the door, wondering what to do. By the time she dragged Plato back here from Cliff

House, the rain would have started and the intruder would be gone. Along with the rifle, probably.

On the other hand, maybe Cal could catch a glimpse of the intruder before he saw her. After all, he probably didn't know she was here.

Cal paced over to the hallway and mounted the steps. The broad staircase curved in two directions. Halfway up, she paused to catch her breath and peer up into the darkness at the room where the intruder waited.

Cal ascended each step slowly, testing it for squeaks before resting her full weight on it. She felt her ears twitching, the way they always did when she was frightened. Like on those trips to the attic in the old house in Chicago, back when she was growing up. Mom often sent her up there, for a box of papers or some old books that she didn't use frequently enough to keep in her office. Cal would force herself to climb slowly, calmly up the ladder. Once inside the musty dusty darkness, she'd feel around until she found what her mother wanted. Only then did she allow the fear to bubble up inside her as she scrambled to the access door and swarmed down the ladder, heart pounding, ears twitching, and lungs aching from swallowed screams.

"Cally," Mom always called in that singsong voice that meant she needed a favor. Up in her office working. Cal would have just gotten home from school. Curled up with a book in the family room downstairs, she waited for Mom to finish so they could start dinner together.

"Yes, Mom." Cal always bounded up the stairs to see what her mother wanted. It was lonely in the old house with Dad gone. And toward the end, Mom got more and more involved in her writing—more and more cross with herself and with her daughter.

But that last time, she wasn't cross at all. Just a little

anxious—she smiled at her daughter, held an arm out, gave her a hug. "You're a good girl, you know that?"

"And you're a pretty neat lady—the best reporter in Chicago," she remembered telling her. Mom had looked out the window distractedly, stroked her hair, kissed the top of her head. Outside, Cal was sure she heard a car door slam.

"I need the—umm—*Tribune* crime file ... the one from 'seventy-one. I think it's up there somewhere—in the corner by the window."

Later, she learned that the file had been in Mom's office all along. Cal hadn't suspected a thing until she heard the shot.

Now, that same scream was bubbling up in her throat. Cal slid her hands along the railing, clutched it tightly until the fear crested over her and died away.

Beyond the open doorway, the noise started again. A thumping, mechanical sound that stopped just as the wind died away.

Cal mounted the last step. A wide balcony swept around in a full circle, casting off doors and hallways in several directions. She stepped along the balcony and peered into the open doorway. The enormous bedroom had several chests of drawers, a wardrobe, a fireplace, a narrow brass bed, and an excellent view of the night sky through a gaping hole in the roof. The wind kicked up, and a loose shingle flapped against the rafters with a sound like hopscotch.

Relieved, Cal slipped inside and shone her flashlight about the room.

A few pictures hung on the walls—faded, dusty, and shrinking in their frames. A painting of a man and woman in their Sunday best, sitting before a curved window that Cal recognized from the dining room. Several yellowed photos of the growing family—one child, then two, then four. A larger photo, less ancient, showing the man and woman decades later, gray-haired and careworn and alone.

Thunder grumbled again, closer now. Behind her, the floor popped and crackled under a sudden fusillade of raindrops. Cal broke from her trance and hurried to the stairs. Back in the parlor, she stopped for one last look around, shrugged, and headed outside.

The sky opened and spilled like a cracked egg. Cal darted through the downpour, skidding to a stop at the cliff's edge, picking her way down the ridge and praying she didn't slip on the sodden path. Far below, the river hissed as rain churned its surface. Gusts of wind bullied the branches overhead; they clattered and clanked together with the hollow sound of death. Huddled against the chill, ears twitching wildly, Cal raced onto the footbridge just as her flashlight winked out.

She hurried on anyway, remembering to step around the gap on the left side of the bridge, forgetting to reverse her directions since she was coming back the other way, and stepping off into nothingness just as she realized her mistake. Like walking down a flight of stairs, thinking you'd reached the last step when you hadn't.

But no landing was waiting for her six inches lower than expected. Her foot met nothing but air. The bridge surface rushed up at her. Cal's shoulders slammed into the gravel and stone, and her legs slipped down through the gap as she clawed the concrete, the broken rail support, *anything*.

And then her right foot caught and held in a crack somewhere below, twisted past where any foot should be twisted. She scrabbled for a hold on the crumbling pavement, waiting for the pain but misjudging its degree. A searing brand scorched her right ankle.

The pain stitched a fiery path through her calf and leg, up her spinal cord, and exploded in her brain. For a full minute she dangled there, suspended between safety and death, fighting down a tide of pain and nausea that set her head pounding in time with the frantic beats of her heart.

She forced her gaze down to the ravine, to the white water and jagged rocks below. Her head still pounded, her ankle still burned, but the nausea was frightened away. Her left foot frisked the bridge for a toehold. A weird mewling sound came from somewhere in her throat; she willed it to silence.

Deep breaths. One, two, three, four. Pretend you're running. Except my hand is slipping on the damned concrete and when it goes, I'll be lucky if whatever's holding my foot doesn't twist it right off before I pitch down and kill myself on those rocks.

Quiet. What would a rational, logical person do in a situation like this?

She took another deep breath, and did the rational, logical thing.

"HELP! *H-E-E-E-L-P!*" Another deep breath. "Some-one! Anyone! PLEASE!"

Nobody heard. Nobody came. The Cuyahoga below would swallow her tattered body. She wondered where she'd surface. Maybe down in the Flats—she hadn't been to Shooter's lately. An awful cackle escaped her lips.

Her hand was slipping across the flat concrete, faster now. Her other hand scratched and tore at the wet gravel and dirt and mud, and started a small avalanche that tumbled onto her head.

She gathered breath for a final scream. *"HELP!!"*

"Hold on, Cal. Just hold on." The voice was level, calm, cool. Footsteps pattered across the bridge.

And just as her hands skidded off into air, a vise clamped around her wrist, held her fast.

"You okay?"

"My-my foot is caught. I think something's broken.

I'm afraid to move it." Cal heard herself sobbing. She sounded like a little girl. But she didn't care.

"It's going to be all right, Cal. I've got you." The grip shifted, then tightened. "I'm going to start pulling up now. Try to loosen your foot."

She tried. "It *hurts!*"

"I know." There was no strain in her voice, though she was supporting half of Cal's weight. "But I can't lift you by myself. And your foot won't stop hurting till you're free. Let's give it a good hard tug—one, two, three, *now!*"

Cal tried to protest, to ask her to wait, but a sudden jerk came from above. Like a steel elevator cable, it pulled slowly, relentlessly upward. Cal clenched her teeth, boxed her knee against the side of the bridge, and heaved. Her foot tore loose from her shoe. The swelling ankle rattled painfully against the crevice but pulled free.

The woman above her squatted on the cliff edge, grabbing an elbow, then a shoulder. Cal tried to help, but with only one foot, she nearly overbalanced and dragged them both down into the ravine.

Finally she was up and out, sitting on the edge, cradling her ankle and gazing into the face of her rescuer.

Evelyn Baker's teeth shone through the falling rain. "Guess it was a good night for a run after all."

"It's on the lateral side—I doubt that it's broken." Evelyn ran a finger over the plum-sized lump on the outside of Cal's ankle and pursed her lips. "Not that I'm an orthopedic surgeon. But breaks on the lateral side are rare—the ligament usually tears first. Of course, you might have chipped the bone—you could go and have it X-rayed."

Cal looked at Evelyn, then shrugged at Plato. Nested in the easy chair before a roaring fire in their room, she didn't feel like moving for the next three days. "I don't think so. Besides, the treatment probably wouldn't be much different."

"Probably not. You'll need a pair of crutches, though."

Plato stirred. He'd been standing there, arms folded, watching Evelyn Baker since they had arrived. Mouth and eyes gaping, as though Wonder Woman had just flown in through the window. "I called the front desk. They've got some."

He handed Baker an Ace wrap and watched her weave it over and under the arch of Cal's foot, around and behind her ankle. Over and under again, binding it tightly to keep the swelling down. She glanced up at him. "I hope you've got plenty of ice."

"No problem. Miguel is running over to the lodge; he'll bring some with the crutches." He still hadn't closed his mouth. "Tell me again—what happened?"

"I was just cooling down after my run," Baker explained. "Up on the cliff edge, I heard a strange noise—like a cat stuck in a tree."

"That was me," Cal interrupted. "You'd be surprised at the funny noises you make when you're about to die." Her laughter had a sharp edge.

"When I got closer, I heard Cal shouting, calling for help. So I reached down and pulled her up." She made it sound simple and mundane, like picking up a pretty shell at the beach.

"You just 'pulled her up'?" Plato's eyes measured the older woman crouched on the floor. With her wet hair, nylon running pants, and gray sweatshirt, she looked old and frail. "Did you have a crane or something?"

Cal's good foot found his shin.

"Not that she's overweight," he quickly amended. "But, my God! To pull a grown woman over the edge of a bridge with your bare hands? I don't know if *I* could do that."

Baker clipped the bandage tight, then fixed a piece of surgical tape over the clips. She looked up at him. "You're right. I doubt that you could."

"Thanks a lot."

Cal grinned happily.

"No offense." Baker's knees crackled as she stood. "Unless I were trained, I'm quite sure I couldn't, either."

"Don't tell me," Cal said. "You took a summer off, traveled to Tibet, and learned how to rescue idiot females who fall off bridges."

"Not far off the mark, really. Except that you're not an 'idiot female.' That fall could have happened to anyone."

Cal had thought she was just being polite, but Baker shuddered. She was staring at the end table beside the recliner. "Sorry. Someone just walked over my grave, I guess. Anyway, the course wasn't in Tibet—it was at a survival school in Colorado. You learn a lot of tricks and techniques, certain things about leverage and so on."

Cal gestured to the sofa. "How about staying for some coffee?"

"I'm afraid I have to be going." Evelyn glanced at the black diving watch strapped to her wrist. "I've got a morning appointment at the bank—I need to be there at nine-thirty."

"No problem," Plato replied. "We've got a car—I'll take you in if you'd like."

"Thanks anyways, but I've got my rental. I'm spoiled, I guess. I hate being without a car, even if there's other transportation available."

"Well, if there's anything else we can do—"

Baker was out the door before they could thank her again.

Cal was still sitting in her recliner an hour later. Miguel had brought the ice and crutches, gawked at her ankle, and heard the saga of Evelyn Baker's rescue before he left. Plato had gallantly stayed by her side, fussing with her blanket and her Ace wrap and generally annoying her until he finally drifted off to sleep on the sofa.

The fire was dying down. Though it was past midnight, she wasn't drowsy. Her hands were still clammy, her head was still throbbing, and she was still shivering despite her warm clothes. Maybe if they went to bed, she'd fall asleep. Maybe she needed a shot of Macallan's from the room's liquor cabinet.

She leaned over and reached for her crutches, knocking Plato's notebook to the floor. It had been resting on the end table beside her. Curious, she turned it over and glanced at the top page.

The paper was covered with Plato's notes from his telephone conversations yesterday afternoon. It was mostly an illegible mixture of cartoons and sketches. But he must have thought he had something. Down near the bottom, he'd bothered to write clearly for a few lines:

"E. Gates—New York!! Malpract. case 17 yrs. ago. Gates off case, partner guilty, died after trial." And then nothing. Except a weird little sketch of the sun and the planets. And something else, a little dot coming in on a sharp parabola, circling the sun, and shooting back out into space. It had a little tail. A comet—

The shivers started at her ribs, spread to her shoulders, her legs, her arms. Her whole body was quaking. She grabbed another blanket from the floor and covered herself, pulled it up over her head. Huddling in the darkness and warmth, she felt the chills gradually diminish. The title of an old Elton John song flitted across her mind:

"Someone Saved My Life Tonight."

It was hard to think. Her mind was filled with a thousand questions. Most would never be answered.

Maybe it didn't matter. She didn't want to do anything, anything at all.

But she thought of Victor Godwin, and Miguel, and the hole in the side of her golf cart. And she thought of her mother.

It still didn't make any sense. She didn't really *want* it to. But Cal knew what she had to do.

CHAPTER TWENTY-TWO

"Pretty awful weather we're having," Kelvin Lorantz said to no one in particular. The group was gathered in the dining room again, picking at the sumptuous breakfast and wincing at each crack of thunder. "I guess it doesn't matter much that Ames is making us stay an extra day. Front desk says most of the flights out are grounded."

He was probably right. The low clouds, pounding rain, and frequent lightning would make most people reluctant to drive this morning, much less fly. Despite its windows, the dining room was dark and gloomy. Even the light from the huge chandelier seemed muted and gray.

Ames had made the announcement last night, shortly after they all returned from the Osler lecture. The sheriff's office would appreciate it if they cooperated with the investigation by remaining in Cuyahoga County for at least one more day. The additional night's stay at Cliff House would be handled at county expense.

"By the way, I got a page for you during the Osler lecture last night," Plato told Lorantz. "Bertie said he might be out of the house Friday afternoon, so you should look for the key in the fake rock."

Lorantz reddened slightly. "Sorry about that. We're visiting some friends this weekend—I gave them my pager number."

"I wouldn't count on going *anywhere* this weekend,"

Harlow Fairfax muttered. He chomped a croissant in half and continued. "We'll be lucky if Ames doesn't make us stay here until the case is solved and the murderer is tried and convicted."

Judith Lorantz groaned. "I certainly hope not. We've considered bringing our lawyer out here. Kelvin, I really think we should."

Plato studied them closely. If his hunch was correct, they would need a lawyer very soon.

"At least the police are paying for it." Jessica Novak was the table's only other occupant. She looked healthier today, her skin was less translucent, her hair fell neatly to her shoulders, and she'd even smeared on a bit of lipstick. She looked almost pretty in the dim morning light. When she smiled, she *did* look pretty. "After all, they could have stuck us in a cheap motel or something."

"We simply wouldn't stand for it," Judith declared. But she looked worried. "Kelvin, maybe we—"

He patted her hand. "Just give it another day, dear. The detective said that's all he needs. I'll call Rosenblum this afternoon and let him know what's what."

Jessica Novak tapped Plato's elbow. "Maybe your wife knows a little more about what's going on. Is she having breakfast?"

"Just coffee—in her room," he answered. "She's in the middle of a migraine."

Jessica frowned sympathetically. Her reply was drowned out by a blast of lightning that struck somewhere nearby, piercing the gloom, rattling cups and saucers, clattering silverware, and rumbling through the walls and floor before slowly dying away. The chandelier above the table jiggled and swayed crazily, blinked once, twice, then winked out.

"Looks like we might have been better off in a cheap motel," Fairfax observed wryly.

Plato rose and tried the other lights, but the power was out completely. He drifted over to one of the front windows. Most of the puddles in the parking lot had joined to form a small lake. The wheels of the lodge's van were submerged. The Chevette was parked on a small mound of gravel, but water had already risen to the hubcaps. Farther off, a man in a poncho was trudging through the woods and up the driveway. It was Ames. The detective skipped gingerly across the islands in the parking lot, then waded through the shallowest part of the lake.

Plato hurried from the room to meet him at the front door.

"You folks are going to need a boat pretty soon," Jeremy announced. The black rain poncho stretched down to his pantlegs, which were rolled up at the knees. The veins in his thick, pale calves looked like drowned earthworms. His shiny black galoshes were unbuckled; muddy water trickled out over the gleaming hardwood floor.

"No problem—we'll just paddle home in the Chevette." Plato watched him slip his boots off and dump the water onto the porch. "Where's your car?"

"Parked on the other side of the landslide. I left the flashers on." His shoes sounded like bags of kelp as he slogged across the alcove and glanced into the empty library.

"Landslide?"

"Remember that rough spot where part of the driveway was missing?" He lit a cigarette and leaned against the doorjamb. "Apparently the rest of it fell into the river last night; I nearly went for a swim in my patrol car."

He took a long drag and blew smoke rings at the ceiling. "Speaking of which, how about paddling your Chevette out to the near side of the gap and putting your flashers on so no one gets hurt?" He glanced outside. "Though I doubt many of the other guests are going anywhere today."

"In a minute," Plato replied. "I want to talk to you first, before you question anyone. Last night, I picked up some gossip that you might find interesting."

"Good." He walked into the library, flopped into a leather wing chair, and snatched a book from a shelf. "Then I'll just warm up and do some reading while you move your car. Milton—what luck. *Paradise Lost* and all that."

He thumbed through the book and Plato got his jacket and keys from the closet in the alcove. He hurried out and started the Chevette, weaving around the biggest lakes and darting through puddles he couldn't avoid. Sure enough, the narrow part of the roadway had finally fallen into the Cuyahoga. Far across the gap, Jeremy's patrol car was running, flashers barely visible through the downpour. Seventy feet down, a few tons of gravel and earth formed a tiny new peninsula.

No one was going anywhere today. Maybe a jeep could get through the woods inland from the cliff, but not much else. Once the rain stopped, the management might be able to clear a path through the trees and ferry luggage and guests around the cut.

Plato left the car running and hazards flashing, then turned away and slogged back up the road to Cliff House. Jeremy was still waiting in the library. He looked up as Plato squished into the room, closed the double doors, and fell into the other wing chair.

"Pretty awful out there, huh?" He glanced at Plato's dripping tennis shoes. "You should have said you didn't have any rain gear—no sense both of us getting wet."

"Thanks, Jeremy."

The detective replaced the book, sat back and folded

his hands across his chest. "So what have you got for me?"

Plato sighed. "First of all, I'm curious whether you guys really think that was a hunting accident on Monday."

Ames shrugged and gave a half smile. "No sense alarming you folks. But we've been looking into it."

"Looking into it?"

He stubbed his cigarette into an ashtray and pulled another from his pocket. Lighting it, he explained. "Same problem as with the tanning lotion business—we couldn't get a warrant to search the whole lodge. Even if we had, the killer probably wouldn't have hidden the gun in his room. So we ran ballistics, and checked out the trash and the river and some of the woods—the usual things you do when you can't get a warrant. We're assuming the killer ditched it somewhere, expecting us to do a search."

"So you think it wasn't an accident, but you don't have enough evidence for a search warrant."

"We think it *maybe* wasn't an accident." He drummed his fingers on the arm of his chair. "And the reason we can't get a search warrant is because we can't say exactly which rooms we want to search. Right now, there's not enough evidence to implicate anyone—not even your friend Miguel."

"Forget about Miguel. Listen to this." He told Jeremy about Lorantz's page last night, Bertie's comment about Judith's shooting ability, and the conversation between Lorantz and Victor on the first day of the conference. He explained his theory that Gates might have been blackmailing Lorantz over Victor's murder.

Jeremy nodded his head. "Sounds interesting, though I think you're reaching with the blackmail bit. But how come you never brought this up before? You've known Lorantz had it in for Godwin ever since Friday afternoon."

Plato squirmed. "I don't know—it's pretty damaging information. I didn't even tell Cal about it until last night."

The detective shrugged. "Well, we couldn't have done much with it until we had harder evidence. Like finding out that Lorantz was prescribing Euphecin for his wife."

Plato acted surprised. "Really?"

"Found out yesterday. We were going over the pharmacy records at Riverside General for another case, and Lorantz's name popped up." He frowned at the cloud of smoke circling his head. "You know, I never did understand Cal's explanation about that narcotic—Euphecin. Which drug killed them—the narcotic or the nitroglycerin paste?"

"Probably both, at least in Victor's case." Plato glanced out the window at the patio and pool. Tiny whitecaps were dancing on the surface and water was sloshing over the edge. "Nitroglycerin dilates the blood vessels—expands them so the blood pressure drops. At first, the heart gets more blood and doesn't have to work as hard. But when there's too much nitroglycerin, the blood pressure drops too fast and too far. Important organs like the brain and kidneys are starved for oxygen and even the heart doesn't get enough blood."

He nodded. "So where does the Euphecin tie in?"

"Nitroglycerin often causes a whanging headache, and an overdose of it would give almost anyone a migraine. Godwin would probably have called for help, might even have lived, except the Euphecin deadened the pain and put him to sleep. It also strengthens the effect of the nitroglycerin."

Ames considered. "Then why wasn't Euphecin used on Gates?"

"The killer was probably worried about it showing up on a tox screen." Down the hill and through the trees, the clay tennis court was visible as a square red pond. "Since Cal was already suspicious about Victor's death, the killer couldn't risk having a narcotic show up on another screen."

"Wouldn't the nitroglycerin show up, too?"

"Probably not on a routine screen. And even if it did, Gates was already taking nitroglycerin for his heart problem."

Except he'd unwittingly taken a fatal dose of the drug. One of their group of physician-editors was doing a little moonlighting, gratis. Professional courtesy, so to speak. Murder by prescription.

They sat there in silence for several minutes, Ames puffing through another two cigarettes and Plato watching the wind whip the trees, hearing the rain spatter the windows, wondering if it really was Kelvin Lorantz or his wife. Now that he'd come clean with Jeremy, voiced his suspicions aloud, it all seemed much more flimsy and tenuous.

The detective finally stirred, squashed his cigarette into the ashtray and didn't pull another from his pocket. "So you think it's Judith?"

"Or Kelvin."

"Couldn't be—he was with you when someone shot at Cal." He sounded more certain that it wasn't an accident now. "Had to be Judith. Except we don't have much of a motive for her."

"Judith's pretty invested in her husband's career. She wants him to move back to New York." It seemed like a trivial reason for killing someone. "He's interviewing at Cornell. But if his suspension becomes public, he'll be a pariah—at least in the big-league Eastern schools."

"Who knows—maybe it was both of them." Ames stood. "Anyway, it's worth sitting them down for a good long chat. Is Cal around? I'd like her to be with me when I question them."

"She's probably still in bed." They walked to the doorway. "She's got an awful migraine this morning."

"A *migraine*?" The color drained from Jeremy's face.

"Yeah—why?" Plato was puzzled. "She gets them all the time."

He pointed to the phone sitting on a desk in the far corner. "Maybe you'd better call up to her room and see if she's all right."

"Of course she's all right. She—" His own words echoed in his head—*an overdose would give almost anyone a migraine*. He scrambled for the phone and picked up the receiver, dialed their room. "No answer."

Ames grabbed his shoulder. "Come on!"

They raced for the doorway.

CHAPTER TWENTY-THREE

Cal staggered to the phone and picked it up just as the ringing stopped. "Hello? Hello?"

Nothing on the other end. It was just as well. The barrage of thunder outside felt like cherry bombs popping in her head. Overnight, her brain had grown too large for her skull. Earlier this morning, it had throbbed with each beat of her heart while she showered and dressed. Cal pictured the top of her head pulsating with angry red light, like a space-alien in a B-movie.

She really didn't feel like talking to anyone.

But she had to. Cal tottered back to her chair, bent over to tie her shoe, and instantly regretted it. All the blood in her body suddenly inflated her brain, stretched her skull thin as a soap bubble. She'd do without the shoe; she didn't need to walk far.

At least Plato had left the curtain drawn. When Cal had a migraine, she shunned the light like a vampire. She hefted herself up on the crutches and staggered over to the bathroom sink, studied her shadow in the mirror. The top of her head wasn't glowing, but her eyes were. Cal reached for her sunglasses; she kept a pair in her makeup case for days like today.

The lights were off in the hallway. She kept her sunglasses on and blundered ahead through the darkness. Downstairs, the maid was arguing with someone about why her cart was blocking the stairwell. Cal stumbled down the other stairway and hobbled down another dark corridor. She finally stopped and knocked on Evelyn Baker's door.

"Good Lord, Cal!" Evelyn Baker's forehead creased with concern. "What's wrong?"

"Migraine." Cal hobbled inside and across the room. "Can I sit down?"

"Certainly, certainly." Baker cleared a stack of clothes from the armchair and gestured. Her open suitcase lay on the bed, half full. Most of the drawers in the antique walnut bureau were empty. "You should be back in your room, in bed."

"If I didn't have to be here, I wouldn't."

"Does the light bother you?" Cal shrugged and Baker drew the curtains together. "Bob used to get migraines—horrible things. Even Darvocet couldn't take the edge off. He found that meditation, and cutting out red wine and meat, could actually—"

"I wanted to talk with you before I meet with Jeremy Ames," Cal said. Even speaking hurt; her voice set off a buzzing from somewhere deep in her skull. "I felt I—owed it to you."

"What are you talking about?"

Cal closed her sandpaper eyelids as a spell of nausea set the room spinning. She opened them again and glanced over at the bed "I didn't think you needed a suitcase to go to the bank."

Baker was wearing jeans and a khaki button-down shirt: good traveling clothes. She fussed with the neckerchief. "I was just getting ready for tomorrow."

A shampoo bottle and a toothbrush topped the stack of clothes inside the suitcase. "And you're not going to brush your teeth until then? Come on, Evelyn. I've figured it all out."

"Figured what out?" She crossed her arms and leaned against the bureau.

"From the beginning, I was pretty sure it was a

woman." Cal swallowed heavily and continued. "Victor Godwin was poisoned Saturday afternoon—shortly after we first arrived. The killer had only one opportunity for poisoning Godwin's tanning lotion—while we were all in the parlor and the luggage was being stored near the front desk."

"That makes sense." Baker nodded. "But why does that mean it was a woman?"

"Judith Lorantz is a royal pain, but she can be pretty observant." Cal leaned back in her chair and remembered. "She ranted at Miguel about black scuff marks in the ladies' room that day. I saw them myself—they looked like wheel marks from a suitcase. I think the killer dragged Godwin's suitcase in there so she wouldn't be caught doctoring the tanning lotion."

"Or maybe one of the lodge's guests simply brought her suitcase with her to the ladies' room. Why are you telling me all this?"

Cal took a deep breath. "I didn't suspect you until the Euphecin tipped me off. Victor's skin tested positive for nitroglycerin and Euphecin, but Gates's skin was only positive for nitroglycerin." Even her *thoughts* rattled in her head like gravel. "I kept wondering why. I assumed the killer knew that two positive narcotics screens would look suspicious. But how did she know I even *did* a tox screen on Godwin? It's not routine in most cases—especially in older people."

"I'm worried about you." Baker gave that concerned frown again, the one that reminded Cal of her mother. "Your color is all wrong."

Cal ignored it. "You were there, Evelyn. It started to rain and everyone else headed back inside, but you hung around Godwin's body for a few minutes while I talked to Marcus. You knew about the tox screen."

"Who's Marcus?" Baker smiled a little, as though to humor her.

"My assistant. You heard me ask him to run a tox

screen. No one else was there. I didn't want to believe it, hoped it was just a coincidence."

"Evidently that's what it was." Her smile was thinning.

"And you were there when Gates died." Cal dredged up her memories of the tennis match. "You suggested playing women against the men, knowing Gates would take the bait. And every time we pulled a little too far ahead, you started playing poorly."

Baker shrugged and recrossed her arms. "I've always been inconsistent."

"That's what it seemed like."

"I thought we were friends, Cal. I understand that you need to check every angle, but *really*—"

"Believe me, it's not the solution I was looking for."

The older woman turned away and fussed with a breakfast tray resting on the wardrobe. Her hands shook, and she dropped a saucer. "I was just having some tea and muffins—would you care for some?"

"No, thank you." She swallowed again. The thought of food made her stomach flutter ominously. "I'm doing all I can to keep my coffee down."

Evelyn perched on the edge of the opposite chair, held her teacup in two hands and carefully sipped. She smiled. "This is all very silly. But I'm sure I can *show* you I didn't do it. For instance, if I murdered Eldon Gates, when did I poison his tanning lotion? I wasn't at his party the night before he died, but a lot of other people were."

"So the police let you off the hook as a suspect. But I remembered that you mentioned your hike with Gates Sunday morning, before the tennis match. You could have told him you were worried about getting sunburned, borrowed his bottle, and added the nitroglycerin. Or maybe you visited him in his room that day. You might even have added it during one of the breaks on the tennis court, though that would have been risky."

Baker laughed bitterly. "It really doesn't matter, does it? You seem pretty convinced that I'm guilty."

"I wasn't, until last night." Cal shaded her eyes with her hands. Even with the blinds drawn and the sunglasses on, it still wasn't quite dark enough. Her eyelids were too thin. "The murderer was apparently someone who knew Eldon Gates long ago. Gates was a vain man, and he hid his heart problem very well. But somebody knew about it—maybe they were around when his rheumatic fever started, or when he had his valves replaced—he couldn't very well hide *that*."

"So now I'm an old friend of Eldon Gates's." Her teacup rattled as she set it on the wardrobe. "You're right, Cal. He was interested in Eskimo healing rituals and we spent a few months together up in the Arctic Circle."

"You weren't friends." Cal ignored the sarcasm. "But your husband was—or at least he and Gates were partners. I got a copy of Gates's curriculum vitae from Jessica yesterday."

Evelyn's lips pressed together. Even in the darkness, her healthy tan seemed to suddenly fade.

"In the research community, a CV covers most of a person's associates from the beginning of their career." Cal watched the old woman shrink a little, saw her shoulders slump, her head bow. "An R. Halley was listed as a coauthor on two of Gates's papers, over seventeen years ago. Robert Halley? Your husband? Maybe. But I couldn't be sure. And even if it *were* him, I couldn't imagine any motive, just a link."

She took a deep breath. "But then I saw Plato's notebook. The same one you were looking at last night—when you said someone had walked over your grave."

Evelyn was silent, motionless. Her eyes were fixed on Cal's knees.

"Plato likes to draw pictures when he takes notes. It took me a minute to recognize the sun and the solar system, and Halley's comet." Cal sat and waited for a reply. Baker didn't stir. "The rest of it fell into place— Gates was sued for malpractice seventeen years ago, and his partner—Halley—died after the trial. Your husband died seventeen years ago, too. That's not a coincidence, is it?"

Evelyn shook her head.

"Gates probably made him the fall guy," Cal guessed. "Just like he did with Miguel."

"It wasn't that simple," the old physician croaked. She finally lifted her head. Her eyes were shiny stones on the bottom of a dark river. "Bob had Alzheimer's disease. It came on very suddenly."

Cal sucked in a breath. "I'm sorry. I—I think I understand."

"No, you don't." Evelyn's shoulders straightened. "It's a long story. The patient—Anderson—died before Bob's memory problems ever started."

She looked back at Cal's knees and gave a little shrug. "Bob was on call one evening—my birthday, of course—when Gates telephoned from the office. Gates was working evening hours, and one of Bob's patients had shown up. He was a severe diabetic who was going into ketoacidotic shock. Gates sent him to the hospital, told Bob everything was stable, convinced him not to go in and see the patient. So we went out to dinner."

Her voice cracked, but she struggled on. "Later that night, Bob called to check on his patient. Gates had been in a hurry to get home. He forgot to order insulin, of all things—the man was nearly comatose. Bob rushed in, but it was too late."

Cal was indignant. "So why wasn't *Gates* sued for malpractice?"

"He admitted the patient to Bob's service. There was no resident coverage that night. Technically, it was Bob's responsibility." Her hands clenched into fists. "When the suit was filed, Gates denied telling Bob that the patient was stable. He insisted that he'd asked Bob to call with the insulin order."

"Still, that's pretty flimsy. He should have had to take at least part of the blame."

She gave that little shrug again, a hopeless gesture. "Maybe he would have. But by the time the suit was filed, Bob had been diagnosed with Alzheimer's disease. The malpractice firm found out about it, claimed he was mentally ill and focused all their efforts on him. They dropped the lawsuit against Gates."

She paused.

"I'm so sorry," Cal breathed.

But Baker hadn't finished. "That wasn't enough. Bob didn't want to plead guilty, but the Alzheimer's disease progressed very quickly. When the trial finally began, Bob was a wreck. The malpractice lawyers got him up on the stand and gave him a mental status examination, in front of about a hundred people. It was a circus. People laughed. By then, he even had trouble remembering *me*."

She remembered Baker's words from their walk yesterday morning. *Just an empty shell, with nobody home.*

Evelyn's voice fell to a murmur. "Bob still had some of his mind left, though. The night the jury ruled against him, he snuck down to the garage and started the car with the door closed. I found him in the morning."

"I'm sorry," Cal echoed again. She blinked, and something trickled down her cheek.

Evelyn looked up at her. "The worst thing was, toward the end, he really believed he had killed that patient. He didn't *know*."

She lowered her gaze again and hunched her head down between her shoulders. "At first, I was angry at Bob."

Cal understood that feeling. Her mother's death was ruled a suicide. Nonsense, of course—her mother didn't even own a gun. Up in the attic that afternoon, Cal had thought it was an engine backfiring, or maybe a kid with a firecracker in the street down below. Until she came down to her mother's office and found her.

She never believed it was suicide, but she was angry all the same. As a reporter, Cal's mother should have known better, should have known who she was dealing with.

Some stones are better left unturned.

"Then I was angry at Gates," Baker continued. "Bob's illness wasn't enough. He was reduced, publicly humiliated. His dignity, his *humanity,* was taken away. He had nothing to live for."

"I'm surprised Gates didn't recognize you," Cal said softly.

"He and Bob had only been partners for a couple of years." Her hands were unclenched now, folded neatly in her lap like the rage she'd shown and tucked away again. "We never saw each other socially and Gates almost never went to the trial. His lawyers told him to stay away—like avoiding sharks in a feeding frenzy. It was almost twenty years ago anyway; he'd have forgotten what I looked like. He probably forgot all about Bob, too. But I haven't forgotten."

She lifted her head and pressed her lips together. "I saw Gates's echocardiogram report once—he'd left it out in plain view when Bob was working late one night. I remember the exact words—'Calcific mitral and aortic stenosis, adhesion of chordae tendinae, valve replacement recommended.' I felt sorry for him then, can you believe it? But after Bob died, I kept wondering why it couldn't have been Gates instead."

"That's how you knew about Gates's heart problems."

Baker nodded, then frowned at Cal. "You were looking for the gun last night, weren't you?".

"Yes. I didn't find it." She had still been hoping it was a hunting accident, that Evelyn wasn't trying to kill her.

"I came across an old well during one of my hikes. I dropped the gun in there, along with Gates's suntan lotion. It was easy enough to grab it from his gym bag during the commotion after he died. I tried to get Victor's tanning lotion, but it was too late. Someone had already collected his belongings by the time I realized you were investigating his death."

Cal frowned. "So why did you save my life last night?"

"I wasn't trying to kill you, Cal. I was hoping to scare you off, but I didn't know it was hunting season already." She chuckled hollowly. "I commit the perfect untraceable murder and get caught, but when I shoot at someone, I can't get anybody interested or frightened."

"*I* was frightened," Cal assured her. Now she understood why Baker kept warning her to be careful. All that worry and concern was just an act, an effort to scare her off the case.

"I'm ashamed to admit it—for just a second last night, I thought about letting you fall." She reached over and touched Cal's knee. "But even if I didn't feel close to you, I'm human. I couldn't help reaching out."

She stood and walked over to her suitcase, then watched Cal struggle to her feet. "Victor's death was an accident, something I will always regret. I really thought Victor had died from natural causes. Then I heard about your suspicions, and I realized I must have opened the wrong suitcase. I felt absolutely terrible."

"You should have."

Baker ignored her. "I guess that's part of being human, too. I even have second thoughts about Gates sometimes. But then I think about who he was and what he did. And I realize that I didn't really kill a human being. I killed an animal."

Cal lifted her crutches and hobbled over to the bed. She watched the old physician load the last of her clothes into the suitcase. "But who decides which of us are human beings and which are animals?"

Baker shrugged and snapped the latches shut. "That depends on the society. Among the Netsilik, insults or gossip were taken very seriously, but homicides were often ignored."

"That doesn't make it right."

Evelyn stared down at her suitcase and folded her hands again. She took a deep breath. "So you're going to turn me in."

Cal was thinking of her mother, the reporter. "I wish I didn't have to."

"You don't."

In one fluid motion she whirled, pushed Cal onto the bed, and sprinted through the door. Taken by surprise, Cal nearly rolled off the far end of the mattress before recovering her balance. She crawled back across the bed, dragged her crutches from the floor, and limped over to the telephone. Holding it in her hand, she heard an engine starting and faltering, starting and faltering. Cal stood and thought for a long minute, then slowly cradled the phone again. She lumbered to the hall and down the back stairs.

Evelyn Baker's engine caught just as Cal reached the side door. She watched the little tan rental race around the puddles and lakes of the parking lot, spitting gravel and screeching through the turns, then finally tearing away down the driveway and out of sight.

Seconds later, Cal heard a dull thud, then a series of

sickening crashes. Barefooted, ignoring the pain in her ankle, she dropped the crutches and broke into a sprint.

It took a full minute to sink in. The car was gone. The road was gone. Something flickered through the mist from the far side of the gap. Cal reached the edge and peered down at the destruction below. Through the fog and rain, she saw the wreckage of Baker's tan rental, crumpled in a heap at the base of the cliff. Farther out, something glinted above the surface of the water.

Flat, shiny, silver. A huge bubble broke the surface, and the Chevette rolled over on its side.

"Oh, God—*Plato!*"

When did it happen? How? Maybe he was still alive. The mewling sound welled up in her throat again. She hobbled to the edge, wondering if she could slide down the hill and swim into the water. Or should she go back to the lodge for help?

Plato's disembodied voice echoed from the fog behind her. It sounded almost real. "What happened, Cally?"

She whirled around. His very real arms swung over her, pulled her close. He stroked her hair, then muttered something crazy: "Then it really *was* a migraine."

Behind them, Jeremy emerged from the fog.

"I'll get a rope and radio the rescue squad—not that it'll do much good." A few seconds later, Ames caught sight of the drowning Chevette. "I think you two are going to need a new car."

CHAPTER TWENTY-FOUR

"I've, um, got a little surprise for you," Plato told Cal.

"Hmmph." She was sitting in the leaky recliner, reading that morning's *Plain Dealer* and sipping coffee. Two days after Evelyn Baker pitched into the Cuyahoga, the story no longer dominated the front page. Cal flipped to page three and scanned the headlines.

Plato watched her from the doorway. She'd been like that ever since he found her on the cliff Wednesday morning. Solitary, preoccupied. Not quite herself. It didn't help that she had spent most of the past two days at the sheriff's office, or the morgue, or talking on the phone with Jeremy or Davis or the mayor. They'd hardly had a minute together.

"What is it?" she finally asked, still studying the paper.

"Just a little something." He grinned and plunged his hand into his pocket.

The ring was gone.

Frantically, he checked his other pockets. Nothing. He had hidden it in one of the zipper pouches in the garment bag before they left the lodge. He'd unpacked it this morning, put the box in his right hip pocket. He was certain of it. Almost certain.

It must have fallen out somewhere. He studied the bare hardwood floor, peeked under the sofa.

"You know something?" Cal asked. "I just can't figure out how Evelyn got to be an editor. It seems like such a wild coincidence that Miguel picked both Gates *and* Evelyn to work on the book."

"Not really." Plato slid onto the sofa and casually poked his fingers between the cushions.

"What do you mean?" She sipped her coffee without looking up.

"Miguel met Evelyn at the American Geriatrics Society conference this past May. They were seated together at one of the dinners, and he told her who his boss was." Plato pulled his hands from the cushions and examined his catch: a jingly cat toy, three M&M's, and a limp tortilla chip. He poked around some more. "When Miguel told her about the book, she acted very interested. He met with her the next day and asked her to be an editor. Miguel's pretty sure he had mentioned our upcoming meeting."

"So she probably *hadn't* been planning it for seventeen years. But when opportunity knocked ..." She glanced over at him and frowned. "What are you doing?"

"Me?" He yanked his hands free and glanced down at the goodies in his lap. "Oh, just looking for some change."

"Let me know if you find any—we could use some." She shook the paper and turned the page. "The mortgage payment is due, but with the money we spent having the roof fixed, I'm not sure we'll make it."

She was right. Tension gnawed at the pit of Plato's stomach. He never should have bought the ring. She'd be furious when she found out how much he'd spent. *We made a decision,* she'd tell him. *We agreed.* Maybe he could get his money back, if he ever found the thing.

Money. Plato couldn't help thinking of Gates, and the four hundred thousand dollars he'd siphoned from Hartman's research funds. Small amounts skimmed from dozens of grants, a confusing trail of withdrawals and deposits and interest and credit that would keep the accountants busy for months. Dozens of times, he had invested research funds, skimmed the profits, and slipped the principal back into the accounts. He might have gotten away with it if he hadn't lost his shirt on the stock market last fall. To cover his losses and square things with the IRS, he'd had to make some big withdrawals from the research accounts. Too big. So he tried to throw suspicion on Miguel.

The thought of that much money made Plato's head spin. It was like one of those horrible word problems in math class: how many engagement rings would four hundred thousand dollars buy? How many research projects?

He spied a small black object on the floor, just under the recliner. Casually he shuffled over, picked it up, and jammed it into his pocket.

She looked up and scowled. "What are you doing *now*?"

Plato jerked his hand free. It was covered with syrupy goo and little black dots.

"It's an ant trap," Cal explained. "I saw a couple of those big black ones yesterday, when we came home."

"Oh." He grabbed a tissue and wiped his hands, placed the trap under her chair again.

Cal peered at him curiously. "Are you all right? You're acting kind of funny this morning."

"I'm fine." He turned away, heart in his throat. What if the ring was lost? What if he never found it again?

It couldn't have just walked away, he told himself. Unless maybe one of Cal's field mice—*Arvicola*—had stolen it. Poetic justice. A mound of tiny bones had greeted them at the front door when they returned home yesterday.

She tapped the newspaper. "It says here that Evelyn's bank wired up a large sum of money Wednesday morning—probably all her ready cash. I guess she wasn't lying about going to the bank that day."

"And then where?"

"Canada, maybe," she said softly. "She might have been hoping to hide among the Eskimos."

"Eskimos?"

Cal sighed. "It's a long story. I'll tell you all about it sometime."

Footsteps clumped on the back porch. Cal squinted out the window and shuddered. "Oh, no. It's *him*."

"Who?"

"Tommy Jorgensen." She leaned back from the window and glanced up at Plato. "You deal with him, okay?"

"Fine." He didn't understand Cal's attitude; she was great with most kids. "I don't see what the problem is. He did a good job taking care of Dante."

"I don't know." She frowned. "He reminds me of that kid in *The Omen*. You know—the pointy ears and weird smile. Anyway, he should have cleared the bones off our porch."

"But Dante wanted *us* to have them," Plato protested. "He knows how much you appreciate them."

The doorbell rang.

"He's just so shifty-looking." Cal sniffed. "And I noticed that one of our basement windows is broken. Do you think he—"

"He's a good kid, Cal. Perfectly honest." Plato walked through the kitchen and opened the door.

To Plato, Tommy Jorgensen looked far more like an *elf* than a demon. Pointy ears and nose and chin. Stick-thin, like a tree that grew too fast, even though he was still shorter than Cal. But it was the smile that really did it—a pumpkin grin with dimples and lots of teeth.

The cat-sitter shrugged the newspaper sack from his shoulder. "Hi."

"How's it going, Tommy? Come on in."

The boy ducked inside, wiped his feet on the mat. He tiptoed across the linoleum and glanced into the living room. "Hi, Doctor Marley."

Cal folded her paper and glanced over the top. "Hello."

"How's your ankle?" he asked hopefully.

"Fine, thank you." She returned to her reading.

Tommy turned back to Plato and grinned shyly. "She's awfully nice."

"I think so, too." He pulled out his wallet. "You did a great job taking care of Dante and watching the house for us. Let's see—that's five days, times—"

"Plato?" Tommy interrupted.

He stopped counting and looked up. "Yes, Tommy?"

They were on a first-name basis. Even at the hospital, Plato wasn't very comfortable being addressed as "Doctor Marley." At home, it seemed ridiculous.

The boy reached into his canvas sack and pulled out a black velvet box. "I found this when I was riding up your driveway. It was sitting in the grass, over by your mailbox."

Plato remembered it now. He'd checked the mail this morning, dropped one of the bills and bent over to pick it up. The box must have fallen out then.

Cal limped into the kitchen.

"Uh. Gee. Thanks, Tommy." He took the box, tried to slip it back into his pocket, but the ant trap had glued it shut.

"What is it?" Cal snatched the little box from Plato's hands and opened it. He winced.

She just stood there, lips pursed in a little "o" of surprise, not moving, not blinking, not saying anything at all. The calm before the storm. Plato glanced over at Tommy, wondering if he should hurry the little elf outside before his pointed ears got singed.

"It's so *beautiful*."

"What?"

"Oh, *Plato*," Cal breathed. She hobbled toward him and snagged her crutch in the buckled linoleum. When he caught her, she pulled his face down to hers and met his lips in a passionate kiss. Her body melted like chocolate in the sun. "Thank you."

Tommy coughed delicately.

She pulled away from Plato, leaned over and hugged the boy close, kissed his cheek. "You, too, Tommy."

A crimson flush started at his neck and ears and swept across his face. He blinked, swallowed twice, wiped his cheek with his sleeve.

Cal grabbed Plato's wallet. "How much were you going to give him?"

He told her. She counted the money out, added half of what was left in the wallet, and handed it to Tommy. "That's your reward."

The paperboy raised both hands and shook his head. But his wide brown eyes were glued to the money. "Doctor Marley, I couldn't. I mean, I just found it on—"

"Just call me Cal, okay? And take the money. If you knew how much the ring was worth, you'd ask for even more." She shooed him out the door, then turned to Plato. "I always liked that boy."

"I think he has a crush on you." Together, they watched him amble down the driveway, still cradling the money in his hand. He finally pocketed it and broke into a sprint. Plato grinned. "You've always been a great judge of character, Cal."

She shot him a strange look.

He took the box from her and opened it. Even in the dim light trickling through the kitchen window, the sky-blue sapphire sparkled brilliantly. He lifted her small hand, slid the ring onto her finger. The jeweler had sized it down for her, and it fit perfectly.

Cal stared at her hand for a moment, then slipped into his embrace. She nestled in the hollow between his neck and shoulder, slid up to nuzzle his ear, finally tipped her head back and found his lips.

The telephone rang.

"It's probably Jeremy," Cal muttered, lips still pressed to his. "He wants to set up a press conference."

"Do you want to go to a press conference?" Slowly, he brushed his lips across her cheek, her forehead, the bridge of her nose. His fingers danced down to the small of her back, touching, stroking, caressing.

"Not really. I want—*mmm*." She purred like a cat.

Cradling her waist with one hand, Plato reached back and dragged the phone to the edge of the counter. He reached up, opened the freezer, and carefully placed it inside. With the door closed, the phone was almost silent. It made small sad sounds, like a lost lamb in a snowstorm.

"You're so romantic," Cal finally breathed. She slid back and looked up at him. "Lets go upstairs, hmm?"

"Uh-huh." He slid his fingers through her hair.

"We can bring up some of that pizza from last night." She purred some more. "We can have breakfast in bed, after."

"I'll bring the whole thing." He opened the refrigerator and grabbed the box. "We can have lunch in bed, too."

"And dinner in bed." She smiled and tugged his hand, led him toward the stair. "It'll be just like a second honeymoon."

Behind them, the telephone bleated one last time and was still.

Author's Note

Dementia, the gradual and progressive decline in mental functions, afflicts 5 percent of people over age sixty-five and 25 percent of people over age eighty. With the graying of America, these percentages translate to a staggering number of victims suffering from Alzheimer's disease and other dementing illnesses. But dementia is not only a disease of the elderly, just as it is not always incurable or inevitable. Up to 15 percent of dementing illnesses stem from treatable causes, including depression and other reversible diseases. So rather than assuming that a loved one's forgetfulness stems from simple "old age," we should consider consulting a geriatrician or other physician qualified to evaluate the causes of memory and cognitive impairment.

Unfortunately, the majority of dementias are incurable. Ongoing research has revealed much about the chemical and cellular biology of the disease, and our improved understanding has led to some modestly promising therapies. But we still have a long way to go. For now, treatment of irreversible dementias focuses on managing symptoms, slowing cognitive decline, and supporting patients and their families. Dementia is a bewildering, crippling disease that tears at the fabric of relationships and lives, but support and guidance can help patients and families cope and survive.

The Alzheimer's Association (Alzheimer's disease and related disorders) is a national organization providing guidance and support for victims of dementia and their families, as well as research funds for investigations into the prevention and treatment of Alzheimer's and other dementing illnesses. The Alzheimer's Association publishes several free brochures, including "10 Warning Signs of Alzheimer's Disease." For a brochure or other information, call the association's toll-free number: 800-272-3900, or write: Alzheimer's Association, P.O. Box 5675, Chicago, IL 60680.

"I hated my cadaver," Plato told his wife.

They were on their way down to the anatomy lab. Twenty-four granite steps worn smooth by the passage of generations of medical students. A stairwell ripe with the fruity smell of embalming fluid, soap, and rubber gloves. The lab was two stories below the main level of Siegel Medical College and fifteen degrees colder. The lights were dimmer, too. By the time they reached the bottom, it was as quiet and chilly as an abandoned mine shaft and almost as dark. The cold air helped keep the bodies fresh.

They were moving so quietly, so furtively, Plato felt like a grave robber.

Cal stopped and fumbled for the hallway lights. Fluorescents whined to life, casting a greenish glow across polished tile, washtubs, and banks of lockers. She turned to Plato and frowned. "What are you muttering about now?"

"I said, 'I hated my cadaver.'" Down there, next door to the lab where the bodies were waiting, it sounded like sacrilege.

Cal seemed to agree. "That's not funny, Plato. It's a *terrible* thing to say."

"It's true." He followed her over to a locker. She pulled out a tiny blue smock for herself and a large one for Plato. They were already clad in their grubbiest jeans and T-shirts and their most ancient tennis shoes. The pocket of Cal's smock featured some fancy embroidery: *"Cal Marley, M.D.: Forensic Pathologist, Cleveland Riverside General Hospital."* She was a regular guest lecturer for the anatomy department at Siegel Medical College. Plato's borrowed smock didn't say anything; he was a geriatrician at Riverside and hadn't visited the anatomy lab since his sophomore year in medical school. Cal had volunteered to tutor some failing medical students down in Siegel's anatomy lab, and she'd talked Plato into coming along and helping out tonight.

Her shoulder-length blond hair was pulled up in a bun. She grabbed a bathing cap from the locker, pulled it over her head, and explained. "Keeps the smell from getting in my hair. It takes *days* to wash it out."

They moved across the corridor to the sink and donned two pairs of extra-thick surgical gloves apiece. Time to enter the lab.

"I was very fond of Harriett," Cal mused. "She taught me an awful lot."

Harriett was Cal's cadaver back at Northwestern, but she might as well have been a friend. Some of Plato's fellow students had felt that way about their cadavers, too. Usually the nerdy ones who spent hundreds of hours meticulously tracing every artery and vein and nerve and putting little flags in them so the instructors would use *their* cadavers for most of the practical exam questions. A lot of them had ended up as surgeons. Or forensic pathologists.

"That's how I thought I'd feel about mine," Plato replied. "But it didn't turn out that way."

They entered the anatomy lab, and Plato was lost in a fog of memories. Freshman year: the first day with the cadavers, listening to the instructor's benediction, the ritual cutting of the plastic and the shroud, coming face-to-face with death for the very first time. Long days and nights in the lab, going home smelling like a cadaver and usually feeling like one, too. Counting the days before the practical exams, a thousand Latin names swirling through his head like dead autumn leaves. Failure. "My cadaver had something against me, I swear to God."

"What do you mean?" Cal led him past dozens of stainless steel coffins to a niche near the front of the darkened room. Each coffin rested on a gurney parked near the walls. Four medical students per cadaver, so each gurney was surrounded by four dissecting manuals propped open on music stands. Chamber music for a grisly quartet.

"He must have weighed over four hundred pounds." Plato watched her flick on the lights over one of the tables. They eased the steel doors down and furled the plastic, folded back the oily shroud. She grabbed a spray bottle and anointed the body with a fresh layer of embalming fluid.

"Our group was always the last to leave the lab, Cally. It took us half an hour just to bundle him in and get the lid closed."

This woman didn't have a weight problem, Plato saw. Five-three, maybe five-four, but people always look taller when they're lying down. Gray hair, thin as a rail, but with overdeveloped arms and shoulders. Wasting of the legs, with that oddly smooth skin you see on paralyzed limbs—atrophic changes. Probably used a wheelchair. Her hands were big and callused and vaguely familiar. But it was hard to tell what she looked like, since the skin of the face on Plato's side had been carefully peeled back to show the lacework of facial muscles and nerves. Someone had done a good job with the dissection. Facial skin is quite thin, and the muscles beneath are as many and varied as the expressions they make.

"Poor you," his wife clucked, sarcasm dripping from her voice. "Your cadaver donated his body so you could get a medical education."

"I bet your Harriett was young and slim—an exercise fanatic, probably." Not that Harriett was her real name, of course. Cadavers are generally anonymous; the door of this one's coffin was labeled with a simple blue tag: 65 Y.O. FEMALE, CARDIOPULMONARY FAILURE. But a lot of students named their cadavers. To Plato, it seemed a little too cute, too possessive. As though the body never had an identity of its own.

"Slim, yes. But Harriett was pretty old. I had trouble finding some of her muscles." Cal stared down at the body, reminiscing over an absent friend. "Sometimes I wondered what Harriett was like, when she was alive. I pictured a very gentle lady. Maybe a music teacher. Her fingers were long and delicate, like she played the piano."

She patted this cadaver's gnarled, ropy hand. Beside it, Cal's gloved hand looked small and smooth as a child's.

"Most of the time, I was wondering how my cadaver had managed to live so long," Plato griped. "Everything was either broken or an anatomic variant. He had a horseshoe kidney and three ureters, and half his arteries started in the wrong places."

"Then you'll make an *excellent* tutor, since you're familiar with all the normal variants." She swung her brown eyes up at him and smiled tightly. "You didn't *really* hate your cadaver, did you?"

"No. I hated anatomy class. I was a terrible dissector." Reluctantly, Plato was doing a little reminiscing of his own. "I was always cutting through nerves and arteries. My lab partner, Jerry Flint, got pretty good at sewing them back up."

"Jerry's a vascular surgeon now, isn't he?"

"Yeah. I gave him lots of practice."

She turned to the cadaver's head, retracted the gray scalp flaps and lifted the cranial cap, the bony lid of the skull. "Good. The surgery students started the head for me."

"I thought you were teaching the thorax today."

"We are." She replaced the lid and smoothed the flaps back down. The way the gray hair hung like ivy over the vacant blue eyes reminded Plato of one of his patients. "We'll concentrate on the thorax today. But these kids had a lot of trouble with the skull practical. So we're going to drill them on it every evening."

Her repetitive "we" had Plato worried. "Listen, Cal. I didn't mind coming tonight and helping out. But it's just this once, okay? I don't have enough time, and I've forgotten half the stuff, and anatomy was my worst subject anyway."

"You don't have to be a genius just to tutor some medical students." She folded her arms and glared at him. "You told me you didn't mind. 'No problem,' you said. Last week, you were griping about how we need to get out more."

"Get *out* more? You call *this* getting out?" Plato slapped his hand against the steel table. The loud *clang* shattered the stillness of the room. Thirty-six cadavers stirred in their cold and oily sleep. "Other people go to movies or see a show. My wife, the forensic pathologist, likes to slice up dead people in her spare time." He flapped his arms. "Maybe I should get some candles and wine."

"That's not fair, Plato. I'm just trying to help these kids—" Her voice broke off, and she stared at the floor.

She was right; it wasn't fair. Plato took a deep breath and decided on the truth.

"Cally. I was *really* bad at anatomy."

"How bad?" She sniffed, and wiped her eyes against the shoulder of her smock.

He glanced down at the cadaver. It was discreetly looking the other way, pretending not to hear. "Bad enough to flunk."

Cal shrugged. "*Lots* of people flunk a class or two. It's no big—"

"I flunked all three quarters. I had to take the entire *year* of anatomy over again with the freshmen, while I kept up with all my sophomore classes."

"Oh, Plato." She reached across and squeezed his shoulder. "That must have been *awful.*"

He stared at the cadaver's face, admiring the tidy dissection once again. "I wanted to be a plastic surgeon."

A quiver started at the corner of Cal's mouth. "Really? You never told me that."

"Yeah. But flunking anatomy ruined my chances of landing a residency spot."

"You're kidding me, aren't you?" The quiver turned into a smirk.

"What? What's wrong? Just because I'm lousy at anatomy—"

"It's got nothing to do with anatomy, Plato. It's your *hands.*"

"What about them?" He plucked nervously at his gloves. "With enough practice, I could have—"

"Practice? Pah-*hah!*" Her laugh burst out like a shotgun blast. "Put a scalpel in your hands, and you'd be worse than Jack the Ripper. Whenever you get hold of something sharp, your hand shakes like a jackhammer."

He held up his hands and glared at them. "A little tremor."

"Tremor, huh? You were practically *anemic* until you grew that beard. And look what you did to the Christmas turkey."

"Thanks, Cal. You're all heart."

"You're much better at talking than cutting—that's why you're such a good geriatrician." She smiled and patted his arm.

"Flattery won't help. I think my little ego is bruised beyond repair."

"*Little* ego?"

Plato shrugged. "Anyway, you see why I can't tutor these kids. They probably know more than me already."

"I doubt it, I really do." She stared up at him and her eyebrows met. "You passed anatomy the second time, right?"

"I *had* to."

"Some of these students may not be so lucky. All four of them have been bombing anatomy all year—and not for lack of trying."

Cal served on the Academic Advisory Board at Siegel, the medical school's version of Mount Olympus. Years ago, Plato had appeared before the board, when he flunked anatomy. It was the worst experience of his life; he'd gone into the meeting fully expecting to be kicked out of medical school. His stomach had tied itself in knots, his voice had tightened up until he squeaked like a cartoon mouse, and his wits had taken a leave of absence. But still the gods had smiled on him, given him another chance.

"Randolph Smythe the Third was ready to can all four of them," Cal explained. She always called the board chairman "Randolph Smythe the Third," even though "Dean Smythe" or "Randolph"—or just "God" would have been so much shorter. But it wouldn't have been nearly so accurate. Smythe was the crown prince in the Siegel aristocracy. Dean of Research, chairman of several boards and committees, and probably the next provost of the medical college—once Dean Fairfax retired. Most of the faculty already saw him as the power behind the throne.

"Smythe agreed to let them take a makeup exam in two weeks," Cal continued. "Provided that I tutor them, *personally*. They're good students—I know all of them from my lectures here. Maybe if someone had put some time in to tutor *you* when you failed anatomy, it might have made a difference."

"Well . . ." Maybe a couple of tutoring sessions wouldn't be so bad after all.

"Besides, I made a little bet with him."

"You made a bet with Randolph Smythe the Third?" Plato's jaw dropped.

"It was the only way he would give these kids a second chance."

"So what's the bet?"

"I told him they were all smart enough to pass their anatomy finals." She smiled and shook her head at the memory. "He said if they did—all four of them—he'd nominate me for the chairmanship of the Academic Advisory Board. He's stepping down anyway, and he said I would deserve it. All the other members agreed. Of course they think it's impossible. They think these kids are hopeless."

A board chairmanship would be a real feather in Cal's cap, Plato knew. She would have the power to soften things up at Siegel and cut down on some of the pressure. Make the College a little more humane.

But Smythe was a hard bargainer—and he certainly didn't plan on losing. The alternative had to be something truly awful. "And if they don't all pass?"

"They flunk out, I'm off the Academic Advisory Committee, and we both have to tend bar at Smythe's next fundraiser. He's running for Congress, you know."

"I know," Plato groaned. Randolph Smythe the Third wasn't just running. He was already favored to win, before the primaries had even been held. Like many successful maverick politicians, he had a unique administrative style—a cross between Machiavelli and a Kirby vacuum cleaner salesman.

"I can't believe you told him—" Plato began, but he was cut off by the squeak of tennis shoes on the linoleum in the hall.

"Hello?" A woman's voice sounded in the doorway, low and husky, more like a whisper.

Cal peered off into the darkness and smiled warmly. "Hi, Samantha. Come on in."

Samantha hurried through the darkened lab to their circle of light. She was one of Siegel's older medical students—early forties, Plato guessed. Dark eyes, long dark hair with a hint of gray that shimmered in the eerie light. Standing near the feet, she smiled at Cal and shot an inquisitive glance at Plato.

"Samantha Ricci, meet my husband. Doctor Plato Marley." Cal gestured with a scalpel. "He's a family doctor and geriatrician at Riverside General, and he's pretty good with anatomy. He's going to help out with the tutoring."

"Pleased to meet you, Doctor Marley." Samantha was dressed like her tutors—tattered jeans and sneakers, a faded Cleveland Indians T-shirt, and the standard blue smock. And a pair of yellow Playtex kitchen gloves—the kind used for cleaning ovens. Plato had worn the same kind when he was a student; they kept the smell off his hands better than the disposable latex gloves.

"Just 'Plato' is fine," he told her. "Otherwise, we won't know which Doctor Marley you're talking to."

Before she could respond, they heard the clatter of lockers out in the hall. A rumbling voice was met by a high-pitched laugh like shattering crystal. Two more students straggled over to join the group, and Cal made more introductions. The laugh belonged to Tiffany Cramer, a tall willowy blonde with eyes like blue half-dollars. A rich kid, obviously— dressed in ballerina flats, jabot blouse, and a pleated skirt that matched perfectly with the blue dissecting smock. A small diamond solitaire ring dangled from her gold rope necklace. A rhinestone hair clip and a pair of pearl earrings completed the ensemble. Plato had someone like her in his anatomy lab back when he was a student—dressed to kill for every class. At the end of freshman year, she had her wardrobe dry-cleaned and donated it to Goodwill. Daddy probably took it as a tax write-off.

Raj Prasad didn't look old enough for medical school; he hardly looked old enough to vote. He was even shorter than Cal, with coal-black hair and thick glasses like a pair of fish-bowls perched on his nose. He shook Plato's hand and grinned. "Pleased to meet you, I'm sure."

His sonorous baritone was way too big for his body. Talking with Raj gave Plato a queasy little feeling, like talking with a disk jockey, or a politician.

Cal glanced at her watch. "Has anyone heard from Blair Phillips today?"

"I saw him in the library this morning," Samantha replied. The others just shrugged.

"We'll go ahead and start without him." Cal folded her hands in front of her and gazed around at the students. "I understand that you folks all did pretty poorly on the head and neck practical."

"I passed all the other parts," Raj rumbled.

Tiffany nudged him and grinned. "There was only *one* other part, silly."

The others laughed. Because the head and neck were so complex, most of the fall quarter had been spent dissecting and reviewing those structures. The thorax had been the only other area covered on the exam; it was quite easy to learn.

"This time, all of you are going to pass the entire exam, *including* the head and neck practical. And we'll review the abdomen while we're at it, since this quarter's first practical will focus on that area. But I want you folks to study the skull every day. It's by far the hardest area to learn." She reached down to a shelf below the body and retrieved a rubber model of the head. It opened in the midline to show the sinuses, oral cavity, and cranial vault. The brain and most of the other soft parts were removable. Tiny hinges swung open to reveal all the little outlets and inlets, nooks and crannies, the beehive that houses the human soul. Like a Chinese puzzle box but even harder to fathom. "Today and every day, I'm going to drill you on this model as well as the real thing."

She tapped the model and gazed at each of them in turn, her voice rising and falling like a revival preacher's. "You'll never graduate if you don't pass anatomy. And you'll never pass anatomy without knowing the skull. Tape a drawing of the facial muscles to the back of your cereal box so you see it at breakfast. Hide your television in the closet for a few weeks and put a model of the skull on the television stand instead. Buy some review tapes and listen to them in the car. You'll be able to name these fossa and foramina with your eyes closed."

"That's what I was doing before the exam," Samantha complained. "My roommate said I was speaking Latin in my sleep."

"Good—then we'll start with you." Cal swung the roof of the skull open and held it up for Samantha to see. "My fingers are in the middle cranial fossa, aren't they?"

"I guess so," Samantha replied doubtfully.

"Here, in the middle, we have a bone with a funny shape, don't you think?"

"That's the sphenoid bone."

"Exactly. Do you know what sphenoid means?"

"Umm."

"Wedge," Raj intoned. "Sphenoid means wedge-shaped."

"That's right, Raj. Looking at the bone, you can see how it got its name. But most people think the sphenoid bone looks more like a bat in flight." She traced the edges of the bone and looked up at Samantha again. "Can you see the shape?"

"Yeah—except it has four wings."

"That's right." Cal's voice was soothing, encouraging. "Which are bigger?"

"These, down here." She pointed at the lower pair of wings.

"Excellent—you've just identified the greater wings of the sphenoid."

Samantha gawked. She held up her index finger and stared at it. "Why, that was so *easy*."

"Not all of it will be this simple," Cal warned. But she had won their attention, and at least a little of their respect. She passed the skull around the circle, touring them across shelves and plates, piloting around tubercles, navigating through canals, trolling and cajoling for answers or guesses. By the time she put the skull down again, Plato's head was whirling with names and terms he thought he'd forgotten, like fluttering snow in a Christmas paperweight.

"Any questions?" Cal asked. The students shook their heads. Already, Plato could sense a change in them— dejection and cynicism brightened by a glint of hope. "All right. For the rest of this session, my husband will work with you on the thorax while I finish dissecting the neck."

Last night, after Cal had asked for his help, Plato had dusted off his old dissecting manual and reviewed the chapter on the thorax. It's a simple area to learn—far fewer muscles and nerves than the arm or leg, no three-dimensional confusion like the skull, and the structures are much easier to find than those of the pelvis. Luckily, most of the dissection had already been done during Christmas break by junior medical students who were taking surgical anatomy and vying for residency positions. Cal had used her influence as a part-time instructor to have a fresh cadaver prepared for the tutoring sessions. Otherwise, it could have taken months to simply complete the dissection.

Blair Phillips finally showed up just as Plato began his lecture. A tall, lanky kid with long hair and bleary green eyes. He came in panting, like someone had just called a code on the cadaver. Plato half expected him to start compressions. But he just mumbled an apology and muttered something about car trouble.

After that, everything went pretty well; even Plato's confidence grew. They worked through the muscles, focused on the relationships of veins, arteries, and nerves at the ribs, and finally entered the pleural cavity. Samantha had trouble mo-bilizing the left lung, so Plato stepped around to the other side of the table. He slipped his gloved finger down into the space between the lung and ribs. Stripping the adhesions away felt like popping Velcro.

Meanwhile, he mulled over how the poor woman must have felt when she was alive. Ordinarily, the pleura lining the lungs and ribcage are slippery and smooth as greased Teflon; the lungs expand and contract eighteen times a min-ute over an entire lifetime with less friction than any piston. But the whole base of the woman's left lung was scarred down as if it had been rubbed with sandpaper. Pleurisy is ex-tremely painful; each breath must have been agony.

Sliding his finger down farther still, Plato thought about Marilyn Abel, one of his patients. Before she died, Marilyn had pleurisy like this, down at the base of her left lung. Ex-cept hers had been caused by an old Vietcong sniper round planted back in the sixties, when she was an army nurse. The bullet showed up on all her chest X rays; Marilyn was rather proud of it.

And then Plato felt it, a tight little knob lodged at the bot-tom of the costodiaphragmatic recess, like a marble wrapped in cotton. And everything rushed together to make a horrible sort of sense—the familiar callused hands, the gray hair, the pleurisy, Marilyn's death last December.

Plato glanced up at the face. The dissectors had left this side untouched; the skin was a smooth and sallow gray. He saw Marilyn's high cheekbones, Marilyn's wide smile, even Marilyn's *wink*—one deep blue eye closed, the other dis-sected and lidless.

Plato pulled his hand from Marilyn's ribcage and stag-gered away, stumbling into the wall and knocking a reading stand to the floor. Across the body, Tiffany Cramer glanced up at him with concern. Samantha mined her hand deep into the chest again, excavating with the oven cleaning gloves, her face a mask of concentration. She felt it, jerked her head, and gestured for Raj to hand her a scalpel.

The others craned their necks to peer into the thorax and help mobilize the lung as Samantha wrestled with her prize. Finally, the long yellow kitchen glove emerged triumphant. Marilyn was already dead, but she was free of the bullet at last. Samantha held the object up to the dissecting light—a tiny pellet wrapped in scar tissue. Cal grabbed a tray and they hacked away to discover the secret of the pearl.

"It looks like a bullet!" Raj exclaimed.

"Oh, my God!" Tiffany Cramer had forgotten her clothes for the moment; her oily glove was pressed to the neck of her jabot blouse. "Do you mean she was—she was *murdered*?"

"It doesn't make sense," Blair Phillips was saying. He stared back at the body. "There should have been blood—a big clot or something, right?"

Samantha turned the body slightly. She explored the landscape of Marilyn's back and found the scar just where Plato knew it would be—one centimeter below the tip of the scapula. When she was shot, Marilyn had been bent over, examining a wounded soldier. Miraculously, the bullet had threaded the gap between ribs 7 and 8, just clipping the intercostal nerve but leaving the vein and artery intact. An excellent demonstration of clinical anatomy. The bullet had been fired from quite a distance, Marilyn had explained. Instead of hurtling on through, it had nestled in near the apex of the heart. The doctors hadn't wanted to risk removing it.

"This is an old wound, Tiffany. She wasn't murdered." Samantha pointed to the scar. "Right, Doctor Marley?"

Cal looked at the bullet again and peered down at the scar.

"You're only half right, Samantha. That looks like an old entrance wound." Being a forensic pathologist, Cal had seen a lot of entrance wounds, both new and old. "Small-caliber rifle bullet, probably an old war injury."

Plato nodded, impressed but not surprised. His wife was an expert in her field. But then she said something that made him wonder.

"I'm afraid you're wrong about the other part, though." Cal glanced at the neck again; her dissection there was almost complete. She raised the shroud, folded the plastic over the body, and gazed around at the group. "This woman was almost certainly murdered. I'll need to take her body down to the morgue for an autopsy."